Seducing the Earl

DANGEROUS LORDS BOOK TWO

BY
MAGGI ANDERSEN

Print Edition

Published by Dragonblade Publishing, an imprint of Kathryn Le Veque Novels, Inc

BOOKS FROM DRAGONBLADE PUBLISHING

Dangerous Lords Series by Maggi Andersen
The Baron's Betrothal
Seducing the Earl
The Viscount's Widowed Lady

Also from Maggi Andersen
The Marquess Meets His Match

Knights of Honor Series by Alexa Aston
Word of Honor
Marked by Honor
Code of Honor
Journey to Honor
Heart of Honor
Bold in Honor
Love and Honor
Gift of Honor

Legends of Love Series by Avril Borthiry
The Wishing Well
Isolated Hearts
Sentinel

The Lost Lords Series by Chasity Bowlin
The Lost Lord of Castle Black
The Vanishing of Lord Vale
The Missing Marquess of Althorn
The Resurrection of Lady Ramsleigh

By Elizabeth Ellen Carter
Captive of the Corsairs, *Heart of the Corsairs Series*
Revenge of the Corsairs, *Heart of the Corsairs Series*
Shadow of the Corsairs, *Heart of the Corsairs Series*
Dark Heart

Knight Everlasting Series by Cassidy Cayman
Endearing
Enchanted
Evermore

Midnight Meetings Series by Gina Conkle
Meet a Rogue at Midnight, book 4

Second Chance Series by Jessica Jefferson
Second Chance Marquess

Imperial Season Series by Mary Lancaster
Vienna Waltz
Vienna Woods
Vienna Dawn

Blackhaven Brides Series by Mary Lancaster
The Wicked Baron
The Wicked Lady
The Wicked Rebel
The Wicked Husband
The Wicked Marquis
The Wicked Governess
The Wicked Spy

Highland Loves Series by Melissa Limoges
My Reckless Love
My Steadfast Love

Clash of the Tartans Series by Anna Markland
Kilty Secrets
Kilted at the Altar
Kilty Pleasures

Queen of Thieves Series by Andy Peloquin
Child of the Night Guild
Thief of the Night Guild
Queen of the Night Guild

Dark Gardens Series by Meara Platt
Garden of Shadows
Garden of Light
Garden of Dragons
Garden of Destiny

Rulers of the Sky Series by Paula Quinn
Scorched
Ember
White Hot

Highlands Forever Series by Violetta Rand
Unbreakable
Undeniable

Viking's Fury Series by Violetta Rand
Love's Fury
Desire's Fury
Passion's Fury

Also from Violetta Rand
Viking Hearts

The Sons of Scotland Series by Victoria Vane
Virtue
Valor

Dry Bayou Brides Series by Lynn Winchester
The Shepherd's Daughter
The Seamstress
The Widow

TABLE OF CONTENTS

Prologue

Linden Hall, Yorkshire
October 1817

THE ELEGANT BALLROOM was filled with guests enjoying the Hunt Ball. Laughter rose in the heated smoky air as decorative ladies mingled with the more soberly dressed gentlemen.

As they danced, Lady Sibella Winborne smiled mischievously at her host, John Haldane, Earl of Strathairn. "This is a splendid ball. I feel I should congratulate you, except I know Eleanor arranged it."

Strathairn's gray-blue eyes twinkled. "Come, am I not deserving of a little praise? But yes, my sister excels at these affairs."

"Eleanor is remarkably efficient. Indeed, a wife could hardly do better."

Strathairn's hand tightened at her waist. "Eleanor intends to live in Devon. She dislikes London life since her husband, Lord Gordon passed away. I fear my grouse will now breed unchecked."

"You do plan to marry at some stage?"

"I accept the need for an heir." He arched his eyebrows. "Your brother still seeks a husband for you?"

Sibella sighed. "Yes. Chaloner is committed to marrying me off sooner rather than later."

"Don't allow him to push you into a marriage not to your liking."

She lowered her lashes. "I should like very much to choose my husband."

He grinned. "You will have quite a list to choose from. A man would be lucky to have you." His matter-of-fact tone belied the warmth of his gaze.

Sibella feared that her hand trembled in his. She studied the tall blond man who led her gracefully over the floor in a waltz. Did he suspect her of encouraging him to propose? She was, in all likelihood, although she knew it to be a lost cause. Hopeless at flirting, she doubted he would fall for it. They had been friends for years. Before the war, John might have married her, but those years away on the Peninsula had changed him. Something held him back from marriage now. She wasn't sure what it was, but he desired her, she could recognize ardor in a man's eyes when she saw it, it was just that he didn't want her enough it seemed.

"It's desperately sad about Catherine, Harrow's wife," she said to change the subject. "The duke is a friend of yours, is he not?"

Strathairn sighed. "Yes. Tragic to lose your wife in childbirth. The babe survived. A daughter."

"I've heard he's devastated."

"Dreadfully cast down. Andrew plans to leave England. He has taken up a diplomatic post in Vienna."

"Are the children to accompany him?"

"No, that would be unsuitable. He is leaving them with his mother and the nursery staff. I believe a governess has been employed for his heir. Young William is now six."

The dance came to an end. Sibella took John's proffered arm, and they joined her sister Cordelia.

He bowed. "Viscountess Bathe."

Cordelia curtsied. "Lord Strathairn."

"You dance very well together," Cordelia said after the earl left them. "Can't you get him to propose?"

"Apparently my charms are not sufficient to lure him into matrimony," Sibella said and puffed at a wisp of hair on her forehead that had escaped her coiffure.

"Well, you'll have to stop mooning over him," said her annoyingly pragmatic sister. "And find a husband."

WHILE WANDERING HIS ballroom, speaking to guests, Strathairn encountered Sibella's brother, the Marquess of Brandreth, who had made a beeline for him through the crowd.

"I hope we bag a few more birds tomorrow," Chaloner said.

Strathairn eyed him. He had something on his mind. "One trusts so. My chef plans a grouse dish flavored with juniper berries for our dinner."

"Sounds delicious." Chaloner raised his glass. "I'm willing to rise at the crack of dawn for that." He took Strathairn's arm and drew him away into a quiet corner. "I don't wish to strain a friendship I value, John, but I feel I must offer a word of advice."

"Oh?" Strathairn had liked Chaloner better before his father died. The man seemed to lose his sense of humor after inheriting the title.

"You are often seen in Sibella's company. Don't get too fond of her."

Faintly irritated, Strathairn glanced over at Sibella in her white muslin, talking earnestly to Mrs. Bickerstaff. "Your sister is intelligent and good company. I enjoy our conversations. Nothing too scandalous about that."

"I struggle to believe it is just conversation. I may not be privy to the details of the work you perform for the military, but rumors do float about the House of Lords. You must admit that due to those circumstances alone, you would not make her a good husband."

Chaloner's determination put him in mind of a robin with a worm. Pointless to argue. With a sigh, Strathairn acknowledged that he only strove to protect his sister from possible hurt. "No need for concern," he said. "I have no plan to marry your sister, or anyone else for that matter. I do intend to ask Sibella to dance again though. Unless you think my dancing with her will ruin her reputation."

Chaloner huffed out a laugh and rubbed the back of his neck. "Only among the biddies. I don't enjoy having to say this to you, Strathairn, but it befalls me as head of the family. Sib has a love of home and hearth. She looks for a husband who will sit by the fire with her at night. That isn't you, is it?"

"She deserves the best, and no, that isn't me, Chaloner."

Chapter One

London Docks, Summer
1818

A GUNSHOT SHATTERED the quiet air. The Earl of Strathairn dropped into a crouch as another ball whistled overhead, followed by a thud as lead bit into the wall above him, showering him with fragments of brick. A bead of sweat trickled into his brow. Hell's teeth—not the first time he'd been shot at by a long chalk, but he hadn't expected it to happen tonight. In fact, he'd been sure this was a fool's errand. The moon sailed free of the clouds. It cast the new dock in silver light, revealing it empty. Where was Nesbit?

Breath held against the stench of low tide, he listened. Nothing but the surge of the swell and the creak of ships moored out in the middle of London Pool waiting to unload their wares. The faint voices of the sailors aboard carried over the water.

When the slap of running feet echoed into the distance, Strathairn gripped his pistol, hunched over, and rushed forward. He leapt over a pile of crates and flattened himself against a wall, his pulse a drumbeat in his ears as he edged around the corner.

Nesbit lay spread-eagled on his back. Strathairn rushed to his stricken friend, fell to his knees, and groaned. Blood seeped from his partner's head onto the ground. Nesbit's eyes, a lively brown only moments before, stared blankly up at him. A prickle of foreboding climbed Strathairn's spine. Had Nesbit been as surprised as he was by this attack, or might he have recognized his killer?

Aware it was futile, he placed his fingers against Nesbit's throat and searched for a pulse, then cursed effusively under his breath. He'd witnessed the death of too many good men. As bitterness twisted in his gut, he rose to his feet determined not to allow his sadness to weaken him. His mind focused on the business at hand as he moved stealthily through the shadows, sure that whoever committed this dastardly act was gone.

Apart from the scamper of rats, the rest of the dock stood empty and silent. The moonlight picked out something shiny on the ground. Strathairn stooped to pick up a finely wrought gold cravat pin in the shape of an eagle, just like the one Count Forney favored. A familiar restless energy and heightened alertness sent his heart racing.

A calling card? Word had come that Forney was dead. But was he? A flowery scent lingered in the air. Strathairn held the pin to his nose. Parisian, and a lady's fragrance, if he was any judge.

BENEATH GLITTERING CHANDELIERS, the dancers spun over the floor to the strains of a Handel waltz. Strathairn smiled down at his partner, her slim waist beneath his hand. Lady Sibella Winborne looked like a delicate flower in a gauzy pale gown covered in amber blossom. White ostrich feather plumes adorned her luxuriant dark locks. He enjoyed looking at her. Her serene, oval face lifted and she smiled at him, her mouth wide and full. Too wide for beauty some might say but perfect for kissing. She had inherited her mother's famous eyes, a delectable mix of blue and green, but her quiet nature lacked the vivacity of her mother in her youth. The dowager was said to have had men fall at her feet. Strathairn admired Sibella's calm beauty, but she was oh, so much more: practical and intelligent with a delightful sense of humor. Yet still unmarried, which surprised him.

Her blue-green gaze met his. "You arrived late tonight. I wasn't sure you'd come."

"I was tied up with business."

"Parliament?"

"No."

She tilted her head. "Your horses, then?"

He grinned at her blatant curiosity. "No."

"You won't tell me."

"No."

Sibella laughed in good humor. "Very well. Might I find you riding in Hyde Park tomorrow?"

"I hope to. Shall I see you there?"

"Yes." Her delicate brows rose. "If business doesn't keep you."

He chuckled. "Precisely."

The music faded away. Strathairn escorted her back to her chair where her mother, the Dowager Marchioness of Brandreth, sat fanning herself among the other ladies. He bowed with the intention of removing to the gaming rooms. As much as he might wish to dance with Sibella again, it would place them under scrutiny, and faro was an effective release from the tension he always carried with him.

"Don't rush off, Strathairn," her sharp-eyed mother said. "We have seen little of you of late. You rarely frequent these affairs." She waved her fan to encompass the ballroom. "Where have you been hiding?"

"Not hiding, my lady, merely dealing with business."

Lady Brandreth adjusted the silk shawl over her shoulders. "Did you visit that pile of yours in Yorkshire? I enjoyed the Hunt Ball, but it's cold as charity in winter up in those parts."

"Not this time. I miss it. There's a wild beauty to the dales in winter, quite unlike southern England."

"I daresay." Her purple turban wobbled as she nodded. "You are a fine figure of a man, Strathairn, well into your thirties. You should marry and set up your nursery." She gestured toward her daughter sitting beside her. "Sibella will bear you healthy children. The Brandreths come of good stock, and the Wederells even better."

"Mama, please!" He caught Sibella's apologetic gaze with a wry smile. Her plea would have little effect. The marchioness was known to be one of the most colorful and outspoken members of the *ton*.

The dowager batted her daughter's protest away with her fan. "I am merely stating a truth, Sibella."

"Your daughter is a credit to you, Lady Brandreth," he said. "She has inherited both your beauty and intelligence."

"Now you are toad-eating." A roguish smile flitted across Lady Brandreth's face. "You always were a charmer. Sibella *is* intelligent. Walk with her on the terrace to discover it for yourself."

Strathairn bowed. He held out his arm. "I should be delighted."

Lady Brandreth was a crafty woman. Sibella's friendship was one of the few reasons he came to these affairs. In the dangerous world in which he played his part, her friendship had become an anchor. Had his resolve to remain single begun to weaken, what happened to Nesbit earlier served only to strengthen it, for the same fate could befall him. He was hardly in a position to enter into a domestic arrangement. Better she marries someone else. She could be hurt if she came to love him.

SIBELLA FUMED. HER mother was as subtle as an ox. No one could accuse Strathairn of being a toad-eater. At least he wasn't offended, for she caught a spark of humor in his eyes.

Sibella had met him in her first season when she'd refused two unsuitable offers of marriage. Now at six-and-twenty, she was in danger of being left on the shelf. No wonder her mother was giving any likely candidate for her hand a push. Unfortunately, Mama didn't push; she shoved.

Had her father been alive, she would be married now, but he had been dead for five years. Luckily, her mother had been distracted bringing out the last of her three sisters and fussing over her grandchildren. Now that her youngest sister, Maria, was engaged to her childhood sweetheart, an heir to a dukedom, her mother focused her full attention on Sibella. Her luck at being overlooked had run out.

Sibella walked out onto the terrace happy to snatch a little time with the earl. The evening was divine. Braziers glowed like fireflies through the gardens, the sky a deep purple, and the air soft and sweet, like a summer bouquet.

His arm felt strong beneath her gloved fingers. Her mother was right; Strathairn was a fine figure of a man in his black and white evening clothes. He wore them with such elegance, but she preferred him in riding breeches. He was over six feet tall, and the top of her head barely reached his shoulder, even though she was quite tall herself.

He smiled down at her. Must his smile be quite so beguiling? As if he read her mind. But she rather hoped he couldn't. In the moonlight, his fair hair took on silver lights, his eyes a deeper and more mysterious blue. An inner cautionary voice cut into her thoughts. *He will never be yours*.

The rakish Lord Montsimon emerged from the garden, escorting a lady. His partner had a glazed look in her eye and hair in need of rearranging. She curtsied to Sibella, excused herself, and hurried inside while the men paused in conversation.

They discussed the news from abroad. The Duke of Harrow had written to Strathairn from Vienna.

"He enjoys the post, but is still burdened with a deep sadness," Strathairn said.

"What of his children?" Sibella asked.

"They remain in good health."

The men's conversation turned to another matter.

When she wasn't required to contribute beyond the occasional nod of her head, Sibella was caught by Strathairn's big hands as he gestured. A man's hands were important. She liked the elegant shape and long, tapering fingers. Not soft, like a gentleman's, there was a ridge of a scar along one thumb. She employed her fan at the thought of him stroking her flesh. Annoyed, she sought to distract herself by comparing the two men. They were both good looking, but very different. Where Strathairn was more of a serious bent, the viscount was a charming, witty man known to have left many broken hearts in his wake.

Strathairn accepted invitations infrequently. He always set up quite a titter among the debutantes and their mamas when he appeared even though he'd made it clear he wasn't in the market for a wife. Some saw it as a challenge, she supposed, while others turned their attention to more amenable gentlemen. Why was he so averse to marriage? Had his heart been broken when he was young? When Chaloner had warned her off him, he'd let slip that it was Strathairn's manner of living which made him unsuitable. He bred horses and ran his estates, what could be unsuitable about that?

"Don't you agree, Lady Sibella?" Strathairn asked turning to her.

"Um. Sorry. What was that?"

"The Prince of Wales's patronage of The Royal Literary Fund. It has enabled them to rent a house as their headquarters."

"A good thing certainly," she said. "While I don't believe Prinny cares deeply for the arts and sciences, he has recognized their importance."

Strathairn nodded, his gaze appreciative and warm. Was she reading more into his manner than there was? Did he look at every woman the way he looked at her now?

When Montsimon left them, Strathairn tilted his head toward the garden path. "Shall we?"

Her pulse raced as they descended the stone steps. She had never been entirely alone with him.

They strolled along the gravel path bordered by a hedge of camellias a talented gardener had coaxed into flower.

Strathairn picked a full creamy bloom and held it out to her.

"Thank you." She held the flower to her nose, aware it had little scent.

"I always enjoy seeing your mother," he said as they strolled on.

"Do you? Not everyone does. She is very plain spoken."

"That is what I appreciate about her."

"She likes you it seems." Sibella bit her lip and blushed. Her mama had just tried to get him to propose. "Have you been visiting your estates or were you just evading her question?"

He leaned over her to brush away a branch, scattering petals. "You're remarkably inquisitive this evening. Why do you ask?"

"Perhaps because you're mysterious. You intend it that way, I suspect."

"A mystery? We've discussed most of my past: my schooling, Eton, Oxford, and the army."

"That sounds so conventional and yet…you aren't, are you?"

He cocked a brow in surprise. "Am I not?"

"Conventional men are an open book. You are not, sir. I know only what you want me to." She suspected his life held more excitement than he revealed. Somehow, she couldn't believe his life was one of mundane routine. "Breeding horses must be satisfying." A keen rider herself, but surely even horses had limited appeal. "Do you miss the army?"

"Some men find it hard to settle down. I admit to suffering that for a while."

"But you're settled…now?"

"As much as I wish to be."

She glanced at his profile for a sign of annoyance. She *was* dreadfully forthright tonight as if her mother's blatant speech had stirred up her restless desire.

A couple greeted them as they passed. The gardens were filled with people enjoying the warm night. At a smothered giggle, Sibella turned to see a pair close together in the shadows. Strathairn caught her gaze, eyebrows raised.

"Lady Gladwin's affairs tend to flout convention," she said, warmth stealing over her cheeks.

"More interesting than most," he said with a smile.

She suspected cards drew him more than strolling about with a lady. They had reached a wide stretch of lawn lit by flaming torches with a fountain at its center. A naked marble figure wrestled with the serpent imprisoning him within the tight coils of its tail. Water sprayed from the serpent's open mouth, spilling into a pool of water lilies.

Despite the silent battle, she found it peaceful and reflective there, until he stepped closer.

Sibella breathed in his manly scent as a heavy nervous sensation settled deep and low in her stomach. His proximity always affected her so. Perhaps if she saw more of him, she might grow used to him, but she doubted it.

She twirled the flower stem in her hand and remained silent, listening to the fall of water and the song thrushes calling through the night air.

His eyes seemed to caress her. "What are you thinking?"

"My thoughts were about you. I'm surprised we are here alone. It's not something you would normally risk."

"Is it a risk, Lady Sibella? Am I in danger?"

"One of us might be."

"I like that you're frank."

She laughed. "Do you mean outspoken?"

He grinned. "Sometimes, but at least you're natural. Many young ladies adopt artful poses."

"How unkind. Perhaps you make them nervous."

He sighed heavily. "I may well do."

"You don't care a fig if you do. You're deliberately distracting me." She searched his disturbing smoke-hued eyes. "Something troubles you." As much as she wished to learn what blue-deviled him, she didn't anticipate he'd tell her. "Shall we walk back to the house?"

"Not yet. I like it here. Talk to me."

He *was* different tonight, too. Sensing they had crossed some invisible line, she grew nervous. She licked her bottom lip and found herself rattling on about her nephews and nieces.

"You, a maiden aunt?" His eyes focused on her mouth. "What nonsense. A woman like you should be loved and loved well."

She flushed. "I enjoy the company of children."

He merely shook his head at her, a smile tugging at his mouth. Unnerved, she resisted the urge to rush in to fill the void.

"Your mother is right," he said finally. "You should marry and soon. Have children of your own to love. You are made for it."

"I fully intend to." Was he warning her not to get too fond of him? Pride made her lift her chin. "When the next personable man asks me."

He chuckled. "Personable?"

"Love doesn't need to be a prerequisite for a successful marriage," she said, sounding horribly stiff.

"Perhaps you're right."

He might have argued the point with her. "I am pleased you agree with me." She tilted her head. "You so seldom do."

An appreciative glint lit his eyes. "Marriage is a business contract drawn up by men, but most women wish for romance. It's better that you're not the missish sort. Love is a fanciful notion more ably expressed by the poets."

She narrowed her eyes. "I gather the poets pen their verse from experience?"

He laughed. "Some do most certainly. I suspect Byron does."

"So love is not for you."

"I would make a very poor husband, Sibella."

She wondered why he thought so. What consumed him? His horse stud might claim much of his time. Her two younger brothers lauded his prowess with racing thoroughbreds and buying and selling them for profit. Once prompted, they rattled on about how Strathairn excelled at many sports, racing matches and riding to hounds. None of this explained his reluctance to marry, however. Perhaps a wife would insist on more society. He seemed to avoid a lot of it, rarely attending musical evenings or soirees.

"Why?" she asked, her curiosity unsatisfied. A slight bump marred the perfection of his otherwise imperious nose. She curled her fingers, resisting the desire to touch it.

"Some men don't," he said flatly.

He looked unhappy. It was all she could do not to reach out to him. Her gaze drifted up to his face. His jaw was taut, and what she saw in his eyes troubled her. "You are sad tonight, but you won't tell me why, will you?"

His nostrils flared. "You ask far too many questions." With a swift movement, he cradled her face in his hands, his lips, firm but gentle, covered hers, stifling her gasp of surprise. Coherent thought slipped away as his arm encircled her waist and pulled her hard against him. His hold tightened and the kiss deepened, teasing her lips and stealing her breath.

Sibella stilled as hot flames rushed through her veins. She had no defenses against this man and she abandoned any attempt to push him away. About to encircle his waist and pull him closer, her need for self-preservation stopped her. But then he angled his head to plunder her top lip, and she was lost. Her body was demanding more. Much more. She gripped his coat as her legs grew unsteady.

He released her so suddenly she almost fell. "Lord, Sibella. That was wrong of me. I do apologize."

She stared at him, noting the contrition on his face. There was no declaration of love hovering on his lips. As she fought to gain her breath, a cynical inner voice cut through her thoughts. The kiss was to distract her from probing the reason for his sorrow. Commonsense prevailed at last. "No it wasn't."

His eyes widened. "No?"

"The kiss perfectly fit the occasion," she said almost gaily. "And please don't concern yourself that I might accuse you of compromising me." She was quite pleased with herself. There was no hint of bitter disappointment in her tone.

He shook his head. "I know you better than that, Sibella."

The man was insufferable. Didn't he realize how enticing that sounded? More than anything, it was a woman's wish to be understood by a man, to be appreciated. "I find kissing quite pleasant," she said coolly, as if she was soundly kissed every day of the week. "But I don't think you should do it again, my lord."

"Perhaps you're right. But don't glower at me, Sibella. It was your fault after all."

She gaped at him. "My fault?"

"You look far too seductive in the moonlight. Perhaps we should walk back?"

"I should rightly slap your face," she said faintly.

"Well?" He bent over her and turned his cheek. "Take your best shot." She shook her head at him and couldn't help laughing.

He laughed, too, and offered her his arm.

She rested her gloved fingers on his sleeve. A hot lick of sensation raced along her veins. Did he feel as she did when they touched? If so, he hid it well, drawing the conversation into a safe direction concerning a two-year-old thoroughbred he'd bought at auction and planned to enter in the autumn flat-racing meet at Doncaster.

He returned her to her mother, who paused from her discussion with the other ladies of her set to raise her lorgnette and assess them. Intent on the gambling chambers, Strathairn's broad back disappeared into the crush. Had kissing her left him unmoved? She snapped her fan open. So they were to go on as before as if nothing had happened. "I don't think so, Lord Strathairn!" she muttered.

"Eh, what was that, Sib?"

Her brother Edward stood at her shoulder. "I've come to claim you for the next dance, before any of your admirers beat me to it."

"I shouldn't worry, many are losing interest," she said crisply, rising from her chair.

He eyed her as they entered the dance floor. "Losing hope, more like."

As they moved through the steps of the quadrille, he dropped quiet remarks in her ear.

"Give up on Strathairn, Sib."

"Not you, too! I don't believe, I—" They parted, and by the time the steps brought them back together, she'd given up protesting. Edward had inherited their mother's astute nature.

"It's not that I don't like him. I do very much. But he's not for you."

"You needn't worry. He has no wish to marry me."

Her brother raised a black eyebrow. "Oh, I believe you could sway him toward marriage if you set your mind to it. That's not the reason."

"Then what *is* the reason?"

"Chaloner hears things in the House of Lords. I can't repeat them."

"So he tells you but not me."

Edward shrugged with a smile as he moved away.

"Why does such mystery surround the Earl of Strathairn?" she hissed at him when she next got a chance.

He shook his head. She'd learn no more. What remained with her were his words. Could she sway Strathairn toward marriage?

Sibella danced a country dance with an old admirer, her mind elsewhere. She recalled the first time she met Strathairn years ago. He was different then. There had been a youthful carelessness about him as he lounged insolently against a column talking with two other men. Savagely gorgeous in his magnificent blue hussar uniform, the pelisse trimmed with silver braid and fur edging, and the leather belt with a polished silver buckle and curved honors scrolls circling his slim waist, he had the attention of every woman in the room from widows to girls in their first season.

She'd doubted the thin veneer of calm in his eyes, especially when his slow and seductive gaze slid downward. Impertinent, she'd thought, bristling, and fidgeted as a dizzying current raced through her. There was a maddening hint of arrogance about him. As if reading her mind, his attractive mouth widened in a lazy smile. She turned away and tried to ignore his presence while dancing with others, but her gaze constantly flittered to where he stood. When she returned to her seat, he appeared at her side with her brother Edward, who introduced them, and they shared the last dance of the evening.

The next time they met, Strathairn sought her out. Every time his gaze met hers, her heart turned over in response. They danced twice and talked for an hour until her mother came to find her. Mama was confident Strathairn would ask for her hand, but he'd left for the battlefields of Spain soon after, and she didn't see him again for over a year.

He returned changed from the war, his eyes haunted with unspoken secrets. There was an air of isolation about him as he moved through the *ton*. She suspected his disinclination to gossip and the detached expression he adopted was protective clothing. When she teased him to draw him out, he responded with an easy grin, but she couldn't penetrate the wall he'd built around himself. Her heart went out to him, but she was continually frustrated when, although he sought her company, and they undoubtedly shared an intense physical awareness of each other, he made no move toward marriage.

She had resolved to enjoy what he offered. He confessed his days at university had been filled with active pursuits rather than learning, but he still seemed well-versed on any subject. They rode together in Hyde Park often, along with others of their set. But now, after that kiss! She'd find a way to make him face the truth. They were, after all, perfectly suited.

Chapter Two

RESTLESS, STRATHAIRN ENTERED the library of his Berkley Square home. The house was too quiet now that his younger sister, Georgina, had married the Duke of Broadstairs and his widowed sister, Eleanor, had gone to live in Devon.

He struggled to come to terms with his behavior. That he should suddenly give in to desire and kissed Sibella when he had promised her brother he wouldn't pursue her, was unforgiveable. While she'd put a brave face on it, she must wonder what the devil had got into him.

It must have been the shock of Nesbit's death. Tomorrow, he must visit his partner's wife. She had recently borne the poor man a son. He swiveled on his heel and moved closer to the coal fire seeking to warm his chilled body, but the cold was more visceral than corporeal.

He had never come to terms with the guilt he suffered after William Laverty's death. William had been a good friend and one of his lieutenants on the Peninsular fighting under Wellesley. When Strathairn had sent him on a surveillance mission with a handful of soldiers, they had ridden straight into the hands of the enemy. He'd searched for them all night, finding them at dawn. Gripped with helpless fury, he had taken William's broken body down from where they'd hung him from a tree branch.

Such memories still had the power to inflict deep pain. He'd lost comrades and witnessed death and devastation caused by Napoleon's army during the war, but details of that one scene continually resonated in his dreams. Finding the scattered bodies in a flowering orchard, the sky an arc of vivid blue, the stench of blood blending with the sweet perfume of blossoms, raw flesh, and the buzz of flies in the still hot air, rictus distorting William's handsome face. The letter of condolence he had to send to William's mother.

Strathairn poked the fire as he attempted somewhat unsuccessfully to banish the image of Sibella, gazing at him, lips parted in the moonlight. He continued to roam the bookshelves. His father had assembled an impressive library during his lifetime. A man given more to deliberation rather than action. His father had been against him joining up and had then begged him to resign his commission. Nothing he did impressed his father. Strathairn had long ago given up trying to be what the erudite, elegant statesman wished of him. He preferred an active approach to problems and felt trapped when indoors for any length of time, which only grew worse after the war. The prospect of spending hours in the House of Lords discussing the Corn Laws left him cold. He wished his father's disappointment didn't still have the ability to gnaw at him.

He drew a volume of John Donne's poetry down from the shelf and leafed through, pausing to read a few lines:

"License my roving hands, and let them go–Before, behind, between, above, below..."

A man familiar with love and desire was Donne. He smiled, recalling Sibella's conversation about marriage. He usually had a good grip on his emotions. Perhaps he'd grown too comfortable in her company and acted without thought. She'd asked too many questions he wasn't able to answer. He disliked prevarication, but he had no choice. He'd given in to his need to be drawn into her perfumed warmth, which only made him want more. Sterling woman that she was, she'd handled his outrageous conduct with aplomb, placing them back on the level of friendship.

Friendship? Once, the notion would have been enough, but now...now he wasn't so sure. Disconcerted by his irrational thoughts, he replaced Donne on the shelf and went to the drinks table. He sat in the fireside chair with a glass of whiskey and took a deep sip aware that he must rein in these intense emotions. They made him feel too much. Think too much. They were dangerous, especially now, with a difficult mission ahead of him. One he might not emerge from unscathed.

The candles guttered low in their sconces. *Enough of this.* He downed the last of the golden liquid and leapt to his feet. He hated a quiet house. Despite the late hour, he would visit the George Inn in Southwark. There was always good company to be found there. Molly's arms would obliterate the sight of Nesbit's dead eyes.

He rang for his butler.

"Get my coat and hat, Rhodes, I'm going out. No need to wait up."

On the street, he tamped down an unaccountable surge of disloyalty. Damn, he was becoming irrational!

As the hackney rolled over the cobbled roads, he wrestled his thoughts into some semblance of order. He must alert his friend, Guy, Baron Fortescue, to the possibility of Forney's return. Guy had helped to foil Forney's plans to assassinate a member of the royal family two years before. Now his friend appeared to be relishing the role of country squire. Guy wrote of his modern methods of farming and the house that he'd built for his bachelor laborers. Paid them fifteen shillings a week, which was twenty times the going market rate. It proved to be a success, resulting in increased profits. Fortescue ventured to London only under sufferance when his wife, Horatia, dragged him there. Less often now since their baby son, John, named in his honor, was born. They were besotted parents.

It sounded like an idyllic existence, but it wasn't for him. His intelligence work had filled the hungry ache and sense of loss he had suffered when he returned from the war and gave him a purpose. His years away had changed him. How could they not have, watching his friends and colleagues die, and unsure himself if he would still be alive by nightfall? He'd spent more hours in the saddle than out riding through the rugged Iberian Peninsula with intelligence needed at headquarters. Bad dreams continued to plague him even now, forcing him to relive the worst of those times.

He wasn't sure why, but the surge of excitement and a sense of living on the edge banished the anguish he suffered, which nothing else had thus far been able to do.

When the carriage pulled up, he shrugged away his thoughts like shedding a heavy cloak and pushed his way through the noisy regulars in the busy inn.

AS THEY OFTEN did at her mother's instigation, Sibella and her siblings repaired to their countryseat, Brandreth Park, a few miles from Tunbridge Wells. Sibella welcomed the change. The country air and quiet always helped to clear her mind. When dark clouds heralded an impending downpour, she hurried back to the house.

Had Strathairn searched for her in Rotten Row and suffered disappointment not to find her? He obviously wasn't going to fall at her feet and propose. After the kiss, things might become awkward between them, but she didn't wish it never to have happened. Trouble was, she now had dreams of such a disconcerting nature she would blush to reveal them to anyone, even her married sisters.

In the entry hall their butler, Belton, took possession of her bonnet, apron, gardening gloves, and sketchpad. "Her ladyship entertains a visitor, Lady Sibella."

She expected a neighbor as no one had stated their intention of calling. With the trug of blush pink roses over her arm, she entered the salon, wiping her moist brow with a naked forearm.

A strange gentleman sat talking to her mother.

"Sibella," her mother called from her chair where their cat, Whiskey, played with the fringe of the cashmere shawl on her lap. "Come and meet Lord Coombe. Only fancy, Lord Coombe was up at Oxford with your brothers. I can't think why we haven't met before."

The well-dressed gentleman had auburn hair swept into a careful

Brutus. He rose and bowed. "What a perfect picture you make, Lady Sibella. The roses match those in your cheeks."

She curtsied, clutching the basket close to her chest. "You must excuse me, my lord, I'm a trifle soiled from gardening." Over his shoulder, her mother cast her a dark look.

Lord Coombe hesitated, caught midway across the room. "I have sought your mother's forgiveness for this inopportune visit. I should have left my card, but I came in the hope that I might see your brother."

"Which brother do you refer to, my lord?" She smiled. "I have several." She settled the wooden trug on a mahogany side table and began to remove each rose, careful of the thorns.

"Edward. He suggested I call in when passing on my way to London from Arrowtree Park." Disappointment plowed his brow. "He was to advise me on the purchase of a gelding at Tattersall's auction rooms this afternoon."

Sibella wasn't fooled. Edward an authority on horses? If it was a legal matter she might have believed it. He had arranged this, and by the smug expression on her mother's face, she was part of the conspiracy. At the very least, Edward might have had the good grace to be here.

Her mother rang for tea, and she was caught. She could hardly make an excuse and disappear without appearing rude.

"Give those flowers to a maid, Sibella."

"I like to arrange them myself, Mama."

"Here you are, Belton," her mother said. "We wish for tea. Tell a servant to put the roses in water."

As Belton left the room, Sibella admitted defeat and sank onto a chair. "Is Arrowtree Manor Elizabethan, my lord? The village of Chiddingston has many fine examples."

"How discerning of you, Lady Sibella. Arrowtree Manor is a wonderful example of the period. To preserve it and its grounds requires a great deal of my attention."

"I'm sure your wife is a great help to you, my lord." Her mother stroked the loudly purring cat.

Lord Coombe's eyes rested on Sibella. "I have no wife to help me unfortunately, but I plan to rectify that soon."

Her mother studied him keenly. "Would we know of your fiancée?"

"I have yet to choose a wife, Lady Brandreth."

Sibella sighed inwardly. She could visualize her mother's glee, although she was far too polite to show it. Well-bred and obviously plump in the pocket, Lord Coombe was ripe for the plucking. Sibella intended to give Edward a stern dressing down as soon as she found him alone.

At this point, her nemesis walked in. With a questioning raise of a black eyebrow, Edward took note of the fiery light in her eyes. He adroitly ignored her and moved smoothly on to greet his guest. "I'm sorry to be late, Coombe. Got held up at Brackett's Corner. A careless drayman overturned his cart and spilled his load all over the road, broken crates, and bottles everywhere. Took them an age to clear it."

As the maids unloaded the tea service and seedcake onto the table, Maria appeared. "I see I'm just in time for tea." She offered their guest her pretty smile.

Sibella considered Maria to be the loveliest of her sisters. At twenty, her skin was flawless and her figure exceptional. Most of the children inherited her mother's black hair and green eyes, except her two older sisters who were fair like their father had been.

Under her mother's direction, a servant placed urns of roses on occasional tables around the room. "How decorative, Sib," Maria said. "Their perfume is heavenly."

Sibella nodded and sat back to admire the result. The salon was a family favorite because the chimney didn't smoke. They gathered here on brocade sofas when her eldest brother, Chaloner, was at home. The walls were papered in moss green, the Axminster carpet pink and cream, the curtains at the arched windows of rose silk damask. In gilt frames, paintings of their descendants hung around the walls. Above the carved marble fireplace, where Dresden figurines and a silver-gilt ormolu clock resided, hung a painting of her mother as a beautiful young woman in oyster silk, her hair piled high and dressed in ostrich feathers. Being part of this unruly and at times annoying brood, gave Sibella a strong sense of who she was, but also, what was expected of her.

Sibella narrowed her eyes at Edward. Unruffled, he winked at her.

Maria crumbled a cake onto her plate while she peppered their guest with questions. "Do you know the Duke and Duchess of Lamplugh in Chiddingston?"

"The duke is my neighbor, Lady Maria."

"Well! How extraordinary! They are my fiancé, Lord Harrington's parents," she said as if Coombe was responsible for arranging it.

Lord Coombe explained how a corner of his property ran with the Duke's, although he seldom saw them. "The Duke and Duchess are abroad. I believe in Italy?"

As Maria continued asking questions, he answered her politely. He was not unattractive although not particularly tall and of narrow build. One's appearance accounted for little in marriage, Sibella supposed. She cast a resentful glance at Edward. How annoying that he and Vaughn were under no pressure to marry. If not the heir, sons could wed whenever they chose and to the lady of their choice, provided she was seen as acceptable.

If her foolish head wasn't filled with a broad-shouldered blond gentleman, she might consider a potential husband among those beaus who had yet to desert her, despite her advancing years. She firmed her lips, she simply must banish Strathairn from her thoughts.

Drawn out of contemplation, she discovered several social engagements had been arranged, all of which Lord Coombe accepted.

Before departing to walk to the stables with Edward, Lord Coombe kissed her hand, his deep brown eyes meeting hers.

The footman closed the door on them.

"Wasn't Lord Coombe an interesting man?" her mother said to no one in particular, as Sibella's sisters, Aida, Cordelia, and the children came into the room. "Your expertise in managing a large household would be of advantage to him." Mama nodded wisely at her. "It must be difficult for him to run such an estate on his own. A man needs a wife. To accompany him to social events, greet his guests, and see to their comfort when he holds shooting parties and the like."

"I would loathe it. The boom of guns and the birds falling from the sky." Sibella wrinkled her nose. She'd always hated guns and killing animals.

Sibella glanced at her mother warily. Mama showed too keen an interest in Lord Coombe for her liking. There was little hope of calling upon her sisters for help as she had in the past. Maria thought of little but her coming marriage to Harry, and both her elder siblings were preoccupied. Aida, a year older than Sibella, expected her first child and busily feathered her nest. Cordelia, at one and thirty, had two young offspring. Married to a cello playing viscount, she was obsessed with her harp.

Small feet danced across the carpet. A boy of four and a girl of three, advanced on Sibella, pushing her back in her chair.

She gathered them up in each arm.

"Oh, do be careful of your Aunt Sibella, do!" Cordelia said, with that vague expression she always had when her mind dwelt on her music.

"Bring more hot water, Pearson," her mother directed the footman. "How are you, Aida? You look peaky."

Aida put a hand on her round stomach. "The midwife says I'm very well, Mother."

"It's their nurse's day off, Sib," Cordelia said. "I don't suppose you'd like to take the children for a walk or something? I need a few hours of perfect peace this afternoon and I can't practice with them under foot."

"You know I love to spend time with them." Sibella kissed Anne's cheek and smoothed back Randal's bright golden hair. "Do you want to play draughts?"

Randal nodded and grinned up at her. *Strathairn might father such a child*, she thought, as he slipped off her knee. A strange ache filled her chest. *Damn the man.*

"Who is this Lord Coombe?" Aida asked.

"A friend of Edward's," her mother said. "He displayed a decided interest in Sibella."

Sibella turned her back on her mother and grimaced at her two sisters.

Aida laughed.

Cordelia snorted. "You've certainly gained experience running this house, Sib. The housekeeper defers to you in most matters. And Lavinia is perfectly happy for you to do so."

"I enjoy it, and Lavinia has all her time taken up with the children."

"She allows them to run her ragged, and poor Chaloner, too," Cordelia said waspishly.

"I'm sure Lavinia is most grateful to you, Sib," Aida said.

"If you girls are conspiring to help your sister remain a spinster for the rest of her life, I beg you to stop and think how sad that would be," Mama said. "Randal, don't pull the cat's tail; there's a good boy."

"Come children." Sibella held out her hand to Randal. He stood at his grandmother's knee where her cat gazed at him warily. Little Catherine was on her knees following the flowery border around the carpet. "Shall we search for bird nests?"

After running around the gardens with the children until they flagged, Sibella returned them to their mother and sought Maria, finding her in her bedchamber.

"I subjected Lord Coombe to the usual close inspection," Maria said, winding a piece of pine-green velvet ribbon around her finger, "as I do all of your beaus."

"He's hardly a beau. But what did you make of him?"

"I don't know," Maria said thoughtfully. "He's polite and well-mannered of course, but he gives very little of himself away."

"Dark brown eyes are inscrutable, aren't they?"

"You didn't warm to him then."

Sibella shrugged. "I neither disliked him nor suffered a strong attraction."

"Well, we know why that is, do we not?"

The name Strathairn hovered unsaid between them.

As Maria rummaged in her jewelry box, Sibella was tempted to tell her about the kiss. They shared everything, and it seemed disloyal not to, but for some reason she wanted to hold the heady, sensory details of John's kiss in the moonlight close for a while, not wishing the experience pulled apart in the cold light of day.

When Edward returned to the house, Sibella waylaid him in the front hall. "I'll thank you not to help mother find me a husband," she said.

For once, Edward didn't laugh. He grabbed her hand and pulled her down the corridor and into the library.

She spun around as he shut the door behind her. "What is it?"

"You need to forget Strathairn."

"I..."

He held up a finger. "There's a very good reason for it."

"I know. He doesn't wish to marry. At least me, anyway," she said ruefully.

"A spy cannot marry. That is, a spy with any integrity who doesn't wish to place those he loves in danger."

"A spy?" Sibella's chest tightened. "Are you sure you're not embellishing, Edward?" It did make sense now that she thought of it.

"I had no intention of telling you this, but I sensed your relationship might have taken another step. I trust you'll be discreet. And for heaven's sake, don't tell Maria! She's the worst at keeping secrets." Edward folded his arms and leaned against the door. "He works for the military."

So that was why such mystery surrounds him! "But what if a woman was prepared to marry him anyway and face the risks with him?"

"And subject yourself to a life of fear and heartbreak? You don't know what you're saying. Forget him, Sib, please." He shook a finger at her. "Strathairn appears on the surface of things to be an earl with a passion for breeding horses. But he also inhabits another dark, dangerous world, which is beyond your comprehension. He resists drawing you into that world and exposing you to possible danger. If you set out to seduce him, his resolve may well crumble. I've seen how he looks at you. Leave Strathairn alone. There are other more suitable men in the world."

He leaned forward and brushed a kiss onto her cheek. "Do you understand?"

She nodded mutely as she fought to grasp the truth, the certainty that she and Strathairn would never marry.

Edward opened the door to find a footman standing in the corridor trying not to look intrigued.

WITH A HEAVY heart, Strathairn left Mrs. Nesbit's house, having delivered the grim news that she was now a widow. He promised the distraught woman financial aid would be forthcoming, and he would make sure it was.

When he reached Whitehall, a secretary showed him into Lord Parnham's office, where his lordship sat behind his large desk piled high with files.

Strathairn removed the eagle pin from his waistcoat pocket and tossed it down on the desk.

Lord Parnham picked it up. He poked at the gold cravat pin in his palm. "You think this could belong to Count Forney? Is it possible the intelligence we received about his death is wrong?"

"Possibly. Or this was one of his cohorts."

Lord Parnham's eyebrows rose. "We hung them all." He dropped the pin as if it might bite him. "What is your gut feeling?"

"This was hardly the act of a rational man, but was Forney ever that? He faces the hangman's noose for his involvement in the assassination conspiracy. The target of which may have been Princess Charlotte. Some other purpose would have brought him here sadly since the princess died in childbirth."

Thinking of Nesbit lying dead tightened his jaw. "I'll continue to dig around. Something might turn up."

"Don't bother. There's not enough to go on," Lord Parnham said. "We'll move on to other matters."

Strathairn stared at him, dismayed. "I'd at least like to try to find out who wrote the note that brought us to the dock. And who shot Nesbitt?"

"It might be an enemy of yours. Best you don't, Strathairn. I can assign someone else—" Parnham paused at a knock at the door.

Strathairn fumed as Parnham's secretary entered the room and handed the spymaster a letter.

"The Home Office." Parnham scanned it quickly. "Seems that Sidmouth's spies have followed a Frenchman to York after he was engaged in stirring up trouble against the government in Manchester. They've apparently lost sight of him. It's drawing a long bow, but we best check it out." He leaned back in his chair, his fingers forming a steeple. "It's likely York got too hot for him with the men on his tail. Nevertheless, go up there and see what you can find out about him. You might pick up his trail. Leave as soon as you can get away."

"And if Forney should surface while I'm gone?"

"Rest assured you'll be contacted."

Strathairn had to make himself clear. He leaned forward, his knuckles on the desk. "I want to deal personally with whoever killed Nesbit."

Parnham nodded, sympathy in his eyes. "You'll get that chance."

"I'll leave in a few days. I'll ride in Hyde Park tomorrow afternoon if you wish to contact me."

His spymaster uttered a displeased grunt. "Cannot such a commitment to friends be deferred? Surely a ride in the park doesn't compare with your estate, which I'm sure you'll take the opportunity to visit."

"It's business." He must set things right with Sibella.

A flicker of amusement lightened Parnham's brow. "I see."

"I wouldn't read too much into it." Strathairn glowered at the impudent man.

Parnham laughed. "Women lie behind most of the irrational things we men do." His brows snapped into a worried frown. "But watch your back up north. And send word as soon as you can."

The following afternoon, Strathairn rode his handsome black stallion, Hercules, to the park, wishing he could explain to Sibella how Nesbit's death had affected him. That he hadn't been himself.

The late afternoon sun warmed his back as he approached the park where the *Beau monde* were out in force, driving their carriages along the South Carriage Drive and riding their horses in Rotten Row.

Two women in a brougham laughed and flirted with him from beneath their lacy parasols as they waited to enter the park in the queue of traffic. Both pretty women, he admired their lavender and yellow carriage gowns and their bonnets trimmed with flowers. He pulled his horse up alongside and doffed his hat. "Good afternoon, Lady Bakewell, Mrs. Andrews. You both are the personification of summer."

"Thank you, Lord Strathairn, we were discussing how well you look," said Lady Bakewell, the elder of the two. "I must say, you have the finest seat on a horse I've seen for many a long year."

Mrs. Andrews put her gloved hand to her mouth, unsuccessfully hiding her grin, as Strathairn bowed in the saddle and rode on.

A gallop was frowned on in the Row. Some riders cantered, others ambled along at a trot while in conversation with their companions. Strathairn greeted several acquaintances as he searched for Sibella, but he failed to find her among the crowd. She always rode on Wednesdays. Where was she? He suffered an annoying, disappointed jolt.

He rode the length of the Row and was considering returning home when Sibella's younger brother Vaughn, appeared atop a bay. Strathairn was on friendly terms with all the Brandreth men. He rode over to greet him.

"The family's in the country." Vaughn whipped off his hat and swiped at his coal-black hair. "I'm off to Tunbridge Wells tomorrow.

It's Maria's birthday. Mother has yet to move to the dower house and will gather us all at Brandreth Park to celebrate every little thing, don't you know."

Strathairn laughed. "Please give your mother and Lady Maria my best wishes."

"I will." He scowled. "I'd invite you if I could. We'd escape the women and hunt or play billiards. Tedious business, family parties!"

"Thank you for the thought, but I'm heading north in a few days."

Vaughn sighed. "Off to Linden Hall, eh? Fine property, that."

"You must visit again as soon as we can arrange it. I'm aware of your interest in my horses."

He eyed Strathairn's horse. "I admire the Arabian Turk breed. You promised me one to equal Hercules."

Strathairn patted the horse's neck. "I've yet to find one of Hercules' equal. I do have a couple of promising foals bred from the Byerly Turk. Dark brown, but they have the same large eyes, arched neck, and high carriage of the tail."

"Sounds promising." Vaughn grinned. "Don't forget me." He gathered up the reins. "I enjoyed bagging grouse at Linden Hall last year, but you must come down to Brandreth Park this October. It's going to be a prime shoot for ducks this year. I'd best be off. Edward wrote me he has a chap picked out for Sibella. All of us are to persuade her to take the leap into matrimony. Sib's too special to remain an old maid."

Lord Vaughn rode off.

Strathairn hunched over his horse's neck. He could only agree with Vaughn, but somehow it didn't make him feel any better. He'd thought himself resigned to Sibella marrying some fellow. To watch it happen, however, was another thing entirely.

Chapter Three

When the family returned to Brandreth Court, their town-house in St James's Square, Sibella and Maria took the opportunity to view the Parthenon sculptures at the British museum before embarking on a dizzying round of social events.

They were returning home in a hackney cab when Maria grabbed her arm. "Look, there's Lord Strathairn."

"Strathairn?" Sibella's heart raced as the tall, fair-haired man crossed the road just as their cab drew up behind a town coach.

Maria opened the window. "Lord Strathairn!"

"Maria!" Sibella hissed as her cheeks began to burn. He turned his head and changed direction, coming to their carriage where they remained stopped in traffic.

With a nod, Strathairn tipped his hat. "Ladies. Have you been shopping in Regent Street?"

"Really, my lord, do you think shopping is all we women do?" Maria asked in a teasing voice.

His smiling gaze sought Sibella's. "Not at all. But I have two sisters who have made me fully aware of the importance of shopping."

Maria laughed. "We have been to the museum to view the Elgin Marbles."

"Ah. Then I apologize. What say you, Lady Sibella? Did you enjoy the museum?"

Strangely divorced from the conversation, Sibella's mind still dwelled on their last encounter. Startled, she whipped her gaze away when she discovered herself staring at his mouth, recalling the salty-sweet taste of his kiss. "It was most edifying. Such antiquities are awe-inspiring."

"Indeed. I confess I have yet to see them."

"Then you are as negligent as we are, my lord," Maria said. "Elgin brought them from Greece some time ago."

He laughed. "I have not seen you riding in Hyde Park of late, Lady Sibella."

"My mare developed shin splints and must rest."

"Your brother Vaughn tells me the family celebrated Maria's birthday at Brandreth Park."

"Yes, we've returned because Mama has persuaded the renowned pianist, Maria Szymanowska to perform at our musicale later this week." Sibella placed a hand to her cheek and felt the warmth through her York tan glove. She hoped he wasn't able to guess how his presence affected her.

The traffic cleared ahead, and their carriage jerked forward. "I trust we'll see you again soon, my lord?" Maria cast a quick glance at her. "Although we leave for York next week. Mama intends to visit our brother Bartholomew who is the vicar there."

"I'm about to travel north myself," Strathairn said.

"We plan to attend the York assembly on Saturday. I do hope you'll come. It's a remarkably dull affair." Maria stared at Sibella. "Don't you agree, Sib?"

"Yes, it certainly can be," Sibella said.

"I look forward to seeing you there," Strathairn called as the carriage moved forward. At a shout from a drayman, he dodged a wagon and ran to the pavement.

Maria turned to her. "Well!"

Sibella raised her eyebrows, attempting a casual pose. "Well, what?"

"You are in a brown study. I'm sure Strathairn was enthralled by your scintillating repartee."

"Oh, do stop, Maria."

"What on earth is the matter with you? You two generally talk for ages. Had you nothing to say to him?"

"He kissed me."

Maria's eyes changed from owlish to accusatory. "Why didn't you tell me? And when was this?"

"I'm sorry, dearest. It was of no consequence. At Lady Gladwin's ball. You remained at home that night with a sore throat, remember?"

Maria stared at her. "Of no consequence? Are you mad? Where?"

"On the lips."

Marie huffed out an annoyed sigh. "Where at Lady Gladwin's, you goose. Surely not in the ballroom."

"In the garden. We went for a stroll." She eyed her sister. "Everyone was out that evening, it was so pleasantly warm."

Maria sniggered. "Well indeed! I've long suspected his feelings for you ran deeper than he would admit to."

Sibella shook her head, heat rushing to every part of her body. "That's just it. He made light of it afterward. It was just an impulse which meant nothing to him."

"Oh. The wretch!"

She gave a choked, desperate laugh. "He doesn't want to marry me, Maria."

"Many men think they do not. They must be persuaded."

"As you persuaded Harry?"

Maria stroked her throat with a dreamy smile. "No."

"Exactly. I shan't spend my time longing for a man who doesn't want me."

Maria sighed. "Oh, Sib. I pray you will find true love as I did with Harry. I do believe you will in time."

Sibella gazed out the window barely aware of the vehicles and pedestrians in the busy street, fighting against her feelings, her throat tight, tears threatening. Annoyed, she said firmly, "A woman can fall in love more than once, I imagine."

"I don't believe I could."

"Mama has her eye on Lord Coombe," Sibella said.

"Mama has her eye on any titled, unmarried male under the age of forty-five," Maria said.

Sibella nodded. "Coombe appears respectable enough."

Maria rubbed her brow. "Perhaps you might fall in love with him? When you get to know him."

"Perhaps." If only she could forget Strathairn's kiss. As the prospect of seeing him again in York lightened her heart, she sat back, frowned, and crossed her arms. She would not yearn after him anymore.

WHILE DRESSING FOR a recital her mother was holding, the door opened, and her parent walked in.

"You may leave, Sarah," Mama said to Sibella's maid.

The girl bobbed and left the room.

Sibella turned from studying her reflection in the Cheval mirror. She fiddled with a sleeve. "Is there something you wish me to do for you, Mama?" She knew as she asked it there would only be one thing her mother wanted. St James's Square ran as well as the Swiss Long case clock in the entry hall.

"You're wearing the muslin?"

"Don't you approve?"

"Why not the white crepe with the embroidery and gold fringe?"

"It's a little too decorative for this evening, don't you think?"

"A lady should always wear what suits her best." She sat down and clasped her hands in her lap. "But that is not what I wish to discuss with you, Sibella."

Sibella took the gown from the clothes press and placed it on the bed. She eyed her mother. "Yes?"

"Is it your wish to remain a spinster and comfort me in my dotage?"

She laughed. "Oh, Mama. How dramatic you are. Of course not."

"Good. Tonight, I wish you to give Lord Coombe your full attention."

"But..."

Her mother rose and motioned with her hand to silence her. "Please make yourself agreeable to him." She stepped forward to rest a hand on Sibella's shoulder. "I gave the man you have a penchant for ample opportunity to declare himself, did I not? I even went against Chaloner's wishes because I want to see you happy."

Sibella flushed. "Strathairn and I are merely friends."

"Fiddlesticks! I have eyes in my head! He chose not to propose marriage to you. That's the end of it. You might find Lord Coombe quite acceptable if you give him a chance."

A heavy sigh escaped Sibella's lips. Her mind seemed to agree with her mother's good sense, but her heart refused to bend. "Very well. I'll try."

"Good." She touched Sibella's cheek with a soft glove. "You are more than ready to set up your own household."

THE DRAWING ROOM and dining room doors had been thrown open to enlarge the space for the evening's entertainment. A visiting Polish composer and pianist, Maria Szymanowska, was to perform several piano concert etudes and nocturnes. What her mother did to entice the woman to Brandreth House was a mystery, for her performances to date were before royalty. But nothing her mother did surprised Sibella, which made her decidedly nervous.

After fortifying themselves with champagne and an array of tasty foods, the guests took their places. Sibella sat in the back row near the door to the conservatory. Lord Coombe, immaculate in his dark evening clothes and spotless linen, chose the seat beside her. With her mother's words ringing in her ears, she greeted him with a polite smile.

"I have been looking forward to this," Coombe said. "She performs in the *stile brillant,* I believe. Everyone raves about her."

Sibella applied her fan, the air suddenly close and stuffy. "You're very fond of music, my lord?"

"Certainly, surely everyone is?"

She thought of the interminable evenings spent at home performing with her sisters. "Some more than others, perhaps." She studied his unremarkable profile, annoyed that she failed to find fault with it. If his chin receded, her mother would be concerned about his progeny. Men with weak chins lacked character, she often said. "You might enjoy attending my sister Cordelia's musical evenings. She plays the harp and her husband, Viscount Barthe, the cello."

"Indeed, I would. Do you play an instrument, Lady Sibella?"

"The pianoforte, rather badly, I'm afraid." She offered a regretful smile. "My mother says there's no excuse for it after years of excellent tutelage, but I prefer to ride and potter about in the garden."

"I see."

Did he look disappointed? She had no time to dwell on it, for Madam Szymanowska had taken her seat at the piano and a hush came over the room.

Even Coombe beside her failed to distract her from the virtuoso performance. When Madam finished the last piece and the enthusiastic clapping died away to be replaced with the buzz of conversation, she rose with the rest of the guests.

Lord Coombe held out his arm. "Would you join me in a promenade of the terrace? The rain seems to have held off."

"How pleasant." She took his arm. Where were her sisters when she needed them? Maria was in close conversation with Harry and Cordelia, and her husband stood among the guests clustered around Madam Szymanowska in rapt attention. No help in that direction. Sibella saw no way out of it.

They followed other couples outside. After being shut up in close quarters with a crowd of overly perfumed people, the night air, although hardly equal to the country, was at least reviving. Clouds hung low, hiding the moon. The braziers along the wall were a halo of light enticing moths to a fiery death.

Sibella slipped her hand from his arm and rested it on the balustrade.

"You seem a steady, thoughtful person, Lady Sibella. I admire that."

He made her sound dull. "I suppose I am," she said, with an inexplicable stab of disappointment.

"One can rely upon you never to lose your head and do something silly, or not quite the thing."

"I doubt that I would." It was clearly her downfall to be made this way. Had John kissed her to cheer her up, or horror of horrors, because he felt sorry for her?

She turned toward Lord Coombe, whose eyes were not far above hers. In the dark, he might have been anyone. He was a perfectly presentable man. If he kissed her, would it be out of pity? Or might she stir desire in him? She suffered a sudden need to find out. "Shall we stroll through the Square, my lord?"

He cleared his throat. "I believe it's about to rain."

"Yes, it does." She had to admit he was right. She placed a hand to her throat. "Let's not risk a dousing. Shall we go inside?"

She found his brown eyes unfathomable as he tucked her arm into his. "A wise decision, Lady Sibella."

Sibella found herself disappointed more by his response than her uncharacteristic impulse. Lord Coombe would not seek to steal a kiss in the moonlight as Strathairn had done. Coombe would wait until all the i's were dotted and the t's were crossed on the marriage settlement before taking such a liberty. He appeared to be a highly moral and principled person. Most women would be happy with such a man.

Why was she not most women?

WITH THE SHARP blast of a horn and a blaze of scarlet and black, a mail coach passed Strathairn's carriage at full speed, the passengers on top hanging on, their faces grim. A long night lay ahead for the poor devils. The drizzling rain obscured the road, and the lowering skies turned the day almost to night, but not dark enough for the coach lamps to be effective. Dangerous conditions for traveling. Strathairn would be glad to reach the coaching inn where he planned to stay the night.

The road had become a quagmire. The carriage hit deep ruts and rocked violently on its springs. Strathairn planted his Hessian boots on the floor to brace himself.

His thoughts returned to the gold cravat pin. The Corsican count was a Bonapartist who had never accepted defeat at Waterloo. Forney had gathered a group of conspirators together with the plan to wreak havoc and destabilize England in the hope of freeing Napoleon from his island prison. Such a plan never had a chance of success.

Strathairn rubbed his neck. Might Forney still be alive and have unfinished business in England? His pulse raced at the possibility of crossing swords with him again. Remembering Mrs. Nesbit's sad eyes geared him up, and he tasted revenge, sour on his tongue. He carried a knife in a sheath in his boot and a pair of Manton's pistols buckled into a leather bandolier on his chest, which fairly begged to deal with the count.

Strathairn rasped his hand over his chin and yawned. Might he have lost his objectivity? Had the work become too important? Once the excitement got into a man's blood, he was lost. Some agents became careless, took too many chances, and ended up dead, like Nesbit.

But all that might change soon. With Bonaparte gone, the war department had lost its relevance. There was now a hue and cry to disband military intelligence. Bow Street dealt with crime and government agents with international matters. They rarely worked together with the military.

These changes could have him out of the game whether he wished it or not. But not yet. Was it foolish to want to leave his mark? To have his work acknowledged? Then what would he do? Retire to his estate and his horses, he supposed. It seemed a lonely, aimless prospect. He indulged in the vision of Sibella strolling with friends in the long gallery at Linden Hall, her laughter filling the empty rooms with life. He stretched his legs and contemplated his muddy boots envisaging Hobson's vociferous disapproval.

Strathairn expected he would marry when this job no longer appealed. But Sibella would be long married by then. There was little point in dwelling on it. He gazed out of the window and smiled as the carriage overtook a slow cart on a hill where a faithful dog perched beside its master in the rain.

The coachman slowed the horses at the tollbooth while the groom paid the gatekeeper, and they were away again. The rain beat against the window, running down in rivulets. The Great North Road was one of the better roads on which to travel, but it, too, was potholed and too dangerous to travel by night.

Aiming to reach Biggleswade before nightfall, they made good time. The carriage reached the Crown Inn just as dusk set in. Strathairn climbed down and stretched his legs as an ostler hurried out to greet them. The proprietor who kept a room for Strathairn on a regular basis, greeted him in the warm taproom where smoke, tallow, and hops mingled with the rich aromas from the kitchen.

"Still employ the same cook, Job?" Strathairn asked.

"But of course, my lord." Job chuckled. "Now, why would I sack me own wife?"

Strathairn grinned. "Most unwise when Mary is such a fine cook." He could almost taste her admirable beef pie with its feather-light crust he'd enjoyed when last there, washed down with a tankard of ale.

Chapter Four

THE NIGHT BEFORE the family departed for York, Sibella gazed around Lord and Lady Felstead's dull soiree whilst fanning herself. Strathairn wasn't there. Nor had he appeared in Rotten Row when she hired a hack and rode that afternoon.

Georgina, Duchess of Broadstairs, approached on her husband's arm. Strathairn's pretty dark-haired younger sister was unlike him in appearance.

She dipped a brief curtsey. "Is your son well, your Grace?"

The lady's dark eyes danced. "Bonny, thank you, Lady Sibella. He is fair and has blue eyes like his Uncle John."

"Lord Strathairn does not attend this evening?" Sibella tried hard to sound indifferent and not let her disappointment show.

"No, he visits his Yorkshire estate."

"Come, my dear, we must take our place for the cotillion." Broadstairs bowed and drew his wife away.

So, Strathairn had gone north without suffering the need to speak to her. She'd hoped an apology for the kiss might be forthcoming. He had not appeared at all apologetic at the time, so why expect more from him since? He probably kissed women all the time, at every given opportunity. And she'd certainly given him an opportunity, gazing at him like a fool in the moonlight. She would not do so again.

Sibella's feelings for Lord Coombe warmed as he escorted her onto the floor for the dance. Unlike Strathairn, Coombe had attended every social engagement her mother had dragged her to. And here he was now dancing attendance on her.

They took their places as part of the square and the musicians began to play. Coombe bowed. Why did he always look so solemn? Though she tried in earnest to enjoy herself, she remained awkward in his company.

"Do you like to dance, my lord?" she asked, when they came together.

"I like to perform it well. I trust that I do?"

"Indeed you do." She eyed him demurely. "You've never stepped on my toes once."

He rewarded her with a faint smile, but the lack of flirtatiousness in his nature bothered her. A reserved man it seemed. Might the real Coombe emerge when they became more familiar with each other?

When the dance ended, Coombe politely left her with her sister.

Maria sipped a glass of lemonade. "I am parched!" She gestured with her glass. "Look! Sir Horace Leister is now courting Anne Talbot. Poor Anne. Remember when Sir Horace was a suitor of yours?"

"How could I forget?" Some of her suitors had recently retired. Sibella could only feel grateful.

"Every time Sir Horace revealed a wish for a private audience with you, Aida, Cordelia and I found ways to distract him." Maria giggled. "It was funny at the time. Fortunately, he was easily distracted. Luckily, Mama didn't like him either."

"No, thank heavens."

"An awful prospect." Maria whispered behind her fan. "Black dye applied to his hair doesn't make Leister appear younger." She gave a peal of laughter. "I do believe I heard him creak and suspect he wears a corset."

Sibella spread her fan to hide a grin.

Maria slid her a sidelong glance. "I don't see Strathairn here this evening."

Sibella fluttered her fan before her face. "His sister tells me he has gone to Yorkshire."

"So I gathered." Maria's green eyes probed hers. "A good thing, for it gives you time to deal with your feelings for Lord Coombe. He certainly appears to be an ardent suitor, does he not?"

"It would seem so." How she wished Maria wouldn't carry on so, but her sister was uneasy about her.

"Mama was extolling his virtues to Chaloner."

Sibella sucked in a breath. "Was she?"

"It surprises me, somewhat," Maria mused. "Coombe seems quite staid, doesn't he? Mama had a proclivity for rogues when she was young. I believe she almost married one."

Sibella blinked. "I wasn't aware of that."

"Before she met Father, of course."

Thankful for the change in subject, Sibella laughed. "Who told you that?"

"Edward. In an unusual burst of loquacity. I suspect he was in his cups." Maria giggled. "And that's not all I managed to get from him. Father wooed a famous actress in his youth."

"Pish, where would Edward have learned such a thing?"

"Opera dancers and the like are sought by unmarried men, are they not? Not to marry, however. Oh there's Harry." Maria motioned to her fiancé with her fan.

"Don't wave in that fashion, Maria. You look like a hawker at a fish market."

"Harry has seen us."

Harry approached with a special smile for his fiancée. "Why are the two prettiest ladies in the room sitting alone?"

"This one is waiting for you to dance with her, Harry." Maria put down her glass and rose to tuck her hand in his arm.

Harry bowed in Sibella's direction before he led Maria onto the dance floor to take their places for the quadrille.

Sibella gazed after them fondly. They were so much in love. It did her heart good to see them together.

Edward emerged from the throng to join her. "Not dancing, Sib?"

"I complained of fatigue. Coombe understood."

Edward gave a derisive snort. "He looked dashed annoyed when I saw him." Edward took the seat beside her and beckoned to a waiter. "And you weren't too fatigued to ride in the park earlier."

"I wasn't then."

"Looked like you were searching for someone."

"You are a tease, Edward."

"Not Strathairn, I hope? You have taken heed of my warning?"

"Stop fishing."

Edward laughed. Then he sobered, dark brows beetling over a pair of green eyes like those she saw in the mirror. He crossed one leg over the other and considered one of his black evening pumps. "Might you have seen Vaughn of late?"

"Not since we came back to London, why?"

"Nothing important. I just wondered."

"Edward, don't think you can drop this in my lap and then discount it as nothing." She tapped his arm with her fan. "What concerns you?"

"It's just that I know what a mother hen you are with all of us."

She gave an impatient shake of her head. "This concerns Vaughn?"

"I discovered him at Watier's, Byron's dandy club, a few nights ago. He was in his cups and betting heavily."

She fanned herself. "Oh. I see."

"That club is no place for Vaughn. Reckless all-night gambling goes on. He is too wild. Needs a strong hand, or he's going to get into trouble."

"Vaughn can only lose his allowance. And it wouldn't be the first time."

"He might be tempted to borrow from a money-lender."

She bit her lip and nodded slowly. "Cannot Chaloner speak to him?"

"Our brother is busy with his estates and bills before the Lords. And Lavinia runs to him with every little thing. You know how he's been lately. He only half listens when you speak to him."

"I'm very fond of Chaloner's wife. That's not fair, Edward. Chaloner takes his position as head of the family very seriously. How can you judge what he'll do about Vaughn unless you ask him?"

"All right. I will." He grinned. "Lord Coombe approaches with a glass of Madeira for you. Don't you hate that drink?"

She groaned inwardly and rewarded Lord Coombe's attentiveness with a nod and a smile while addressing her brother *sotto voce*. "Will you visit Vaughn at his rooms at Albany tomorrow?"

"Yes. I plan to."

Relieved, she gave her brother a speaking glance. "Please let me know how he fares."

Edward inclined his dark head. "Are you enjoying the evening, Coombe?"

"I am." Lord Coombe held out his offering as if it was a chalice encrusted with jewels. "An excellent affair."

DRAWN BY FRESH horses, Strathairn's carriage departed Biggleswade after breakfast. He was an impatient traveler and tapped his fingers on the window ledge as the carriage swayed on its inferior springs along the rutted roads. He disliked being enclosed within the confines of a vehicle, and this hackney coach was a less than sterling one at that. His own having a broken wheel.

Some hours later, after stopping again to change horses, they crossed the Wetherby Bridge over the River Wharfe with hours of daylight remaining. Wetherby nestled in a bend in the river. It was good to be home.

Strathairn put down the window. A hint of the dank river carried on the breeze, blended with the aroma of baked goods and meat. Thursday was market day when farmers traded produce in the shops known as The Shambles.

A long-forgotten memory from the history of his discordant relationship with his father rose from somewhere, clear as if it was yesterday. On occasion, as a child, he'd slip away from his tutor and go to market with his father's servants as they traded the estates vegetables for other goods. Once he'd been right next to a pickpocket in the crowd when a red-faced man turned to find his pocket watch missing. Strathairn had been accused, held by the ear and searched until his father's bailiff appeared and explained he was the earl's son. His father got wind of it and had taken the stick to him for evading his tutor. Although he wasn't able to sit down for a week, the lesson hadn't been learned, for it wasn't long before he did something else to cause his father's ire. There was a pattern there, he thought ruefully.

Carts unloading their wares in the high street held up the carriage. Villagers came to his carriage window to welcome him and advise him of the local news until the carriage moved on.

Once free of the town, the horses fell into a fast trot as if sensing they neared home. The gray stone houses left behind, Strathairn watched fields stretch away dotted with sheep and cows, in a lush green landscape. In the distance, the rolling countryside changed to purple moor grass, limestone, and the dark bulk of the Pennines.

The coachman drove through the gates of Linden Hall and entered the park along the road lined with chestnut trees. The carriage stopped on the sweep in front of the columned portico of the majestic house, the westerly sun warming the York stone.

In the great hall, Strathairn's steward, Peters, hurried forward with a smile of welcome. "Good to see you, my lord."

Strathairn shed his coat, hat, and gloves into a maid's hands. "Unfortunately, it's a short stay this time."

A skeleton staff remained in the house all year around, for he came here whenever he could, regardless of the time of year. Once the London season ended, the Mayfair townhouse would have the knocker taken from the door, while the staff repaired to Yorkshire. Strathairn put up at Grillion's Hotel if he had to return to the city.

"Shall you be here for dinner, my lord?"

"Yes. I'll dine at six."

Strathairn called for his bailiff and ascended to his bedchamber. As he walked the long corridor, he yanked at his cravat, eager to change into riding clothes after being confined for hours in the coach. His footsteps echoed across the parquetry floors. He'd expected the restlessness he suffered to leave him here in Yorkshire. His estate had never failed to lift his spirits before. How often had he come here, wounded mentally and physically, and been made whole?

In his riding clothes, Strathairn walked to the stable mews, keen to see his horses. His two hounds, Jasper and Rosy, greeted him with joyful barks, calling for him to admire their new litter. In the stables, he knelt to stroke their silky fur and offer his approval of the sleek, plump puppies. An inspection of his horses along the row of horse boxes followed. "That muscle problem has gone?" he inquired of his head groom, while patting the dark neck of one of his favorite mares.

"Yes, milord. Healed up well," Joseph assured him.

Strathairn mounted Ulysses and rode out over his lands. He urged the horse into a canter and then a gallop, the breeze whipping his face. The cold rush of country air perfumed with summer grasses and damp soil helped to banish the grim reality of his friend's death. Confident in his horse's ability, he took fence after fence, exhilaration imbuing him with new energy. When they both tired, he walked the horse back to the stables. Leggy foals gamboled in the verdant paddocks. Was there anywhere on earth better than Yorkshire?

Back at the house, he spoke with his housekeeper, gamekeeper, and bailiff. Several hours passed before he'd finished attending to business. Alone again, he looked forward to a decent dinner, but the night stretched before him. He was sick of his own company. Even the idea of attending a dull assembly Saturday next, where he would be called upon to do his duty by the young debutants appealed, especially with the opportunity of dancing with Sibella.

Damn. It was going to be a *very* long night.

He stood and walked to the window. A distraction was what he needed. Perhaps he might seek out his neighbor, James Kent. He might be available for a game of chess.

The next day dawned gray beneath a lowering sky. Strathairn breakfasted late having enjoyed his neighbors company into the wee hours. It was past noon when he rode into York, the ancient city of

Roman walls and dark narrow streets.

The magistrate informed him that a Frenchman caused some disruption in Manchester, stirring up the people who were already disturbed by the Corn Laws.

"He encouraged workers to drill with staves with the obvious intent to cause an uprising. The situation is combustible. Orator Hunt is agitating for change and the people are suffering because of the high cost of bread."

After finishing with the York magistrate, Mr. Pugh, Strathairn spoke to one of his informers. "Do you think this Frenchman's still in the town?"

"We don't know, my lord." The shabbily dressed man shifted his feet and lowered his head. "We followed 'im to York, but then we lost 'im."

"Describe him." Strathairn said.

The fellow, one of Sidmouth's spies, undernourished and dull-eyed, shrugged. "Big chap."

"Big? You mean tall?" Forney was tall, but slightly built.

The man nodded. "Huge, the shoulders on him!" He gestured with his hands to a width that Strathairn doubted even Gentleman Jackson could claim.

Whoever the fellow was, he was not Count Forney. Despite this knowledge, Strathairn joined the constable to make a reconnaissance of the poorer guesthouses, hotels, and alehouses. They found no trace of the Frenchman.

"He's likely moved on, my lord," the constable said. "Nothing much to keep him here."

Strathairn dismissed the episode as unrelated to his present concerns and returned to Linden Hall.

At the end of a slow week spent visiting his tenant farmers, Strathairn drove back to York in the evening for the assembly.

Noise floated out from the Assembly Rooms along with the music. The rooms crammed with people. Those prepared to pay the yearly subscription, from farmers to the gentry and a sprinkling of the *ton*, gathered to dance in the ballroom, enjoy the card play, and the supper.

Strathairn entered the ballroom where dancers departed the dance floor, having just performed a Scottish reel. His gaze drifted over the ladies in search of Sibella. He found her with Maria and made his way over to the dowager marchioness. He bowed. "Lady Brandreth."

"Lord Strathairn." Since he'd reached adulthood, the dowager was the only person who could make him feel like an awkward lad in short trousers with one look. "I had not expected to see you at a York assembly." Her ladyship's green eyes drilled into him.

"Seeking an antidote to boredom, my lady."

"It is evident why you have come. It is to see my daughter." Her green eyes narrowed. "I like you Strathairn, always have. But it would be better for you to make yourself scarce where my daughter is concerned."

"Then after tonight, I shall heed your advice." He bowed.

The two sisters came to join them. "Lady Sibella, Lady Maria."

A high color spread across Sibella's cheeks. He cursed under his breath. Usually so composed, it was obvious his kiss had unsettled her. "May I claim the next waltz, Lady Sibella?"

"Certainly, my lord."

When the master of ceremonies announced it, Strathairn took her in his arms and they joined the swirling dancers. "I would hate you to think I don't value our friendship," he said.

"Heavens, are you concerned about our last meeting? I pray you treat what happened between us as meaningless. As I do." The look in Sibella's eyes darkened before she turned away to nod at a friend.

His gaze wandered to the tendrils of ebony hair curling on her swan-like neck. He drew in a breath. "You sound so formal. I suspect you have not forgiven me."

Her eyes sought his with a frank expression. "I have, now that I know the truth of it."

He raised his eyebrows. "The truth?"

She tilted her head up at him. "You believe your work precludes you from marriage."

So, Edward or Chaloner had told her. He should feel relieved. Instead, the hollow in his chest seemed to deepen. "You understand then."

"I don't understand, my lord. I merely know the reason behind your motives."

"Dash it all, Sibella!" A woman dancing past frowned at him. "I wish we might go somewhere where I can explain it more fully."

"We certainly cannot do that, my lord," Sibella said coolly. "And I don't see the necessity for it. You have stated your case. I have accepted it. Nothing has changed between us. Unless we are to become kissing friends?"

He huffed out a laugh. The prospect was most tempting, but of course, she didn't mean it. He couldn't tamp down the pleasure of holding her light in his arms. Her dainty pastel pink dress with its froth of lace around the sleeves and hem reminded him of a dessert made by Marie-Antoine Carême. "I wish to hear you say you forgive my rash action," he said in a low voice, aware that his hand at her waist had tightened.

She raised her face to him. "I do." She sobered. "Of course I do. I just wish…"

He gazed down on her lovely face, concern ruffling her brow. "Wish what?"

"That you would stop."

He had nothing to say to that. He couldn't. Not while this dangerous affair required his attention.

The dance ended, and couples walked from the floor. He offered her his arm and escorted her back to her chair. Their conversation had reached an end. It left him strangely dissatisfied. It was pointless to talk further on this, but still, he would have liked to remain in her company. To laugh and discuss other matters. He wanted to tell her about his foals and the new litter of puppies, to make her laugh and set her mind at rest. To return to the comfortable friendship they'd shared.

A half hour later, the master of ceremonies, a rotund officious fellow, ushered a very young woman with the startled eyes of a young deer toward him. "I'd like to introduce Miss Gudge, my lord. You'll be delighted to dance with so pleasing a young lady, embarking on her first season. You shall lead the dance!"

"Charmed." He bowed over the girl's trembling hand and gave her a reassuring smile as the fiddlers took their places in the musician's gallery. He glanced over at Sibella who was taking the floor on the arm of some callow youth. He would not be able to dance with her again nor seek her company without her mother scowling at him. Here in Yorkshire where his countryseat resided, his behavior came under more scrutiny than in London, and gossip bearing their names would spread like wildfire.

At eleven o'clock, the crowd dispersed. Lady Brandreth left in her son, Bartholomew's carriage as Strathairn assisted Sibella and Maria into theirs.

After saying their goodbyes, he walked down the dark road toward his curricle. He dropped a glove onto the cobbles and bent to pick it up as a gunshot ricocheted around the street. It was followed by the sound of footsteps running away down the alley.

Strathairn ran back to where Sibella stood. Her carriage had stopped, and she'd climbed down onto the road.

"Go home! I'll call on you tomorrow."

She nodded, her face chalk-white in the moonlight. He ushered her inside where Maria was entreating her to take care.

Thankfully, the order was given, and the carriage rumbled away down the street.

Strathairn ran to his curricle where Joseph slumped on the ground. He huffed out a sigh of relief to find him unconscious, but alive.

He grabbed the gun he kept in the carriage and, aware it was useless, went after the shooter. He paused to listen at the mouth of the narrow alley. There was no sound bar the yowl of cats. Nothing moved. Pools of impenetrable shadows, where the moonlight and candlelight from the windows above failed to reach, could hide an assassin. Too dangerous to continue, but he was sure the gunman had got clean away.

Strathairn hefted his groom into his arms and placed him in the curricle. Then he clambered up onto the seat and untied the reins. Once York lay behind them, it remained an uneasy trip home with the young man sprawled semi-conscious beside him. Strathairn kept an eye on the road but no one followed. The fact that they knew where to find him made him growl in frustration. He didn't like dealing with an invisible enemy. He preferred to confront them face to face.

The next morning, he was able to question Joseph, who had little more than a sore head. He was of little help. The scoundrel had crept up behind him as he held the horses and watched for Strathairn.

Strathairn rode Ulysses back to York to inform Mr. Pugh. He continued to the presbytery where Sibella stayed with her brother. He found the family in a flurry of activity, planning to return to London. Sibella, Maria, and Bartholomew's wife, Emily, were in the parlor, the dowager busy upstairs with her maid.

"You must forgive me, Lord Strathairn, the ladies will have arrived with the flowers for the church," Emily said.

"And they are all in love with Bart," Maria said with a giggle after their sister-in-law left the room.

Strathairn grinned. Their brother Bartholomew's appearance could be an inconvenience for a vicar.

"That was a pistol shot we heard last night, wasn't it?" Maria said. "Did you discover who was behind it?"

Strathairn shook his head. "No, some young buck, no doubt, shooting at rats."

Sibella brows were drawn in a puzzled frown. "I saw you ride past on Ulysses. I should like to see him. Shall we take a walk to the stables before we have our tea?"

Strathairn rose. "But of course." He offered his arm. "Lady Maria?"

Maria waved her hand. "I shan't come. I have no great fondness for horses."

As they strolled along the drive, he glanced at Sibella's serious profile. "You leave York tomorrow?"

"I believe my mother is half gypsy," Sibella said. "I shall almost be glad when she settles into her dotage in the dower house."

"That's not likely to be soon. Your mother is still filled with youthful fire." He thought of her fiery gaze on him the previous evening and had a feeling she was watching from an upstairs window.

Sibella turned to face him, her concerned gaze seeking his. "Are you going to tell me the truth about last night?"

He shrugged. "Someone shooting off a pistol. As I said."

She searched his eyes. "You won't tell me then."

"I don't know who it was, Sibella."

She shook her head and fell silent.

They reached the stable where his big, chocolate-brown horse enjoyed a feed of oats. Sibella patted the stallion's nose. "Oh, he is a true beauty."

"Yes. Ulysses is going to be one of my greatest successes." He leaned against the stall, enjoying looking at her in her green and white spotted dress. "So, we are friends again?"

She smiled. "We were ever friends. It shall always be so."

Was he a fool to hope that their friendship would continue? With the knowledge of how precarious his life had become, he felt reckless in the warmth of the stables with the horses shuffling in their stalls. He disliked the distance that stood between them, and would far prefer to pull her down onto the straw and… "We'd best return to the house," he said abruptly.

After casting him a careful glance, Sibella followed him out into the daylight.

As they sat taking tea, the dowager entered the room. She greeted Strathairn with a brisk nod.

"Have you written to Lord Coombe, Sibella?"

Sibella looked startled. "No, Mama."

Lady Brandreth drew her shawl around her shoulders and aimed a pointed glance at Strathairn. "I'm sure he is keenly awaiting your return to London."

Bartholomew, their tall, dark-haired brother, entered the room and the conversation turned to more light-hearted mundane matters.

As soon as was polite, Strathairn took his leave.

SIBELLA STOOD AT the window watching a hawker selling oranges below in St James's Square.

"I can't understand why Strathairn doesn't propose, Sib," Maria said as she brushed her hair before the mirror. "The way he looks at you shows he cares very deeply for you."

"Perhaps he looks at many women that way."

"I've never seen him do so. In fact," Maria paused. "I've never seen him show any interest in another woman."

Sibella drew in a breath as a quiver of sadness passed through her and turned away from the window. "Perhaps he prefers the ladies of the opera."

"Or has a *chère-amie*," Maria said as if she was a great authority on the subject. She shook her head. "No, I don't believe that. Might his heart have been broken?"

"It's possible, dearest." Sibella almost wished it were true. That was something she could fight.

"I don't believe that either. He loves you, Sib. I'm sure of it," Maria said in a tragic tone.

Sibella hated to keep the truth from her sister. She took the brush from Maria's hand and began to brush her long black hair. "He's fond of me, I think. But I can't force the man to marry me, now can I?"

When they settled in the drawing room later in the afternoon, the door opened and their youngest brother, Vaughn, walked in. "Vaughn!" Both his sisters jumped up to kiss him.

Maria hurried away to tell their mother after Vaughn collapsed on the sofa beside Sibella. She studied him as she put a stitch in her embroidery. At one-and-twenty, and the youngest male in the family, he was indulged, rootless, and restless. Right now, he looked haggard. "Are you going to tell me what worries you?" she asked. "Can't you pay your rent at Albany?"

"Don't you start, Sib. I've been harassed by Edward and Chaloner until I'm numb. Chaloner disapproves of my friends."

"Might he have reason to disapprove of them?"

He shrugged. "They are young bucks, a bit wild at times."

"You agree with Chaloner then? Won't you heed his advice?"

He unwound his long limbs and climbed to his feet to stalk the carpet, swiping at his thatch of black hair. "Advice? That depends on how you look at it. Have I seen the error of my ways? I expect so." He returned to stand before her. "Don't worry so much, Sib."

Sibella sighed. "Have you given any more thought to a commission in the army, Vaughn? The light cavalry, wasn't it? Edward is in the law, Bart in the church. You must find something to do. The devil makes trouble for idle younger sons."

"I sought Strathairn's opinion about the army. They have reduced the size of the army because we are not at war. Who wants to toil for half rations?"

"Yes, but surely when Chaloner buys your colors—"

"An officer does better, I know." He fell back in a sulk on the sofa. "I wouldn't wager a groat on me ending up in the army. In fact, nothing appeals to me."

"In a year or two you might marry, but until then, you should find something to occupy you which does not involve gaming."

His green eyes widened. "Do you mean court an heiress? I never expected you to urge me to do that, Sib."

"I didn't. I'm merely making suggestions." She tamped down her annoyance at his freedom to decide, a luxury not afforded to her.

"Well, they are most unhelpful."

At the sound of the front door knocker, Sibella tucked away the handkerchief she embroidered in a silk bag with relief.

"Are you at home to Lord Coombe, Lady Sibella?"

She hesitated. She could find little reason to refuse him. "Yes, Belton." She rose and smoothed her skirts as Henry Coombe walked into the room. "How nice of you to call, my lord."

Coombe bowed first to her, then Vaughn. "We are fortunate to have a perfect summer day, Lady Sibella, and I hoped to persuade you to enjoy a carriage ride."

If only an afternoon in his company appealed to her more. Despite her disinclination, she had promised Chaloner she would try. Besides, she'd accepted that Strathairn was lost to her and refused to pine.

"What an excellent suggestion." She glanced back at her brother, who had returned to his seat, frowning in contemplation, his thumbs tucked into his waistcoat. "Why not join us, Vaughn?"

Vaughn leapt to his feet. "Ah, no thank you, I just remembered something important I must do. Your servant, Coombe." He bowed and left the room.

"Well," Sibella said. "Where shall we go?"

"I thought we might drive to Richmond for luncheon. I had a picnic basket prepared, which awaits us in the landau."

"Only fancy, Maria was saying yesterday that she hadn't been to Richmond in an age. I shall go and ask her."

Lord Coombe inclined his head, his face thoughtful. Was he disappointed because they were not alone? Or didn't it make the slightest difference? Sibella went in search of Maria. Whether she liked it or not, Maria was coming to Richmond.

Chapter Five

ONCE THEY WERE settled in the park, Maria wandered away to seek the shade of a copse of trees. A footman poured wine into crystal glasses. Sibella took the proffered glass and sipped the cold liquid while she watched her sister pick wildflowers. A warm breeze fanned the damp curls beneath her bonnet, offering little relief. The weather was too hot to be pleasant.

Clearly determined that nothing was to ruin his picnic, Lord Coombe tempted her with all manner of treats from the well-filled basket, from scotch eggs to ham pie and fresh strawberries. The blazing sun had turned the landscape colorless and parched. Even the ducks left the water and tucked their heads beneath their wings. Hot air gathered beneath the umbrella the footman held over them. When the umbrella's shadow wobbled, she glanced up. The poor man's face was puce, and a river of sweat ran down his cheeks.

"Are you, all right?"

"Yes, my lady," he said swallowing loudly.

"Give me the umbrella and sit in the shade." She poured out a tumbler of water and held it up to him.

"Gather yourself together quickly, man," Coombe said roughly. "I expect you to do your job."

The footman who was very fair skinned, staggered into the shade and drank the water before hurrying back again.

Sibella could do little but return the umbrella to him, with a glance at Coombe who seemed to have lost interest.

Not always so agreeable then. Coombe's enthusiasm had driven her to taste everything put before her, when she'd preferred to rest rather than eat. Slightly ill, she wondered when they might leave.

He leaned closer to dab with his napkin at the droplets threatening to spill from her glass. His lips parted as if to speak, then he closed his mouth and pulled away.

"Maria, come and drink wine with us," Sibella called.

He glanced up at her. "May I ask you a question, Lady Sibella?"

She swallowed and nodded politely as dread curdled her stomach.

"Do you wish to marry?"

"Yes, of course."

"And children? You must want a family." He flicked a crumb from his cuff. She failed to find fault with the way he dressed, immaculate as always in a drab coat and brown breeches, his red hair carefully arranged.

She couldn't imagine his hair ruffled as it must be when he first woke. She took a large gulp of wine and broke into a fit of coughing. Croaking out an affirmative, she turned to her sister who took her time returning.

"I confess, I do wonder why you're unmarried," he said. "I'm sure many have sought your hand."

"How flattering, my lord," she murmured.

Maria finally strolled toward them, ending their conversation. Relieved, Sibella smiled up at her as she took a glass of wine from the footman.

"Really, it is far too hot to be out, don't you think?" Maria asked, showing a remarkable absence of guile, for which Sibella could have kissed her.

When Lord Coombe escorted them back to the carriage, his piqued expression left no doubt as to his dissatisfaction with how the day had gone. Sibella couldn't really blame him. He had planned this picnic to please her. She sat beside Maria who was fanning herself furiously. As the carriage crossed the Thames on its way to London, Sibella recalled their conversation. It appeared he was intent on asking for her hand. And would do so soon. She was no longer an *ingénue.* Ballrooms were filled with fresh young faces each season. She yearned to hold a baby of her own in her arms and had to face the fact that her chances of that grew less with each passing year. Would marriage to a man she didn't love, who could give her a child, make up for everything else?

STRATHAIRN HAD NOT long returned to Grosvenor Square when Baron Fortescue was announced. Guy's face was lightly tanned from spending time out of doors. He smiled as he shook Strathairn's hand.

"Country life seems to agree with you," Strathairn said, surprised to find himself a little envious.

"I plan to be more often in London next year when I take my seat in the House of Lords, now that matters at Rosecliff Hall are in better shape." His dark brows snapped together. "You mentioned Forney in your letter. I thought he was feeding the fishes."

He filled Guy in on what had happened the night Nesbit was killed and how an anonymous note had brought them to the dock.

"He and his cohorts had those gold cravat pins specially made," Guy said. "There is definitely some connection although it may not be Forney himself."

"Except that they were all rounded up and hung."

Guy shrugged in his Gallic fashion. "Might there now be others who have taken up Forney's cause?"

"Possibly, someone took a shot at me in York."

"*Tiens!* If it is Forney, why return to England? It's too dangerous for him here."

"Parnham believes Forney and his cohorts consider the time ripe for revolution. It would serve them well to see upheaval in England. Revenge could drive them."

"After all this time?"

"Revenge is a dish best served cold, is it not? To be on the safe side, you should take precautions."

Guy clenched his jaw, the muscles jumping in his cheek. "I don't care for myself, but I have a family now."

"Where is baby John tonight?"

"At my house in Mayfair with his nurse."

"Would you like me to assign a man to watch the house?"

Guy huffed out a sigh of relief. "*Merci.* It would ease my mind. I can't always be there."

"Are you returning to Rosecroft Hall soon?"

Guy's nostrils flared. "No, my friend. I intend to join you in your search for Forney."

"I welcome your company, but your wife may not wish you to become involved again."

"Ah, yes, Hetty," Guy said thoughtfully. "I shall have to be very creative, no?"

"BRANDRETH WISHES TO talk to you, Sibella." Her mother eyed her cautiously. "You'll find him in his study."

A flicker of apprehension coursed through her. "What does Chaloner want, Mama?"

"Go and find out, child."

Her mother knew, and she did, too, unfortunately. Sibella made her way to her brother's study. Whatever he wished to tell her would be significant. Chaloner found less time for idle conversation of late.

When she entered, he glanced up from his satinwood desk loaded with papers. "Ah, there you are. You may go, Pettigrew."

His secretary nodded to her as he left the room.

"Come and sit down, Sib. I hardly see you these days." He bent his dark head over a document.

That was not her fault. She settled on the ornate satinwood chair and waited.

Minutes passed before he cast the paper down and leaned back to study her. "I've just received the best news."

She widened her eyes. "You have?"

"Lord Coombe has requested permission to ask for your hand."

"Oh." She sucked in a deep breath, sure her heart missed several beats.

"You don't look pleased."

"I'm not ready, Chaloner."

"Not ready? At six-and-twenty? At what age do you think you might be?" He rubbed a bloodshot eye and glowered at her. "Childbearing age one would hope."

She scowled back at him. "You chose your bride, did you not?"

"Dash it all, Sib! You might have done, and indeed, I have waited for you to do so. You've given the *congé* to every suitor who pursued you."

Sibella chewed her bottom lip and fought the urge to cry. She stiffened her spine and leaned forward. "I'm not going to marry a man I don't know."

"You'll get to know him better once you're engaged. Spend more time with him, even alone. Briefly, of course," he amended hastily.

"I don't want to spend time alone with him!" Sibella jumped to her feet to tread a path over the Turkey carpet to the window. A carriage rattled past in St James's Square. "I can't explain exactly why, but I feel little fondness for him and I certainly don't love him."

"Love? You'll need to do better than that," Chaloner said. "Lord Coombe is an excellent match for you. Your first season was years ago. This might be your last opportunity to marry well."

She came back to the desk, clutching her hands in front of her. "There's something about him. I feel a little apprehensive in his company."

"He hasn't been rude to you? Not too forward one would hope."

Remembering John's kiss in the garden, she huffed in a breath. "Certainly not."

Chaloner seized a pen, testing the nib on the paper in front of him. "What then?"

"It's…just a sense I have. I doubt he's a kind man."

"He's unkind?" Chaloner shook his head. "What has he done to make you think this?"

"Nothing exactly. It's just a feeling."

"I can hardly explain that to Lord Coombe, can I? I don't understand it myself. You're being too dramatic." He smoothed his hair back with a hand, a gesture that reminded her of Vaughn, but Chaloner's hair had whitened at the temples. She suffered a sudden fondness coupled with pity for him. He carried the whole family on his shoulders as well as everything else a marquess of considerable fortune must do. No wonder he looked tired. "It's not as though he's never married," Chaloner continued. "His wife died before she provided him with an heir."

"I know that," Sibella said. "But beyond a certain sympathy, I can't make myself care."

Chaloner tapped the end of his pen again with a heavy sigh. "Rather than turn the fellow down flat, how about I put him off for a month? In the meantime, spend time with him. I'm sure you'll find that he's not an ogre but quite a decent chap who will make a good husband. Is that reasonable?"

"You're a dear, Chaloner." With any luck, Coombe may seek another bride in the interim. Hot with relief, she rushed to give her elder brother a warm hug.

He looked surprised and pleased. "I'll write to him today."

Sibella walked to the door.

"But he may decide to look for a bride elsewhere," Chaloner called after her. "Are you prepared to lose your chance to marry a man of your equal in fortune? Of reasonable age and in good health?"

"And with all his teeth?" She laughed at Chaloner's grimace. "I will chance it, dear brother."

Sibella left the room feeling a good deal lighter. Her mother's maid waited for her around a corner of the passage. "Your mother would like to see you in her bedchamber, Lady Sibella."

"Thank you, Plumley." Sibella eased her tight shoulders. This really wasn't her day. No doubt her mother would be impatient with her, but she would still defer to Chaloner.

Sibella's relief dissolved two days later when Lord Coombe apparently undeterred by Chaloner's letter, called to invite her to the opera. Aware of her promise to her brother, she accepted. Her music-obsessed sister Cordelia and her husband, Roland, were more than happy to accompany them. Settled comfortably in Lord Coombe's box at the Theatre Royal in Covent Garden, Sibella enjoyed the first act of *The Marriage of Figaro*. It was amusing, and the audience revered Mozart as she did and were reasonably well behaved, most remaining in their seats.

The soprano was both beautiful and in excellent voice. Sibella almost forgot Coombe beside her. She watched through opera glasses as the swelling *aria* lifted her spirits. When it was over, a glance at his serious face reminded her of his sad lack of humor. She should, she supposed, admire his dogged determination. Perhaps it was just that he was not Strathairn. But then, no one was.

While at interval, Cordelia and Roland talked to friends, Lord Coombe brought her coffee. As she sipped the tepid brew, he leaned close. "I received your brother's letter," he said. "I understand you require more time before we might announce our engagement."

The cup rattled in the saucer. "*Oh*. Yes, I'm relieved you understand, Lord Coombe."

"I've come to the opinion that you're a woman of finer feelings, Lady Sibella. And I plan to devise many pleasant outings on which you can grow in confidence as to my impeccable conduct and manners."

"I have no doubt your manners are exemplary, Lord Coombe," Sibella said. "I worry that our natures may not suit."

He raised an eyebrow. "You dislike something about me?"

"No…it's not that at all."

"Then what?"

"I'm…not in love with you."

He sighed with evident relief. "Many successful marriages are not love matches. Most, of our class, I would say."

"I believe love is essential for a happy marriage."

"You are a romantic," he said. "I'm surprised but not deterred by that."

Sibella almost sighed with frustration. "Surprised, my lord?"

"I would expect to find such feelings in a green girl, not a mature lady. Do not despair; such a notion does not deter me."

"No, my lord?"

He patted her hand encased in its white glove. "I rise to a challenge."

A challenge? "I'm not sure what you mean."

His gaze shifted away from her. "I plan to win you, Lady Sibella. Make no mistake about it."

Sibella sucked in an annoyed breath. She couldn't understand this man at all. Greatly relieved, she greeted Cordelia and Roland when they entered the box.

At breakfast the next morning, Sibella told Maria about her conversation with Coombes.

Maria paused in the act of taking a bite of toast. "Coombe said exactly that?"

"Yes. Exactly."

"Well that's good isn't it, dearest? It means he loves you passionately."

She eyed Maria uneasily. "You think so? I can't believe it. He seems so…forced." If Coombe was passionate, he'd hidden it well until now. And he'd made no mention of being in love with her. In fact, she doubted he was. He was exceedingly polite. But she'd begun to suspect he was a bit of an actor. What lay behind it, shyness?

Maria shrugged. "What else could he mean?"

"Am I being unfair, Maria?"

Maria shook her head violently. "You are never unfair, dearest. Never."

Sibella held a hand to her breast. "Then why do I feel this way?"

"Have you no inkling?" Maria sighed. "You simply must find a way to get Strathairn out of your system once and for all."

Frustrated, Sibella prodded a kipper then laid down her fork. "A comment of Edward's did make me think."

"Oh? What did he say?"

Sibella had never turned from a fight in her life. Why be a wimp now when it mattered more than anything in her life? She pushed back her chair and rose, crossing the room with a determined tread. She needed to rethink her wardrobe. "I'll tell you later."

"You are *so* annoying," Maria called as Sibella quitted the room.

That evening they were to attend the Regent's soiree at Carleton House. Strathairn was sure to come, for the prince would expect it.

Sibella's hands trembled as she put on her earrings, silently pleading for Strathairn to be there. He must, for this was her last chance.

There was only one way out of her present predicament. She must persuade him to marry her. Edward had planted the seed in her mind. Strathairn wanted her; she had sensed it as they stood together in the stables in York. She couldn't be wrong about something like that. She would never expect him to give up his important work. Indeed, she may well be able to assist him in his duties.

With this in mind, she had chosen her most seductive gown, a scoop necked, sea-green silk satin, the tiny puffed sleeves embroidered with silver leaves. Ivory tulle flounces embroidered with the same silver lamé leaves decorated the hem. To complement her ensemble, exceptionally fine aquamarines hung on a chain around her neck and at her ears. She turned in the mirror, pleased with the result. She intended to play the flirt tonight to devastating effect. Picking up her gloves, shawl, and beaded reticule, she prayed Strathairn would be unable to resist her.

She walked downstairs while pulling on long white gloves, the silver shawl draped over her arms.

Maria waited on the black and white marble floor of the entry hall. "How beautiful you look in that."

"I do hope so."

"Mama is waiting in the salon." Maria grinned. "You are up to something, sister dear. Might it have something to do with Strathairn?"

"What makes you think so?"

"You still have the blossom he picked for you, pressed into your Bible. He won't be able to resist you tonight." She grinned. "If it is Strathairn we talk about."

"I am not nearly as clever with men as you, dearest," she said evasively, while admiring her sister, a vision in Indian muslin, which featured a Grecian pattern, embroidered in gold thread and a low neckline. "I pity poor Harry. He can hardly wait for your wedding day."

Maria smoothed her low bodice. "Mama was a bit cross with the dressmaker." She gave a cheeky grin. "But she merely followed my instructions."

After the carriage deposited them at Carlton House, Sibella, Maria, and her mother moved through an entrance hall of yellow marble Ionic columns. Light filtered down from above. A footman showed them into the drawing room, which was the epitome of elegance with French decor and furniture, and Rembrandt, Rubens, and Van Dyck's oils gracing the walls. Sibella took a glass of champagne from a waiter as they maneuvered through the crush. Both the drawing and music rooms were already crammed with well-dressed guests, the women in colorful finery.

Lord Coombe came immediately to her side. "You look radiant, Lady Sibella," he said. "A man would be proud to have you at his side."

"Very prettily put, Lord Coombe," her mother said. "Don't you agree, Sibella?"

Sibella curtsied. "Indeed. Thank you, my lord."

Lord Coombe's brown eyes warmed. He did appear to approve of her in his stiff, formal manner. Might his cool reserve and strict sense of propriety mask an affectionate nature?

She excused herself and followed her mother through the throng.

When the ladies of a similar ilk claimed her mother, Sibella went in search of Strathairn. She found him deep in conversation with the Regent, the eccentric Sir John Lade, who managed the Prince's racing stable and dressed like a groom himself, and the Irish diplomat, Viscount Montsimon, who was often at the Prince's elbow on these occasions.

A warm glow flowed through her as Strathairn's searching gaze alighted on her. He dipped his head with a brief smile. She met his gaze before her friends, Lady Somersmere and Miss Greville, came to draw her away.

Once the ladies moved on, Sibella searched again for Strathairn. The Regent had left. Strathairn stood with Viscount Montsimon and Baron Fortescue. She located the baron's wife, Horatia, glamorous in bottle-green taffeta and threaded her way to join her.

"Lady Fortescue," Sibella said. "How wonderful to find you in London. I hope this isn't to be a brief visit."

The tall willowy redhead laughed. "Only fancy, Lady Sibella, the baron has opened the townhouse for the rest of the season. And here I was fearing we would rusticate in the country until little John was ready for Eton."

"How delightful. I shall see more of you."

"Thank you, my dear." Horatia took her arm, and they strolled about the room. She nodded in her husband's direction where he talked to Strathairn. "I wish I didn't suspect something going on with those two. My husband tends to keep me in the dark about some matters."

"Men tend to believe women will break like fragile china under the slightest pressure," Sibella said, gazing in Strathairn's direction. He had not made a move to greet her.

"Until we show them just how strong we are," Horatia said forcefully.

A fair young lady dressed in the first stare of fashion approached them. "Hetty!"

"Fanny! How splendid! Lady Sibella, this is Mrs. Bonneville, a dear friend of mine." Horatia said.

Fanny bobbed. "Please call me Fanny, Lady Sibella."

"Fanny's husband, James, has just come into an inheritance from an aunt," Horatia explained. "And they have bought a new house in Mayfair."

"It shall have all modern conveniences," Fanny said. "But it's not quite finished yet. We hope to move in next month." She giggled. "It will be such a relief not to have to live with Mother in Digswell any longer. One tires of being told what to do when one is grown up."

Sibella silently agreed.

Horatia gestured toward a group of vacant seats. "Let's sit in that alcove. We must arrange a time for you to come to tea and meet Master John."

With a glance in Strathairn's direction, Sibella moved with the two women toward the chairs. Her heart pounded hard and she feared she would lose her breath. For what she intended to do went against every notion of etiquette.

Chapter Six

WHILE STRATHAIRN TALKED to Viscount Montsimon and Guy, he was constantly aware of Sibella's slim figure in her green dress moving through the room. Earlier in the evening, her brother Edward had told him Sibella refused Coombe's offer of marriage. The family hoped she would change her mind. With Chaloner present tonight, it was best Strathairn keep his distance.

Horatia came to claim her husband. She gave Strathairn a shrewd glance before they strolled away. Guy would need the angels on his side to convince her to return to the country without him.

Strathairn's plan to avoid Sibella had failed, for she stood before him. He tensed and caught his breath. She was very beautiful tonight. The fine material of her dress clung to her curves, making him dwell on what lay beneath.

"My lord." Sibella curtsied. "How agreeable to find you back in society." She fluttered her painted fan in a manner that emphasized her eyes. He drew his gaze away from her tempting mouth.

"Lady Sibella."

She smiled coquettishly and tapped him on the arm with her fan. "So many ladies here tonight will be glad you have come."

"Most focus on Viscount Montsimon," he said with a grin, taken aback by her flirtatiousness which was out of character.

"We had hoped you would call on us at Brandreth Court."

He raised his eyebrows. "Not your mother surely?"

"Mama enjoys good company as much as I."

"Lord Coombe's company, perhaps?"

"Yes, he has been attentive of late." She frowned at him and nibbled her bottom lip, something he wished to do to her himself. "Don't you want to talk to me?"

He caught a thunderous expression on Chaloner's face where he stood within a small group and sighed. "Of course, but your brother seems to seek your attention."

Sibella arched her slender eyebrows. "One might suspect you are avoiding me."

"Not at all. How well you look. Your few days in the country have brought color to your cheeks."

"Thank you, but my health is a poor topic for conversation."

"Then shall we change it? Are you not on the verge of announcing your engagement to Lord Coombe?"

"I never expected you to listen to the gossipmongers."

"Is your brother Edward a gossip?"

The music swelled to a deafening crescendo. The prince liked music to dominate a room. Sibella narrowed her eyes. "Might we go somewhere where we can talk without raising our voices?"

"Would that please your brother?"

"I don't care what Chaloner thinks or does. I am a grown woman with a mind of my own."

"You'll get no argument from me," he said.

He'd never seen Sibella like this. Her vivacious beauty made his pulse race. How her mother was known to be in her youth, perhaps. He fought the strong pull of attraction, the desire to take her in his arms, to whisk her away. To thumb their noses at society and be damned. But a dangerous man dogged him, and he would never risk Sibella. She was far too precious. Wives could be held to ransom. They would weaken a man. He would not break her heart nor leave her a widow. He glanced casually around the room. "Where is the elegant Lord Coombe?"

She nodded toward the far corner. "In conversation with Lord Southern."

"Ah, I see." He must stop this now. "I'm afraid I must leave you, the Regent—"

"Is it because of what happened in York, John? Are you in danger?" Her wide green eyes, made greener by the large aquamarine decorating her deep décolletage, assessed him, making him feel like glass.

Her use of his first name here was reckless. Afraid for her reputation, and aware that merely conversing with him in this manner could shatter her life and remove her from all she held dear, he took her arm and led her to a quiet spot behind a pillar. Fortunately, most of the guests had ventured into an anteroom to partake of the lobster patties, thinly sliced ham, and exotic foods they'd come to expect from the prince's table.

He gazed down at her imploringly. "Sibella, have a care..."

"Are you in danger?" she asked again.

"You must not concern yourself with me." He was caught by the emotion behind her words. She deserved an explanation if only he was able to give it. He braced himself and lowered his voice. "You will please not repeat any of what your brother told you. Not to anyone, do you understand?"

"Do you really believe I would?" A high color flooded her delicate cheekbones.

He struggled with his feelings, suddenly helpless. His breath exploded out of his lungs. "Not even to Coombe, Sibella."

The fervor in her eyes faded, and they became shadowed, inaccessible to him. Desperate to reach out to her, he put out his hand. Over her head, he spied her brother Chaloner still watching, and fell silent.

He couldn't go after her without causing a scene. Frustrated and angry at the clumsy way he'd handled her, he watched as she turned and was swallowed up by the throng gathered around the prime minister. Jealousy tightened his belly. Coombe had better measure up.

SIBELLA FUMBLED FOR her handkerchief as she hurried to the ladies'

retiring room. Tears blinded her. She was hopeless at acting the femme fatale. What a cake she'd made of herself. Edward had been wrong about Strathairn's susceptibility. He appeared as unmoved as a marble statue. Under that smoky blue gaze, the idea of flirting with him had become embarrassing. Questioning him about his work was stupid. As if he'd tell her. She should feel ashamed of wearing her heart on her sleeve. She didn't, because she feared for him, although it had been humiliating.

She should have taken him at his word. His work meant too much to him. She gasped. Somehow, she must draw strength from somewhere to forget him. She'd been distracted by a man she would never have and was blinded to the possibilities of happiness with another man. Was it Coombe?

She blundered into a strong body. *Edward.*

"Whatever is the matter?" With a concerned expression, Edward stopped her from passing, his hand on her arm.

"I have something in my eye."

"Let me see." He bent his knees to peer into her eyes. "Both of them?"

"I suspect it's those urns of delphiniums. They always affect me this way."

"It wasn't the conversation you just had with Strathairn behind the pillar?"

She glowered at him. "I declare you have nothing better to do than watch me, Edward."

Edward tapped her lightly on the back. "That's better—the old Sibella, showing some spirit."

"You may tell Chaloner I have decided to marry Lord Coombe."

"You have?" Edward gave a slow disbelieving shake of his head. "Are you sure, Sib? It's not a rash decision? Made on the rebound as it were?"

Sibella dabbed at her eyes. "Made with a good deal of common sense I would have thought."

"Perhaps you need more time. Sleep on it. You may think differently tomorrow."

"I thought you wanted me to marry him," she said in an angry tone.

"I want to see you happily married. Not necessarily the same thing."

Sibella shook her head. "Tell Chaloner, please Edward."

She sniffed. How tired she was of vetting possible husbands. But she did want her own home and a nursery full of children. The years were passing her by. She sagged with a sudden fatigue. Now that she'd made up her mind, it offered her little comfort, and she doubted she would sleep tonight.

Out of a corner of her eye, the dependable Lord Coombe approached.

WHILE STRATHAIRN TRIED to convince himself Sibella would be happy with Coombe, Montsimon appeared at his side. "We are expected in Parnham's office tomorrow at eleven," he said in his pleasant Irish tenor voice.

"You bring news from Paris?"

Montsimon inclined his head toward a deserted alcove where they wouldn't be overheard. Strathairn followed him. Blessed with considerable charm, Montsimon hid a serious, thoughtful personality. His mother–an Irish beauty–ran away to Europe with her husband's best friend when he was a child and left him with his father. Perhaps it resonated with John because at ten years old, he'd become a motherless lad after his mother passed away.

The viscount was forced to pause several times when ladies drew his attention. To his credit, Strathairn had never heard him boast of his conquests as some were wont to do, nor had a lady been known to openly disapprove of him.

Montsimon altered his direction and attempted to speak to the blonde widow, Althea Brookwood. She had rejected the advances of several men who hoped to take her husband's place, either in marriage or in a discreet arrangement after he died. Not a happy marriage by all accounts. Brookwood was a nasty piece of work who was killed in a duel after cheating at cards.

After a brief curtsy, Lady Brookwood turned away to greet a lady at her elbow, treating Montsimon with appalling casualness bordering on rudeness. Strathairn noted the almost imperceptible stiffening of Montsimon's shoulders. He doubted it would end there. The viscount would rise to a challenge, and the lady was worth fighting for.

As he and Montsimon reached the alcove, two more ladies advanced on them, seeking Montsimon's promise to attend a poetry reading.

"Tomorrow," Montsimon said to Strathairn. With a smile, he strolled away with the two ladies.

A few yards away, Coombe talked to Sibella. Coombe took her hands in his. Strathairn's chest tightened at the sight. Fool that he was, he had wished her safely tucked away with this man. He hadn't bargained on the conviction that Sibella was his and that no other man had a right to her.

After Lord Coombe left Sibella to engage someone in conversation, Strathairn made his way to her side. "Lady Sibella…" he began, not sure what he would say. The words 'marry me' rushed into his mind. He longed to kiss away the uncertainty in her eyes.

She stopped him, a glove on his arm. "You may be the first to offer your felicitations, Lord Strathairn. Lord Coombe and I are engaged."

He forced a smile on his lips. He would not object, for what reason could he give? The man would give her the life she deserved. "You have it," he said, his throat dry. "I must offer Lord Coombe my congratulations. He is a very lucky fellow." He lowered his head to hers. "Please remember, if you ever need me for any reason, Sibella," he said in an undertone. "Come to me or send word."

"Thank you, my lord. I shall not forget." Sibella's dark lashes veiled her expression. Dear lord, may she be happy. Had he driven her to it?

Chapter Seven

STRATHAIRN WALKED UNDER the Horse Guards archway with a nod to the mounted guard. He hoped Montsimon might offer something helpful. He had a task on his hands to convince Parnell to continue the investigation into the death of his partner, Nesbit.

In his office, Montsimon and Parnell were already in deep discussion, his desk strewn with papers. The sun slanted through the window leaching color from the solemn painting of Wellington hanging on the wall.

Strathairn divested himself of his hat, gloves, and cane into the arms of Parnell's aide. He greeted the two men, took the spare ribbon-back chair, and waited for them to resume the conversation.

Montsimon perched on the corner of the desk. "You'll be interested in this, Strathairn. We've been discussing what I discovered in Paris."

Strathairn folded his arms. "Forney?"

"I spoke to several of Forney's former, shall we say, acquaintances. Word has it he drowned while escaping England back in '16. His boat foundered on rocks and sank in the Mediterranean Sea. He hasn't been sighted since, so it seems likely to be true."

"And that puts an end to the speculation," Parnham said.

"I don't see how." A heavy sensation settled in Strathairn's chest. Aware he'd raised his voice, he took a deep breath. Anger wouldn't work with Parnham. He had the coolest head in the business. When he spoke again, he lowered his tone. "And the Napoleonic symbol, the eagle-shaped cravat pin, identical to the one Forney used?"

"Some mischief maker." He nodded at Montsimon. "Montsimon tells me he saw the countess in Paris. If Forney lives, he would be with her."

Montsimon shook his head. "He wasn't."

"The man's dead. Sidmouth's network has turned up nothing," Parnham said, "and neither has Bow Street. I suggest we let the matter rest."

Strathairn leaned forward. "How about my new partner and I return to the docks? I'd like to discover who shot my man."

"There's trouble brewing in Manchester." Parnham ran his hands through his iron-gray hair. "I can't be responsible for everyone, Strathairn. We need to deal with that. There are agitators stirring up the people. The government must be made aware that the country is a powder keg."

"There are a lot of hot heads, shopkeepers, tradesmen, and publicans who will cause trouble," Montsimon said.

Parnham pursed his lips. "The government is considering the Six Acts which will forbid weapons and public meetings without a magistrate's permit."

"If the Act is passed, it will only stir up more trouble." Strathairn frowned. "If they limit the freedom of the press, it will merely increase the people's dislike of Liverpool's government."

Parnham shuffled the papers on his desk. "You can see why I don't want to spend any resources on Forney. Unless and until he shows himself. We have enough to do stopping these groups intent on provoking a revolution in England."

Summarily dismissed, Strathairn left the building. Agents such as Nesbit were dispensable. Easily replaced. There was no room for sentiment in this business.

SIBELLA ENDURED A harrowing couple of days. Not sleeping well, she was weary of her mother clucking over her appearance. Since their engagement was announced, Lord Coombe came often to St James's Square. So often, in fact, that she yearned for time to herself, and felt suffocated when he was in the room.

He was announced again as she tried to distract herself in the conservatory. Having bid her continue her work, he followed her about as she tidied her plants. The sun warmed the room through the cathedral glass ceiling, drawing out scents from the fruits and flowers. She wiped her moist brow with the back of her gloved hand. "The scents of oranges and lemons are delicious, don't you think?" she asked, desperate to find a congenial subject of conversation.

"Most pleasant." He drew out a wrought-iron chair and motioned for her to sit. "I'd like to talk about our future."

"Oh? Yes, of course." She removed her gardening gloves and sat.

"I am eager to show you our home. When next at Brandreth Park, we could make a day of it. You might bring Lady Maria, if you wish, although now we're engaged a chaperone isn't necessary."

"I am eager to see it," she said, fighting to sound enthusiastic.

"The house is a fine example of the period." Lord Coombs voice rang with more fervor than she'd heard from him before.

"Arrowtree Manor was your family home?"

"Ah, no. Lady Coombe's family home."

"Oh, I see."

"We lived there after my wife's parents died as it is superior in every way to mine."

Sibella brushed away a leaf clinging to her sleeve. She disliked the idea of living in his dead wife's childhood home. Her doubts must have shown on her face, for he leaned forward and took her hand.

"You will love it as I do. I have no doubt."

He began to describe the clever way the rooms were situated and the fine knot garden.

"It sounds utterly charming," she said. "As you have no London property, where might we spend the season?"

Coombe dropped his gaze to his hands. Surely, he would come to

London during the season?

"I prefer the country. My constant traveling for business takes me away from home too often as it is."

"But I shall wish to see friends…my family."

"Mm. I'll give it some thought."

She frowned at him, finding him evasive. It was hardly satisfactory to leave it so up in the air, but before she could argue the point, he rose and bowed. "Unfortunately, I have come to tell you I must take leave of you. Business calls me to Bristol. I shall be away for a sennight."

She rose with him. "I wish you a safe trip."

"Only business would part me from you," he said huskily.

He took a step closer. She stilled. He planned to kiss her. A stiff hand on her arm drew her to him and his mouth settled over hers in a brief, careful kiss. He withdrew with a sharp intake of breath. "I shall count the hours until we meet again."

Although his words were passionate, the kiss was not. It should have sparked something in her other than dismay. She stared into eyes burning with what might have been desire, but also something else, indefinable. Again, the suspicion that he was a man who was hard to know returned to worry at her.

"I'll walk with you to the door."

With a strained smile, Sibella bade him farewell in the entry hall.

As he descended the front steps, a tremor of apprehension rippled along her spine. She could discern no real affection for her in his eyes. True, she may not love the man, but had she made a terrible mistake in accepting him? Was he not the same man who had wooed her? Nothing had changed. And yet…

Maria waylaid her on her way to her bedchamber. "Edward and Chaloner have been closeted in Chaloner's study for hours."

Suspicious, but knowing it unwise to interrupt them, Sibella lingered in the corridor. When Edward emerged, she took his arm and dragged him to the library. "Is it Vaughn?" She shut the door behind them. He grumbled at her and smoothed the superfine cloth of his sleeve where she'd clutched it.

"Is it Vaughn?" she repeated, threatening to grab his arm again.

Edward backed away, palms up. "All right, Sibella. I did not wish to tell you. Vaughn can't be found."

"He's disappeared? How? When?"

"I visited his rooms yesterday. His servant hasn't set eyes on him for over a week. I returned this morning, but he still hasn't appeared."

"Might he have gone off on a jaunt? To purchase a horse, perhaps?"

"I doubt he has the coin for that. I just wish he'd told me. Chaloner doesn't seem particularly worried as it's happened before."

"Yes, but that time he'd fallen in love with a girl in Reading."

"How can you be sure he hasn't tumbled into love with another unsuitable girl?"

She twisted her fingers together. "I suppose we can't, really. But the last time he fell in love, he confided in me." She paused. "He's been a bit quiet of late."

He patted her shoulder. "Best we leave it for a few days."

"You promise to tell me the minute you hear from him?"

Edward nodded. "Lord Coombe just drove off. He's certainly attentive, isn't he? Are you more settled, Sib?"

"You knew him at university didn't you, Edward. What can you tell me about him? Did you meet his first wife?"

"No. Never met her." Edward chose one of the leather chairs by the fireplace and tapped his fingers on the arm. "You're still uneasy, aren't you. Is there a particular reason for it?"

"Not really." Sibella perched on the chair opposite. "I suppose I'm a bit mean to doubt him."

"I didn't have much to do with him at Oxford. Wasn't in my circle of friends. Can't say I was close to any of his companions either."

Sibella eyes widened with interest. "But I understood he was a friend of yours."

"An acquaintance. He approached me about a horse, and as I considered him a fairly solid sort of fellow if his behavior was any judge—"

"I doubt your judgment, Edward, recalling your behavior at Oxford," Sibella said waspishly.

"Well, yes, but that's all forgotten long ago. I must say, Sib, it's not good *ton* to bring the past up now. Chaloner made inquiries about him."

"How did Coombe's wife die, do you know?"

"No I don't. Why don't you ask him?"

"And how do you propose I do that?"

"Just introduce the subject casually into the conversation…"

Sibella jumped up. "Oh Edward, you are no help at all. But we must find Vaughn." The one man she needed now remained unavailable to her. "Strathairn would be the one to find him. But I made a complete fool of myself at the ball." She gasped and tucked her trembling hands out of sight behind her back. "I thought he cared for me."

Edward stood and sighed heavily. "I don't know what happened between you two, but I take my hat off to him. Strathairn is doing the noble thing. It's his belief that your life will be happier with Coombe. He wouldn't want to leave you a broken-hearted widow."

"A widow?" She gasped.

"Well, that is to say… For God's sake, Sib." He eyed her with a raised eyebrow. "What's going on in your mind? I don't like that look on your face. I've seen it before and what follows is never good."

"Last time I poked you with a knitting needle," Sibella said. "And you deserved it. In fact, I believe you deserve it now."

With a chuckle, Edward flung open the door, startling a footman and made his escape.

Strathairn had offered to help her if she ever needed it. Well, she needed it now. When days passed with no sign of Vaughn, Sibella decided to bury her pride and ask him to find her brother. But social occasions passed with no sign of Strathairn either. She hadn't expected to find him at Almack's, he hated the place. She thought he might attend Lady Forest's card party, but he failed to make an appearance there, too.

By the end of the week, no news of Vaughn's whereabouts had reached her. How was she to keep this from her mother? When her unease turned to deep concern, she waylaid Chaloner at the front door as he returned from a special evening sitting at Parliament.

After Belton helped him off with his greatcoat, Chaloner answered her question. "Vaughn has not returned to his rooms." He climbed the stairs.

Sibella followed him. "Has Edward searched in all Vaughn's favorite haunts?"

He sighed wearily. "I believe he has, my dear. Vaughn must learn to take responsibility for his gambling debts."

"How much does he owe?"

He shrugged. "Who knows? I have learned of at least one signed wager of a large amount. As he cannot pay it, I'm sure we'll hear from him in a day or two."

Lavinia appeared at the top of the stairs, her pretty face creased with anxiety. "Chaloner, Freddie is sick. Should we call for the doctor?"

Chaloner put an arm around her. "What does Nurse say?"

"That it's just a cold, but..."

"Dear heart, you worry too much. I'll come and take a look at him."

Sibella suffered a stab of compassion as her tired brother disappeared up the stairs to the nursery.

She returned to the salon where Maria and her mother were entertaining Harry. When her mother mentioned Vaughn's prolonged absence, Sibella made light of it. But something must be done soon to find him.

The youngest of the Brandreth males, Vaughn, had been indulged, which had done him no good at all. He'd been gone for weeks. Where was he?

Chapter Eight

BARELY MORE THAN a week later, Strathairn was recalled to Lord Parnham's office. Parnham had relented to a degree, agreeing to a brief reconnaissance mission to beat the bushes as he put it, hoping to flush out information. If nothing came from it by the end of the week, the matter was to be shelved.

Strathairn left, clenching his jaw infused with new purpose, Montsimon at his side. They walked together along Whitehall.

The Irishman's gray eyes were sympathetic as he smoothed his dark brown hair and settled his beaver hat on his head. "Is it possible they intended to murder Nesbit all along?"

"Nesbit?" Strathairn frowned. "I doubt he had any enemies."

"Then you, perhaps?"

Strathairn shrugged. "I've made a few along the way." They approached a waiting carriage.

"Mine, I believe." Montsimon motioned to the waiting carriage. "May I offer you a lift?"

"Thank you."

The carriage jerked and rattled through Whitehall and turned toward Mayfair. "Has the regent sought your opinion on his intention to seek a divorce?"

"He has ignored my advice." Montsimon shrugged. "Since Caroline's manservant Bartolomeo Pergami gave evidence at Vice Chancellor Leach's Milan commission, the prince is determined to prove adultery. He knows that is his only chance to gain a legal divorce. He's hardly white as a lily himself. Even if a bill is drawn up and can be passed, the people will never approve. The Princess of Wales is a disgrace, but she still has the bulk of the public on her side."

"That won't stop him, despite being sensitive about his excess weight and his unpopularity. He has detested his wife since the day he married her."

"Quite so," Montsimon said. "Prinny can hardly ignore what is said about him. There are boos and jeers wherever he goes. I heard a chant as he passed. Something about *Georgie Porgie, and pudding.*"

The carriage approached Hyde Park Corner.

Strathairn bid Montsimon good day and left the carriage beside Hyde Park. He set out for the walk home. The breeze curled around him cool on his face, stirring the dead leaves over the ground. He had a sudden glimpse into his future. More summers drawing to a close as the years passed. If he survived them, would he end up alone?

A landau drew up beside him. "May we offer you a lift, Lord Strathairn?"

Lady Brandreth with Sibella sitting beside her in an appealing high-crowned hat with crimson and white striped ribbons tied in a bow beneath her ear.

He was about to refuse when Sibella flushed and averted her eyes. "Thank you, Lady Brandreth." He climbed in and sat opposite them with his back to the horses. "Good afternoon, ladies."

"Lord Strathairn." Lady Brandreth studied him through her lorgnette. "No doubt you've heard Sibella has become engaged to Lord Coombe?"

"I've offered my congratulations to Lord Coombe. He is a fortunate man."

"He is indeed. Where shall we take you?"

"I am returning home, thank you."

"Berkley Square, Belcham."

"How is your family, Lady Brandreth?" Strathairn asked. "All are well, I trust?"

Sibella's eyes met his, wide with apprehension and some sort of message. He raised his eyebrows. While Lady Brandreth launched into a description of Maria's wedding plans, he attempted unsuccessfully to read Sibella's expression.

"A ball is to be held at St James's Square, in honor of Sibella and Lord Coombe's engagement. You will receive an invitation in due course." Lady Brandreth's tone suggested it would be of little interest to him.

The carriage jerked to a stop in the street outside the square. He bent over Lady Brandreth's hand, then kissed Sibella's gloved fingers, raising his eyes to hers again in subtle query. She shook her head ever so slightly as if in warning.

"Will you ride in the park tomorrow, Lady Sibella?"

"Sibella will not ride in the park for some time," Lady Brandreth said. "She must prepare for Maria's wedding, she and Cordelia are to be bridesmaids, and then her engagement ball."

"I look forward to your ball, Lady Brandreth." He climbed down. "Always a prized event on the social calendar."

Lady Brandreth gave him a searching look. "Drive on, Belcham," she snapped.

Strathairn stood on the pavement as the carriage drove away. Was that alarm in Sibella's eyes? What would have caused it? After the last time they spoke, he expected a certain coolness, but this? Might she be in trouble? If so, did she need his help? He could hardly scale the wall to her bedchamber to discover what it might be. Nothing for it, he would have to wait for the ball, which could be several weeks away. Frustrated, he thrust his cane over his shoulder and crossed to his front door.

SIBELLA WALKED UP the path of the stone building. A pretty, fan-shaped window sat above the shiny black door, flanked by two Doric marble columns. She was pleased when an invitation came to take tea with Baroness Fortescue at her townhouse in South Audley Street. She liked

Horatia, but her main reason in coming was the hope that she might find out where Vaughn was. The baron was a good friend of Strathairn's, and she might manage to get word to him.

She'd been tempted to write to John, but her mother and Chaloner would learn of it. The butler kept them abreast of every piece of correspondence sent from or delivered to the house. And time was growing short. Her mother would be sick with worry if her youngest son, of whom she was most fond, failed to appear at the ball and no explanation was given.

Horatia, in a morning dress of lavender and white striped percale, rushed forward to welcome her in the marble-tiled entry hall. "Lady Sibella, how pretty you are in that primrose gown, so perfect with your flowery bonnet. I have long admired your eye for color and style. Surely you must draw and paint?" They climbed the stairs to the floor above.

"I prefer my garden." Horatia's energy made Sibella aware of how tired she was. She was seldom calm enough to rest of late.

"Gardening always seemed like hard work to me. I prefer to spend my time writing."

"So difficult for a woman to be published," Sibella said.

"One must write under a pseudonym. Mine is Charles Grey. I have an article published in the Examiner titled: *What is poetry*?"

"It sounds intriguing. I most certainly shall read it."

"Thank you," Horatia said, looking pleased. "The weather is blessedly cool, I'm pleased to say. Baby John was so restless during those hot summer nights."

"Is your baby awake? I'd love to see him."

Horatia's brown eyes warmed. "Nurse has taken him to the park. They'll be back shortly."

Sibella followed Horatia along the passage. "Your home is quite charming."

"We spend little time here. The baron prefers Rosecroft Hall, but I enjoy the season."

"Is Lord Fortescue in London?"

"No, he's away in the country, something to do with his estate. He wanted me to come with him, but I know he will leave me there." She narrowed her eyes. "He is in cahoots with Lord Strathairn and won't tell me about it. So I shall not leave him."

Sibella buried the hope of meeting Strathairn as a footman admitted them to the drawing room. Apricot silk covered the walls and gold damask graced the long windows. She and Horatia sat together on a beautiful French scroll sofa covered in rich chintz facing the Adam's fireplace.

"Lady Brookwood is to join us." Horatia said. "Do you know her?"

"Yes." Sibella liked Althea Brookwood, a widow who struggled gamely with the poor situation in which her husband had left her.

At the scratch on the door, the butler announced Lady Brookwood. A petite, pretty woman with fair curls entered the room. She curtsied. "Lady Fortescue, Lady Sibella. How pleasant to see you both."

"We shall be firm friends I feel sure," Horatia said. "You must call me Hetty."

"I detest Lady Brookwood, please call me Althea."

The maid brought in the tea things. They were unloaded onto a rosewood table at Hetty's elbow.

Althea took the flowery porcelain cup and saucer Horatia offered her. "Have the banns been called for your wedding, Sibella?"

Sibella sighed inwardly. "Coombe and I have decided to wait until my sister Maria is married. Their wedding is to be held at St. Paul's Cathedral. I seem to recall Coombe mentioning your husband, Althea. Were they good friends?"

"Yes. We saw him and Mary Jane quite often," Althea said.

Hetty refilled Sibella's cup with ink-stained fingers. Sibella took the cup and saucer from her with a smile. "I confess, I'm curious as to what Lady Coombe was like."

"Poor Mary Jane." Althea stirred her tea. "She loved her childhood home, Arrowtree Manor, and was meticulous in its preservation. But life was difficult for her. She was often ill. A chest complaint."

Sibella selected a strawberry tartlet from the plate laden with delicious cakes. "It was an illness which claimed her?"

"No, actually it was a fall. They found her at the bottom of the staircase," Althea said. "Perhaps she fainted. She was often quite breathless." She declined the proffered cake plate. "None for me, thank you. I must watch my figure."

Obviously never having to worry about her slender waistline, Hetty added a second cream puff to her plate. "Poor Lord Coombe must have been devastated."

"He was, more so because he has no children. Mary Jane could not conceive, which put a strain on their relationship, she confessed to me."

"That is sad. Every man wishes for a son," Hetty said. "You will make a perfect mother hen, Sibella. Your sister, Maria told me how you cosset your nieces and nephews."

"I can't wait to have my own to fuss over," Sibella said, wishing the prospect of bedding Coombe wasn't so unappealing.

"Then you both seem of the same mind. A marriage made in heaven," Hetty said with a smile.

"Not given to rashness or levity, Lord Coombe," Althea said. "Very upright in his manner."

Hetty cast a sympathetic sidelong glance at Sibella. "Is that the kind of man you wish for, Althea?"

"I don't intend to remarry," Althea said with a tiny shrug of her shoulders. "I am perfectly happy. I can do as I please and I enjoy my freedom."

A small cry came from outside in the corridor. The footman admitted the nurse who swept in with young John in her arms. Nurse placed him on his unsteady feet.

Sibella jumped up and crossed to where John staggered across the flowery Aubusson carpet on his short solid legs.

"May I pick him up?"

"I'm sure he won't mind." Hetty looked lovingly at her son. "John can never get enough cuddles."

Sibella held the small compact body in her arms and put her nose to his soft dark hair. Babies had such a lovely smell. "He favors his father, doesn't he?"

"He has Guy's blue eyes and his black hair, I'm pleased to say."

"Oh, but your hair is beautiful, Hetty," Althea said.

"I never liked mine much." Hetty screwed up her nose. "And I'm not at all fond of men with red hair. They are often bad-tempered." She started and gasped. "I'm sorry, Sibella. Do forgive me. Lord Coombe's hair is so dark a red one might think…" her voice trailed away in embarrassed silence.

Sibella laughed. "Lord Coombe's hair is auburn. If he has a temper, I've seen no evidence of it."

Baby John spied the plate of cakes and wriggled in Sibella's arms. With a demanding cry, he pointed a chubby finger.

"No, my darling." Hetty came to take him from Sibella. She hugged and kissed him as he cried in protest. "You shall go to the nursery for a proper tea."

She handed him to his nurse, and the door shut on the noise the rambunctious baby made.

The conversation drifted to society gossip and the latest fashions.

"I must go," Althea said, putting down her napkin. "I promised to escort my aunt to Debenhams."

Left alone while Hetty saw Althea to the door, Sibella reflected on what she had learned about Coombe's wife. Their marriage had not been a happy one. Had they argued? She suspected Coombe's censure would be hard to bear.

"Althea is like a lovely doll, isn't she?" Hetty said, when she returned.

Sibella laughed. "Just don't let any man try to treat her like one."

"I've only recently made her acquaintance. She certainly seems a spirited woman."

"Perhaps she's had to be. The marriage was arranged and not a happy one." Sibella rose. "But I also must take my leave. Thank you for a lovely afternoon. Please come for tea at St. James's Square very soon."

"Thank you, I'd love to." Hetty descended the stairs with Sibella. "Will you and Lord Coombe take a house in London?"

Sibella tamped down the rush of anxiety tightening her chest. "I'm not sure. He hasn't warmed to the idea."

Horatia nodded and said nothing.

"Your baby is adorable," Sibella said with a pang of yearning.

"Isn't he?" Hetty fingered her necklace. "Guy has a man stationed outside the house. He follows Nurse when she takes John for an airing."

Sibella's eyes widened. "Why?"

Hetty shrugged. "Guy thinks I don't know, but I saw him conversing with the fellow. I watch from an upstairs window. When Nurse pushes the perambulator down the street, the man detaches himself from behind the tree across the road and follows her."

"I'm sure it's just a precaution," Sibella said, attempting to make light of such a worrying development. "Lord Fortescue is obviously an indulgent father. It's unusual among the *ton*, but I find it endearing."

Hetty's lips trembled and her tongue darted out to lick her lips. "I suppose that is the reason for it."

"I'm sure he would tell you if there was something else."

"The slightest hint of something untoward and he'll be determined to send John and I back to the country."

"And you don't wish to leave him."

"It's silly, I know," Hetty said with a shrug. "It's when he's away from me and I don't know what he's up to… But I must put baby John first now."

"Of course, you must, caring for John is of utmost importance. But I'm sure there's no need for you to worry." Sibella hoped she was right. It was odd, and she wanted to discuss it with Strathairn. Where was he? Might he be on a dangerous mission? She paused as she pulled on her gloves and shivered; the breeze had suddenly turned cold.

Chapter Nine

STRATHAIRN'S NEW PARTNER was Miles Irvine. Irvine had been a sergeant in Wellington's army, wounded at the battle of Waterloo. A farmer's son, Irvine chose not to till the soil after the war ended. He was a stocky man, his shoulders broad, his muscular legs too short for his body. He seemed levelheaded and strong. Strathairn had taken to him immediately.

Aware of how little time he had before Parnham called a halt to this investigation, Strathairn and Irvine spent some hours at the docks, conversing with sailors off the boats and barges. An old salt knew of a dockworker who had earned a large amount of blunt from a stranger to the docks. The sailor sucked a quid of tobacco in his cheek as he declared he hadn't set eyes on the man but had heard a French accent when he passed by the alley where they talked.

The dockworker, Joe Dawes, hadn't shown up for work the next day nor had he been seen since.

"Not surprising when someone greases your fist," the old salt said, spitting tobacco onto the ground. "Odd that he hasn't been to his usual watering hole though. He's an elbow-crooker, Joe. I expected him to be straight round to the bawdy house, too."

"Where does this Dawes live?"

"His room is a few blocks from here," the sailor said. "In Falmouth Lane."

Such deals on the docks were not uncommon. Tomorrow, Strathairn would seek Dawes out, but he despaired that this week's investigation would come to naught. It became increasingly likely that Nesbit's death would be buried under a pile of paperwork and forgotten.

He arrived home after several ales with Irvine. He'd missed dinner and considered himself not exactly cup shot, but not entirely sober either. Perhaps he would be spared the bad dreams tonight.

After his valet pulled off his boots, he dismissed him and the rest of the servants, then wandered the library in his stocking feet with a banyan over his shirt and breeches, a glass of whiskey in his hand. Outside, wind driven rain lashed the windowpane.

He heard a carriage stop outside, then a light rap of the knocker. "What the deuce?" The grandfather clock had just chimed one o'clock. He snatched up his swordstick from the table in the front hall and strode over the cold marble floors to open the door.

A very damp lady stood on the doorstep, the hood of her crimson velvet cape pulled over her face. She stepped up to the doorway and threw back the hood.

Soft lamplight fell on a delicate oval face.

"Sibella!"

"I had to come," she said breathlessly.

Strathairn looked past her into the empty street. "Who brought you?"

"No one. I came alone."

"You're soaked through." He took her arm and pulled her inside, her familiar flowery scent making his pulse race.

She wiped a lock of damp hair from her forehead and gazed up at him, eyes wide with anxiety. "I had to see you."

"Come into the library."

The remains of the fire smoldered in the grate. He mustn't touch her. "Take off your cloak and I'll dry it by the fire." His raging blood seemed hotter than the embers he bent to stir. He threw on more coal. "Couldn't this have waited until the ball?" he said, straightening. "If you were seen…"

"No one saw me." She untied the strings of her cape and threw it off, revealing damp white muslin decorated with flowers embroidered in silver thread, which now looked almost transparent. He bit down on a gasp as his body tightened. She was soaked through to her chemise. The cloth clung to the jutting fullness of her young bosom and lovingly framed the gentle curve at the base of her stomach. Completely unaware, she clutched her hands. "I've been to a soirée with Mama this evening."

"I must get you back before you're missed." He averted his gaze, strain evident in his voice. "Come close to the fire. You must be chilled."

"I'm a bit damp, that's all. It's not such a cold night," she said, but she moved closer to the flames.

He allowed himself a brief glimpse of a shapely derrière. "You're shaking."

She turned to face him. "I suppose I'm nervous. This is not something I do often, you understand. But you have not appeared at any of the social events I've been to lately. And I had to talk to you."

He hung her cloak over a chair. "You should not be here." Aware the drink weakened his resolve, he tried not to look at her breasts. He drew a wing chair closer to the fire. "Sit down. I'll get you something to drink."

"Thank you."

Sibella arranged her dress over her legs. She took the crystal tumbler of brandy he offered her and drank thirstily, a flush spreading across her pale cheeks.

John polished off the last few mouthfuls of his drink but resisted pouring another, already fighting to keep a cool head. He drew up a chair facing her. "Are you going to tell me why you've risked coming here in the dead of night?"

She clutched the glass with both hands. "It's Vaughn. He's disappeared. His manservant says he hasn't slept in his bed for almost three weeks. Edward and Chaloner can't find him. I'm afraid Mama will find out."

"You have no idea where he might be?" A sexual encounter, no doubt. Desire was almost impossible to resist at one-and-twenty. Still difficult at thirty. "Might he have fallen in love?"

He watched her take another deep swallow, patently aware of the undercurrent, so much unsaid between them. "I don't think so. I suspect it's a debt of honor. He signed a wager after losing money at Watier's Club in Piccadilly. Edward says it's a wild place for gambling. Old estates have changed ownership there."

"Tavern games are one thing, but clubs like Watier's, where the rich gamble enormous sums at high play, are very dangerous for a young buck. The club will soon close as many of its members are now in Dun territory. Perhaps Vaughn is hiding away, too ashamed to appear before the family."

Sibella seized on the notion eagerly. "Chaloner refused to bail him out this time. He wished Vaughn to learn his lesson."

"Might he have gone to the money lenders?"

"Edward believes so."

"And they've got their hooks into him, no doubt."

"I fear so."

"I'm going to fetch you a towel. Stay there by the fire."

He wrestled his emotions under control while grabbing a towel from the washstand. When he returned, Sibella had finished her drink and roamed the library, clasping her hands in front of her.

He offered her the towel, then turned his back as she dried her alluring décolletage.

"Lady Fortescue tells me some man is stationed outside her house. He follows the nurse when she takes her baby for a walk. It's odd, don't you think?"

"London is a dangerous place."

"She suggested you and the baron conspired in some matter. Is that true?"

"We've been friends for years. You know that."

She sat and arranged her damp skirts about her, dimpling at him. "May I have another brandy?"

She had no idea how seductive she was. "Is that a good idea?"

"Please."

"It's a lot stronger than Madeira."

"You know I hate Madeira." She lowered her delicate brows in a scathing look.

He grinned and moved to the drinks table. "I shall carry you home over my shoulder when you're in your cups. Discreetly, of course."

He splashed amber liquid into the glass from the crystal decanter while dismissing the temptation to keep her here for the night. Ridiculous of course. He smiled as Chaloner's outraged face swam in front of him.

She took the glass from him. "What makes you smile?"

"How your brother would react if he knew you were here. Sip it." With a defiant glance, she downed the drink, coughed, and screwed up her nose, her hand at her throat.

He grinned and shook his head. "Why didn't you ask for Coombe's help to find Vaughn?"

"He's away on business in Bristol, and anyway, what could he do?" She leaned forward, gathering up tendrils of hair escaping down her neck. Such a tender sight, he drew breath. "You are so resourceful that I trust you can find him, John."

He tried to ignore how his name sounded on her tongue, intimate, inviting. "Business? I gather Coombe is fairly flush in the pocket?"

"It appears so. He's heir to an earldom." She fiddled with another stray curl and tucked it behind her ear, revealing a sapphire and diamond earring. "You have the means to find Vaughn at your fingertips."

"Have I?"

"Don't fudge. You can ask other spies to look for him, can you not?"

He shook his head at her. "I believe you think there's a spy around every corner."

"It's why you won't marry me, isn't it?" She gasped and placed a hand to her breast. "I may be a little drunk."

He grinned despite himself. This was so unlike the Sibella he knew.

"I did warn you to go easy with spirits. Shall I wake a servant to make you coffee?"

"No, please don't. I'll be all right."

He sat and clutched his hands between his knees to keep from reaching out to her. "I'm not a fit partner in life for you. You need to understand that."

She raised her chin. "I'm not here to beg you. I'm concerned for my brother."

"I wish I could make you understand," he said, desperate to keep events on an even plane, so drawn to her in this moment that he could easily throw caution to the wind. "You are engaged to Coombe. I don't poach on another man's land," he said, his voice sounding rough to his ears.

She uttered a derisive noise. "It's you who doesn't understand. You're trying to rationalize something that can't be."

"Can't be?" He struggled to make sense of Sibella's tipsy thought processes.

She rose and came to perch on the arm of his chair.

"Sibella please..." His attempt to sound stern faded. He wanted to draw her down, laugh with her, make love to her.

"This feeling...we have for each other can't be explained away," she said. "It's about a deep sense of knowing. It's about emotions...and...senses."

"Senses?" Strathairn's body tightened as he allowed his gaze to wander over the flawless skin of her throat. Lustrous damp ringlets framed her face and her wealth of dark hair had begun to unravel from its artful arrangement. His fingers itched to free the silken locks, slide them through his fingers and breathe in their fragrance. Like an orchard in springtime.

She took his hand and rubbed it against her velvety cheek, making his blood drum in his ears. "It's about touch and smell and...and want." She lost her balance and tumbled into his lap, leaning against his chest with a gasp.

He lost his breath, his body clamoring to draw her close, to feel her under him. To pleasure her and feed his own urgent need. Instead, he stood abruptly with her soft, sweet-smelling body in his arms and placed her on her feet. "You're playing with fire, Sibella," he said, his gruff voice betraying him.

"Tell me why," she said slowly, searching his eyes.

"Because I desire you. Very much."

"You admit it then."

"Any red-blooded male would, and many would take advantage. I won't."

She shook her head but said nothing.

He couldn't tell her how much he needed her tonight. Needed her warmth to sooth the bone-chilling ache and emptiness he'd been experiencing. The temptation to seek a haven in her arms was almost more than he could bear. "You've had no experience of how cruel society can be. And neither are you the sort of woman to flaunt convention."

"You accuse me of having been kept in cotton wool. I came here tonight, did I not?" The delicate pale skin of her inner wrist caught his eye as she tucked an errant wisp behind her ear. Even that small gesture made him gasp.

He hurried on, hating the ponderous way he sounded. He didn't give a damn about any of it; he loved her like this, but he had to make her believe him. "Your concern for your brother has overwhelmed your reason. It has driven you to act recklessly. Out of character."

"You have me all worked out, it seems," she said with a sigh. "I may continue to surprise you, my lord." She shook her head and turned to pick up her cape. "You will find Vaughn, won't you?"

He took the cape from her and arranged it over her shoulders, hiding her tempting body from his gaze. "This is almost dry." He dropped his hands. "You mustn't worry. I'll find your brother. I'm familiar with his favorite haunts." The responding glimmer of hope in her eyes made him determined not to fail her.

"Thank you, John," she said in a small, dignified voice. "Could you hail me a hackney, please?"

Her eyes were shadowed with hurt, making his heart swell. He stifled a groan. How could he let her go like this, believing he didn't care? Without thought, the sensual curve of her hip lay enticing under his hand. He gazed deep into her eyes and drew her slowly to him until she rested snug in his embrace. With a sigh, she settled against his chest as he embraced her, enjoying how well she fitted. "You know it's more than desire. I care for you," he said against her hair. "I'm not going to deny it."

"Yes," she said, her voice muffled against his silk banyan.

He reluctantly pushed her away. "Trust that I know best."

"I shan't ever ask anything of you again, have no fear," she said in a tired voice. "But please find Vaughn."

"I will. I promise." It hadn't hurt this much when they dug a ball out of his thigh.

A dangerous wicked longing diminished his resolve and attacked his carefully built defenses. He cupped her face and rubbed a thumb along her full bottom lip. He moaned her name as he trailed a row of kisses along her neck. Sibella's soft body arched against him. *What are you doing, you fool?* His warnings turned to dust. He breathed in the delicious peach scent of her skin as if it was his last.

God help him, he took her mouth in a long, heated kiss.

SIBELLA'S HEART BANGED when, with a sharp intake of breath, John's mouth claimed hers. His hands swept down over her back, pulling her hard against him. Enveloped in new tastes and sensations, she caressed the nape of his neck and threaded her fingers through his thick hair. John had kissed her before, but not like this. Heat rippled under her skin. Her pulse raced, and she was lost to the overwhelming emotional pull of his body. His lips firm yet soft against hers while his strong hands stroked her lower back. She wrapped her arms around him as much to hold herself up as to draw him closer. She would allow him anything. An insatiable desire to know this man intimately, to have him know her, drove her on. She didn't give a fig about what disgrace might come from it.

But enough of her wits remained to be sure that whatever happened between them tonight would end there. She would never use this as a means to force him to marry her. No marriage would survive that, and he meant too much to her to destroy the affection they had for each other.

Chapter Ten

WITH A SOFT curse, he pulled away. "This isn't right, Sibella."

Released from his arms, Sibella grew unsteady. He reached out for her, but she moved away.

Her eyes were shadowed. "John, I would never ask you to give up your important work for me."

"It's not that simple."

Annoyed with his weakness to have let it go this far, he pulled the cape across her breasts and stepped back before they both landed on the sofa where the war would be lost. "Wait here while I put on my boots. I'll take you home."

She flicked a tongue along her swollen bottom lip, her eyes filled with passionate fire, her rapid breathing matching his. Lord how he wanted her!

"Very well." She moved away from him.

When had he realized he cared so much for her? The revelation sent him reeling. But his life had never seemed more uncertain. It was impossible.

He sat on a chair in his bedchamber to pull on his boots while fighting to forget how she had curled into the curve of his body, pressing her soft breasts against his chest. Pushing away the strong impulse to return and make love to her, he located his coat, attempting to arrange his thoughts into some sort of order. *Hell's teeth, have sense, man!* He could be dead tomorrow. And Sibella was engaged to a man who would offer her the life she wanted—that she deserved. *He was a blind fool.* Determined to return her safely to her home, he hurried back to the library.

She had gone.

A curse on his lips, he ran to the door and yanked it open. There was no sign of Sibella in the square. He ran to the corner as a coach disappeared down Grosvenor Street. Had she found a hackney? Surely, she wouldn't attempt to walk alone to St James's Square through the dark streets.

Yes, she would. Strathairn broke into a run. He'd caught a glimpse of crimson as Sibella passed under a gas lamp. She was hurrying along Upper Grosvenor Street toward the park.

He caught up quickly, grabbed her arm, and swung her around to face him. "Are you trying to frighten me to death, Sibella?"

"I merely wished to go home," she said, her face hidden beneath the hood. "Just find Vaughn for me, John. I don't ask anything more of you."

"You are being foolish." He tucked her arm through his. "We'll find a hackney near the park."

They walked toward Hyde Park, the noise of a night cart rumbling along in the distance. When they neared Park Lane, a shabbily dressed fellow stepped out from behind a tree and approached them.

Sibella gripped his arm. "John, he has a knife!"

"I'll have your valuables," the man growled. "Give me the lady's earrings. What other jewels are hidden beneath that cape?"

Strathairn pushed Sibella behind him. "I advise you not to try," he said, cursing that he had rushed out without his pistols and knife.

"Those rings, too, be quick." The rogue edged closer, slashing the air with a nasty looking weapon.

"I suggest you go on your way," Strathairn said. "Or you may come to regret it." While keeping his eyes on the knife, he planted his feet in a boxer's stance, hands raised to protect his face and neck, elbows close to his body.

His actions appeared to have the desired effect. Unnerved, the ruffian sniggered but backed off a step.

"Why don't you go home?" Strathairn said. "I have no desire to hurt you."

"You see this 'er knife? It will separate your head from your neck in an instant." The thief gained confidence and came at Strathairn in a rush, his weapon raised to strike.

Strathairn avoided the man's lunge and a well-placed kick to the groin stopped his forward motion.

With a shriek, the man crumpled and bent double, the knife skittering away into the shadows. Strathairn punched him hard on the back of the neck. He crashed to the pavement and lay silent.

"Is...is he dead?" Sibella whispered.

"No." Strathairn grabbed her hand. "Best we find that hackney."

When a hackney appeared in the street, Strathairn stepped out and hailed it. He assisted Sibella inside and directed the Jarvie to St James's Square.

In the carriage, Strathairn said, "You're very quiet."

"I'm stunned at how easily you dealt with that armed man."

"Poor fellow was weak and undernourished."

"A man wouldn't want to cross you, John."

"I remain confident that I can handle a thief. It's an elegant dark-haired lady I'm having the most trouble with." He searched her eyes in the dim light cast by the swinging carriage lanterns. "You know I must do the honorable thing, don't you?"

"I know you think you must," she said sadly, "and you've condemned me to a life with a man I don't love."

"But Sibella, try to understand." *Understand?* He was fighting to convince himself it was the best thing. "Marriage to an honorable man. A home of your own. Children. A quiet life..."

"This won't happen again. You make me feel emotions I don't want to feel." She took a deep breath and turned to the window.

He put out his hand to touch her trembling shoulders, then withdrew it, the tightness in his throat rendering him silent. "You'll soon forget me." It hurt him like the devil to say it. He fortified himself with the knowledge that she would be safe with Coombe, a man her brother approved of. If she married him, Chaloner might cut her off from the family. He respected Chaloner too much to believe it, but it could happen.

"I'm going to try very hard to forget you," she said, sparing him nothing as the carriage entered St. James's Square.

He deserved that and more. "I'll get word to Edward as soon as I learn where Vaughn is."

"Thank you, John. I am confident that you'll find him."

He would find that young rascal and give him a piece of his mind when he did. The house was dark apart from the flicker of candlelight below stairs. When the carriage stopped, Strathairn leapt out to help her down.

"Sibella..."

"Please leave me here, John. My maid will admit me through the servants' entrance." She crossed to the iron fence, then paused to glance back at him. "Be careful, won't you?" She disappeared down the steps below the street. Light fell onto the pavement from the open door, and with a swirl of crimson velvet, she was gone.

He stood staring after her at the dark house. When candlelight shone from an upstairs window, he crossed the road. Was he a fool to think he could walk away from the one woman in the world he wanted? He climbed back into the hackney where her perfume lingered.

THE NEXT MORNING, a heavy sensation of sadness dragged Sibella down into the feather mattress before she came completely awake. As no one arrived to chastise her, she was confident her nightly excursion had gone unobserved. An attempt to dismiss from her mind what had passed between them last night failed dismally. She would never forget the touch of his lips, how his tender kisses turned demanding and passionate, how his breath hitched as he pulled her close against his hard body. How he forced himself to break away.

She blushed with the shameful knowledge that she would have lain with him if he'd asked her. But it was he who showed restraint. It was right that John had refused to make love to her, for if he had, he would be hers. She knew him. He was an honorable man. Had she subconsciously hoped to seduce him into marriage? It was too painful to face that possibility. She'd always hated subterfuge. No wonder she was no good at it.

Sarah entered and handed Sibella her hot drink. She drew back the curtains and the gray morning light flooded the room. Sibella yawned and sat up to sip the chocolate. How could she have gone to Coombe's bed with the carnal knowledge of John filling her mind and tugging at her heart and pretend she was an innocent? Living a lie would be an abomination. John was right, he was wiser than she. But he cared for her. That was no lie. She uttered a tiny moan.

The maid who was laying out a morning gown, turned to her. "You spoke, my lady?"

"No, just thinking aloud, Sarah."

She warmed her cold hands around the cup. At least John had promised to find Vaughn, which allowed her to focus on Lord Coombe. She would not go willingly like a lamb to the slaughter. She cringed at the analogy, but was determined to have full knowledge of what she was getting herself into.

After breakfast, Sibella went in search of Chaloner. She found him in the nursery checking on Freddie's condition. "How is he?" she asked over his shoulder as he sat by the bed.

"Just a heavy cold, the doctor assures us, but you know how Lavinia worries."

He sounded gloomy.

"Would you like me to spend some time with him today?"

"I'd be most grateful, Sib. I have a pile of work to do. It's Nurse's afternoon off, and Lavinia is exhausted."

"We enjoy our games together, don't we, Freddie?" Sibella smiled at the young boy who lay in bed looking more bored than sick. "I'll fetch some, shall I?"

Six-year-old Freddie grinned. "Checkers," he croaked.

Clearly relieved, Chaloner rose. He turned to her outside Freddie's door. "Did you want something?"

"Just to ask you what business Lord Coombe has in Bristol."

"He inherited a coffee plantation in the West Indies from an uncle some years ago." He darted a glance at her. "Do you object to him being in business?"

"No, of course not. How ridiculous it is to frown upon gentlemen if they are seen to work in some capacity, like the lower classes, and yet many do work, terribly hard sometimes, attending parliament and managing their estates. You are always exhausted."

They walked along the corridor together. "I'm sure Coombe's past has touched your soft heart. He lost his young wife after only two years."

"That is sad. I wasn't aware his marriage had been so brief."

"When is he expected to return?"

"At the end of the week."

"Then we shall find him here again. He doesn't stay away for long."

Sibella brushed aside Chaloner's attempt to encourage her. "Mama intends to remove to Brandreth Park tomorrow. She opens the village fete on Saturday." She searched his eyes. "That really is something Lavinia should do, don't you think?"

"Try taking it away from Mother."

Sibella laughed. "You have a point there." But she knew Lavinia didn't want to take up the reins of marchioness. She shirked it at every possibility. She must eventually.

Chaloner leaned against the stair rail. "You know, Sib, it's my belief a marriage works better if the man is more in love than the woman."

"Can it not be both?"

"Indeed it can, but painful, I should think, to love a man who does not return your love."

Chaloner left her to go downstairs.

What about a man who loved a woman too much? Did he speak from experience? Chaloner bent over backwards to please Lavinia, and Lavinia, although Sibella was indeed fond of her, needed a good shake. It wouldn't be her that did it, however. Cordelia was the outspoken one. With a shrug, Sibella left and went in search of games to keep young Freddie amused for a few hours.

Chapter Eleven

THE SEARCH FOR Dawes led Strathairn and Irvine to a busy street near the docks crowded with horses and wagons, pushcarts, and pack animals. Dawes had a room in an alley off to the side of the main thoroughfare, rank with the stink of cat urine and something worse. When Strathairn and Irvine were close enough to knock, the smell grew stronger. They eyed each other, recognizing the stench. Strathairn cursed and banged on the rough wooden door. When no one answered, he tried the knob. The door swung open.

Pistols in hand, they entered the dim interior of the windowless room.

They staggered back as a blast of putrid air washed over them. "The devil!" Irvine gasped.

"Damn this infernal window tax." Strathairn cursed and kicked the ill-fitting door wide. "It forces the poor to live in the dark."

Handkerchiefs held to their noses, they stepped inside. As his eyes grew accustomed to the gloom, Strathairn made out a small table with a candle and a chair and a narrow cot in the corner.

A man lay on the bed. Judging by the signs of vermin, he had been dead for some time.

Strathairn took the candle Irvine lit and held it close to the body. The mattress was soaked with blood. "Not a natural death then. How long would you say?"

"In this warm weather it's hard to tell." Irvine's voice was gagged by his handkerchief. "A week at least."

The dead man's pockets yielded nothing of interest to Strathairn's search. Irvine inspected the few clothes hanging on a peg on the wall. The wretched room held little bar a jug of ale, a tankard, and a few crumbs of bread on a pewter plate the rats had missed.

Strathairn checked under the pillow and straw mattress, lifting them with his cane. He swiped at the swarm of disturbed flies. "Nothing here."

They escaped the rancid air into the alley, gasping for breath. "Find a constable and send for the coroner," Strathairn ordered.

After the coroner's inspection of the body, it was removed to the morgue. No autopsy was to be performed. Dawes had been feloniously murdered by persons unknown, his throat cut.

"Dawes could just have been robbed of his recent bounty, but we have to discover who paid him and for what. We'll return to the docks," Strathairn said after they left Bow Street.

In the tavern, one of Dawes's cronies appeared genuinely shocked to learn of his death. He confessed that Dawes was paid to smuggle a wooden crate ashore and deliver it. To whom he didn't know. He never saw the man who paid him.

"Describe the crate," Strathairn said after buying him another pint of ale.

"Twas flat, longer than wide." He took a long swallow.

"Do you think it was heavy?"

"Maybe not, but 'e was strong, was Dawes." He shrugged. "I were tryin' to mind me own business. Don't pay to poke yer nose in anyone else's 'ere on the docks."

"Contraband," Irvine muttered as he and Strathairn crossed the road. "But that's usually foreign brandy, spirits, bolts of silk or tea. A few soldier mates of mine got involved in the business after the war left them injured and unable to work. But they operate in small ships down along the coast."

"Somewhere like Dartmouth, where they can transport their cargo inland? Risk enough to cross the channel with customs preventative boats in pursuit." Strathairn was thinking hard. "The sheer number of ships moored in the Thames makes it easy to conceal contraband brought in along with legitimate cargo. But we're looking at something unusual here. This isn't a tailor merely in need of French cloth or a gentleman after the brandy."

That evening in The Three Crowns riverside alehouse, some of Dawes's friends and fellow dockworkers admitted seeing him with the crate. No one could or would identify the boat. It was a busy time at the docks.

"Did any of you get a good look at the man?" Strathairn gazed around the taproom at the assembled group, softened up by several rounds of ale he'd bought them.

One man with a knitted cap on his head spoke up. "Dawes met 'im in the alley beside the alehouse."

"Did they leave together?"

The beefy dockworker scratched his chin. "Nope. Followed me inside, showed me his blunt, but refused to say more. Dawes was scared right enough." He shook his head sorrowfully. "Said the Frenchie threatened to cut his throat if he talked."

They left the alehouse into a chilly night. Soupy fog drifted off the river and swirled around their legs, threatening to rise to choke and blind them.

"Looks like he did talk," Irvine said as they walked beneath a gas lamp's hazy circle of light.

"Maybe he'd outlived his usefulness," Strathairn said. "Dead men don't tell tales. We'll need to delve further and find out what was in that crate. Where the contents are now. I'll report to Parnham in the morning. You're in charge, Irvine. Get people on it. Talk to the Thames River Police. Go to the Customs House and check the charts for boats arriving from France on or close to that day. I have something else to do."

Irvine straightened his shoulders. "Right, my lord."

Strathairn began a tedious round of the clubs Vaughn frequented during the evening. The fog had worsened. The moist air clung to his hair and clothing as he made his way cautiously along gloomy streets, wary of footpads. Lamps cast a feeble glow from carriages moving at a snail's pace through the soupy air. A linkboy dashed past him, lighting the way for pedestrians.

Vaughn wasn't at Watier's. His search went steadily down from there in the less salubrious smoky gambling hells. No one had seen Vaughn for weeks. He arrived back at Grosvenor Square in the early hours, tired and dispirited. He did not want to let Sibella down. His promise meant a lot to him. It was the only thing he could do for her.

THE DAY AFTER she accompanied her mother to the village fete, Sibella was on her knees digging in the garden at Brandreth Park when Lord Coombe appeared. He was his immaculate self, dressed in an olive-green coat and buff trousers. "Don't your gardeners do that?" he asked with his stiff smile.

Did her messy appearance upset him? Sibella removed her gloves and untied the smock over the cambric gown she always wore in the garden as they strolled back to the house. She suffered again from that fervent desire to do or say something outrageous; to force a reaction from him. His starchy reserve annoyed her, but it also made her guilty. After all, her feelings for Strathairn were not his fault. "Your trip was successful?"

"Quite successful, yes." His smile was a trifle smug whether he was pleased at her question or his trip, she wasn't sure.

"Chaloner tells me you import coffee from your plantation in the West Indies."

"That is correct." He averted his gaze, prodding his cane at a branch of azalea too close to the path.

"Do you go to the West Indies often?"

"When business demands it."

She waited for him to elaborate, but he said nothing more.

"Should I like it there?" she asked. "Quite different to life here, I imagine."

"I will never take you to the West Indies." He grimaced. "It's different in every respect to England. Little morality exists in that hot heathenish country. You would hate the place."

She doubted he had much idea about her likes and dislikes as he'd never asked her about them. Tired of the awkward silences between them, she gave voice to an idea she had been considering. "Remember when you invited me to visit your house?"

"Of course I do." A spark brightened his eyes. "You wish to visit my home?"

"We might go tomorrow," she said.

"We'll need to leave early. Would it inconvenience you should I call after breakfast? Ten o'clock?" He cleared his throat. "I trust that Lady Maria will accompany us?"

"I'm sure she will."

As soon as Lord Coombe departed, Sibella climbed the stairs in search of Maria. "Please come. I can't go alone," she said, "and I need you to distract him while I question the staff."

Maria's brows shot up. "Question the staff?"

"I want to learn more about Lord Coombe and his wife."

Maria turned from the mirror, a new hat in her hands. "Why? Do you have reason to believe Coombe strangled her?" She gave an exaggerated shiver.

"What a horrible thought. No, I just want to learn more about her. Was it a love match? What Lady Brookwood told me led me to believe theirs wasn't a happy marriage."

"I don't know how you intend to find that out from servants. They might gossip among themselves but remain loyal to their masters. If they know what's good for them," Maria said with a chuckle. She turned back to the mirror to consider the hat, spangled-blue velvet adorned with plumes of feathers, now settled atop her dark curls. "It's unlike you to be so nosey."

"I'm about to marry the man. Shouldn't I be at least a little curious?"

"I would never pry into Harry's past. I'm sure I'd discover he'd been with other women. I hope he has. I wouldn't want us both to be virgins."

Sibella's lips twitched. "I shouldn't think you need worry about Harry. The way he looks at you, I'm sure he'll know exactly how to go about it."

Maria laughed.

"But what I wish to learn about Lord Coombe is more important."

"More important than the bedchamber?"

Sibella coughed, a lump blocking her throat. "Don't be frivolous, Maria."

Maria's eyes widened. "Wasn't that why you wanted to marry Strathairn? Because he looked at you in the same way?"

"In the past perhaps," Sibella said crossly as Strathairn's smoky blue-gray eyes appeared in her mind. "I'd rather we didn't speak of him."

Maria bit her lip, shamefaced. "I'm sorry, Sib. Of course, I'll come. And I'll distract Lord Coombe for you, which shan't be easy."

"Bless you, my sweet." Sibella hugged her and eyed the blue affair perched on Maria's head. "I'm not sure about the hat, though."

"No, I agree. It's a little ordinary. Blue suits everyone, and everyone wears it. Unlike orange or olive green. And yellow, which is even more unusual." Maria returned the hat to the tissue paper and replaced it in its round box. "I'll have it sent back."

Early the next morning, Lord Coombe's shiny black carriage arrived with a groom beside the coachman and two fair young footmen riding behind. Just before luncheon, they reached the first tumble-down black and white cottages of Chiddingston.

Maria gazed out the window. "You can see the spires of Lamplugh Abbey from here."

Lord Coombe nodded, pleased. "The duke is my neighbor, as I have said."

They drove on through green fields dotted with wide spreading oaks and black and white cows, for another half hour. Then the carriage turned into a narrow lane.

Arrowtree Manor's gardens were as neat as a new pin with clipped box hedges and raked gravel walks. "You'll be impressed with the house's decoration," Lord Coombe said, with a proud smile.

A black and white half-timbered house, the casement windows had fine latticework. Coombe stepped aside as Sibella and Maria entered the handsomely paneled hall. He escorted them through the house pointing out the decorative touches: symbols of Tudor rose, thistle and fleurs-de-lis featured in the oak woodwork and the stained-glass windows. The theme continued in tapestries and the embroideries which adorned the walls.

"How very fine those embroideries are," Maria said. "Who made them?"

"Lady Coombe." Her name hung in the air as Lord Coombe hurried them past the oak staircase and along a passage to the dining room.

Seated at the table, a footman served them a light luncheon of cold meats, cheeses, breads, and nuts before they embarked on a tour of the house. Then Coombe led them out into the gardens.

Sibella looked about at the ordered grounds, so very unlike Brandreth Park with its banks of roses, flowering trees, arbors, and hot houses. "I look forward to working in the gardens."

"There are several gardeners in my employ," Coombe said flatly.

After returning to the house, they partook of tea, seated on a green-velvet sofa in the drawing room.

Lord Coombe stirred sugar into his cup. "What do you think of my home, Lady Sibella?"

Sibella took a welcome sip of tea, her mouth dry. Mary Jane's presence was everywhere she looked. "The house is beautiful, isn't it, Maria?"

"Exquisite," Maria said.

Aware of how little time remained, Sibella finished her tea and stood. "I wish to be excused."

Coombe jumped up and pulled the bell. "A footman will direct you."

She slipped from the room as Maria asked, "What year was the house built, my lord?"

An older footman escorted her. "What is your name?" she asked him, as they climbed the staircase.

"Havers, my lady."

"Were you in service when Lady Coombe was alive, Havers?"

"Yes, my lady."

"You enjoy your work here?"

"I do, thank you, my lady. It's quieter these days. His lordship seldom entertains and is away a lot."

She nodded sympathetically. "I expect business does take him away often. It would have been livelier before your mistress died, I imagine."

Havers' face suffused with color. "When Lady Coombe enjoyed good health, yes."

They reached the top of the stairs. "So difficult when one is constantly ill. I imagine a certain amount of upheaval would occur."

Havers glanced down at the hall below before speaking. "There was some unpleasantness. But not now, I'm glad to say. Positions such as this are difficult to find, my lady."

She thought Havers apologetic as he bowed and left her. When Sibella emerged from the water closet, the corridor was empty. Taking her chance, she darted down the servants' stairs.

She emerged into the kitchen. "Oh dear, I'm afraid I'm lost." The cook, scullery maid and, a middle-aged lady in a black gown all gaped and dipped in curtsies.

The black-gowned woman came forward. "I'm Mrs. Elphick, the housekeeper, my lady. May I show you the way?"

"I'd be grateful, thank you."

She followed the housekeeper back upstairs to the drawing room. "Lady Coombe must have been house proud."

"Oh she was, my lady."

"Her early death was tragic."

"Poor soul. A maid found her lying at the bottom of the stairs when she went to do the fires."

"How shocking for Lord Coombe."

"He was so distraught he instructed Lady Coombe's pet dog to be shot." She shook her head. "But he was persuaded to give the animal to the coachman."

With a sharp intake of breath, Sibella clutched the banister. "How very sad!"

"Couldn't stand the sound of its whining, said the dog reminded him of her and fair broke his heart," Mrs. Elphick said. "His lordship left for the West Indies straight after the funeral. He was gone for months. We don't know why her ladyship chose to leave her chamber during the night." The housekeeper's face lengthened in distress. "Lady Coombe was ill and took laudanum to sleep, which may have muddled her mind."

They approached the door to the drawing room. "Thank you for showing me the way, Mrs. Elphick."

"My pleasure, my lady."

The door opened, and Lord Coombe's face appeared. He looked annoyed. "There you are. Your sister has gone to find you."

"Has she? I'm afraid I got lost. Mrs. Elphick kindly assisted me."

"We must be on our way. Fresh horses stand waiting. Even so, we won't arrive back at Brandreth Park until after dark. My footmen will need to be armed."

"My goodness. I do apologize."

The trip home seemed interminable. Maria made an attempt at bright chatter and Sibella tried to contribute, discussing everything from the opera to politics. Then Maria, bored or exhausted, slept against her shoulder as the carriage negotiated the appalling roads.

Lord Coombe fell silent, but she sensed he watched her. What would he think if he knew she had been asking questions of his staff? He appeared genuinely distressed by his wife's passing. But the incident with the dog worried her, even if the result of deep sorrow, it seemed unnecessarily cruel. Might he still mourn the wife he had loved? It would account for his serious demeanor. If so, her future as his wife appeared even more challenging. She licked her lips nervously.

Lord Coombe nodded to her. "I hope you enjoyed the day."

"Yes, we did, and the house is perfectly lovely. Thank you for showing it to Maria and me."

He had been attentive and considerate, and she really had no right to be so ungrateful. She had an overwhelming urge to confess her concerns to her mother. She'd been unaccountably emotional of late and a dose of common sense was sorely needed.

When the carriage finally reached home in the early evening, after a tedious, but thankfully uneventful trip, they found the house in uproar. Her mother rushed to hug her and Maria in the entry, a letter clutched in her hand. "We must return to London on the morrow. Your sister Aida has begun her lying in." Her lips twitched in vexation. "And from the sound of this missive from her husband, Lord Peter is the one having the baby."

Chapter Twelve

AFTER A FALSE sighting of Forney led them to a dead end, Strathairn suspected Parnham had withdrawn his support for the investigation. He was soon proved right, for Parnham stated it bluntly and would not be swayed.

Strathairn stamped away from Horse Guards, grinding his teeth. This was tied in some way to his dead partner, of that he remained convinced. He needed to prove it for Nesbit's wife's sake. If he could, It might be possible to convince the War Office to pay some sort of remuneration and possibly gift Nesbit with a decoration for bravery. But not even a little luck had gone their way, and he didn't have the smallest clue as to who killed his partner or Dawes in so ruthless and efficient a manner. Disheartened, he resumed his search for Vaughn.

Strathairn visited the morgue, coming away relieved not to find the young man. As night fell, he went to Covent Garden. The stalls had shut, and the market closed and only a few prostitutes roamed the shadowy square.

He ventured into the brothels in the surrounding alleys and questioned the game girls. No one remembered him. And a good-looking young lord would be remembered. At Haymarket Theatre, King's Theatre, and the Royal in Drury Lane, the actresses and opera dancers could tell him nothing. London teemed with people; it was easy to get lost among them if one chose. He only hoped Vaughn hadn't chosen to.

Strathairn sought out the Black Legs at the gaming houses in

Jermyn Street, Bury Street, and Cleveland Row, but it, too, proved unproductive. Vaughn was known in several places, but no one could say where he'd gone.

Strathairn visited White's Club on St. James's Street. The current arbitrator of fashion since Brummel departed London, William Arden, Second Baron Alvanley, hailed him from his position by the bow window, the seat of privilege.

"You haven't set eyes on Lord Vaughn of the Brandreth clan recently, have you, Alvanley?"

"That young whippersnapper? Not of late."

Alvanley was an inveterate gambler who frequented Watier's. Not a bad sort, he'd supported Brummel and sent him money after he'd fled to the Continent to escape his debtors. If he hadn't seen Vaughn, then it was unlikely he was around. "You haven't lost Underbank Hall, I trust?"

"Not yet." Alvanley gestured to the window with a laugh.

Strathairn grinned and clapped Alvanley on the back. "Send me word if you hear from the youngest Winborne?"

Alvanley nodded, his attention already caught by an offer to take a bet.

Strathairn moved on through the club where laughter and conversation rose from every corner. He located Edward in the card room.

Edward threw down his cards and rose from the table with a worried frown. "Sibella said you were looking for Vaughn."

"Haven't found him yet. Vaughn might be holed up with a woman somewhere," Strathairn said, trying to ease his mind.

"Yes, he'll appear before long. I just wish Sibella didn't take these things to heart."

"She worries about her mother," Strathairn said as a fresh wave of frustration tightened his shoulders. "If we don't find him soon, the dowager marchioness will discover him missing."

"Dear God, let's pray that doesn't happen," Edward said gloomily.

Strathairn feared what sort of condition Vaughn would be in. If he was found. There was nothing more he could do in London; all avenues had been explored. He left Edward to continue the search.

With Parham disinterested in furthering the investigation, and Sibella prevented from riding in Hyde Park, Strathairn had a fervent desire to escape London for a few days. He wanted to bury his woes while watching his latest racehorse perform at Doncaster. He had run out of ideas and his mood had grown too low to bear.

The next day, Strathairn left Irvine in charge of what amounted to the cleaning up of a defunct operation. With a portmanteau packed, he headed north to Linden Hall. His thoroughbred was to make its debut run in the St. Leger. He would return to London in time for Sibella's ball, where he hoped Vaughn would finally appear.

It had rained earlier but was now a fine crisp autumn day, the trees bordering the race course gleamed green, gold, and bronze in the sunlight. A lengthy line of punters trudged along the busy road to the racecourse, the road choked with riders and carriages.

The St. Leger course provided a broad straight gallop for the horses. Strathairn entered the racetrack grounds, keen to see how his horse Ulysses faired, though he doubted the gelding was suited to the distance.

Strathairn fought his way through the crowd and placed a bet on the next race, then he skirted the mob where all manner of betting was taking place from cockfighting to cards. He climbed the steps into the grandstand to wait for Ulysses to be led out onto the track. When the big horse appeared, he rose to his feet along with the well-dressed patrons around him. At the flap of the starter's flag, the five horses sprinted. Ulysses got off to a good start. Strathairn followed the progress of his big chocolate brown horse, holding his breath as excitement kicked in and the crowd's roar rose to an ear-deafening crescendo. Ulysses was well placed, tucked in behind the two leaders. The mighty horse, Antonio, led the way, and he was sure it would win. A lot of jostling took place among the competitors before Antonio galloped home in first place.

He turned away, pleased that Ulysses had run a good race. Next year the horse would have a better chance. He made his way down the stairs, planning to bet on the next race. Someone slapped him on the back and he swung around. "Vaughn!"

Vaughn grinned. "When I heard you had a horse running, I thought I might find you here."

Annoyance fought with an overwhelming sense of relief. "You've been gone from London quite a while. Care to tell me where you've been?"

"Making a tour of race tracks." The youngest of the Brandreth males was unkempt and pasty-faced. Either he hadn't slept or he had been drinking too much. Startled but greatly relieved, Strathairn grabbed Vaughn's arm as if he was about to disappear in a puff of smoke. "Your family is worried about you."

Vaughn cocked a brow. "Are they? I am only doing what Chaloner wants of me, to stand on my own two feet."

Strathairn eyed Vaughn's crumpled cravat, from which a stale unwashed smell arose. "You don't appear to be making a great success of it. Lady Sibella is frantic. She asked me to find you before your mother learned you'd gone missing."

"I intend to stay away from home until I win back the money I owe." Vaughn's green eyes shifted away and his mouth formed a mulish caste.

"An admirable goal." Strathairn raised a brow and hid his pity for the younger man behind a brusque stare.

Vaughn shrugged. "I can see you don't agree. If you'll excuse me…"

"Don't run off." He slung an arm around Vaughn's shoulders. "I need to speak to my groom about Ulysses. I'd appreciate your company."

Vaughn nodded and walked with him past the horses being led onto the track. The thoroughbreds tossed their heads, their glossy coats gleaming in the sunlight. "Love to own one of those beauties," Vaughn said.

After Strathairn saw his horse depart for home, he remained with Vaughn as they waited for the next race to start. The splendid favorite was a very short price.

"He looks a safe bet. I'll wager a monkey on him. I won at billiards last night," Vaughn said.

"Five hundred is a lot, Vaughn. Are you sure? There's no such thing as a sure thing," he said. Gambling seemed an unpalatable way to deal with feelings. It fixed nothing in the end.

"It can't lose." Vaughn firmed his lips.

"You think not?" In response, Strathairn raised an eyebrow, and he fell silent.

Strathairn was glad the favorite failed to win. Vaughn may learn something from it although he already appeared to be a hardened gambler. As they walked away from the track, he found out Vaughn had nowhere to stay.

"Come home with me," he said, wanting to make sure the young man didn't disappear again. "I'll be glad of the company." It would give him time to talk some sense into Vaughn.

Despite readily agreeing, Strathairn could get little out of Vaughn on the way home. He remained tight-lipped about where he'd been or the state of his finances. He gave up asking when the young man scowled and slumped on the squabs, looking profoundly miserable.

At Linden Hall, they visited the stables and then rode out to watch a groom put a horse through his paces over the moor. The handsome black stallion performed impressively, covering the ground with easy grace.

Vaughn rested his arms on the fence rail. "I was impressed with Ulysses, but he's even better," he said, enthusiasm warming his voice.

"You're looking at a champion in the making." Strathairn ran his hand over the horse's smooth neck. "Indigo is the best I've ever had. He's the progeny of Sabre who won the Two Thousand Guineas at Newmarket."

"Good lord! I'd love to see him race!"

"Would you?" He studied Vaughn. Here at the hall, he seemed a different person. The debauched gambler had suddenly turned into an excited young man, his eyes bright with interest as he admired the stud's blood cattle.

Vaughn asked surprisingly intelligent questions about the stud, and he did his best to answer them as they dismounted at the stables, then walked down the avenue of trees, fallen chestnuts crunching underfoot. In the library after dinner, Strathairn eyed the hunched young man sitting opposite him in the fireside chair. "How much money do you owe?"

Vaughn winced. "A thousand guineas."

"You went to the cent per centers."

Vaughn nodded. "The interest is crippling. I had hoped Chaloner would bail me out before it got to this."

"Chaloner's not a mean man. I believe he tried to rein you in."

Vaughn scowled. "I regret being so pig headed. I got myself into this mess, and I'm determined to get myself out."

Strathairn eyed him sympathetically. He might have got into the same trouble when he was younger, had he not chosen the army. "You are genuinely interested in horses, aren't you? Not just betting on them."

"Indeed, yes. One day I hope to set up a breeding stable like yours." His shoulders sank. "If I ever get free of debt." He shoved an errant lock back with an impatient hand. "But I won't come into my inheritance for years."

"You might consider a proposition of mine, then."

Vaughn's eyes widened. "Which is…?"

"You will have to be prepared to remain here and not be tempted to seek excitement in the city fleshpots. You can learn from my man and help with the running of the stables. That will require manual labor. I would be grateful if you'd help me out until things settle down in London."

"But the money lenders are after me—"

"I'll pay them off."

Vaughn gasped. "I can't allow you to do that."

"Yes, you can. You'll earn every bit of it. But you must write to Lady Sibella and tell her where you are. I'll take your letter with me tomorrow."

Vaughn regained some of his lost cockiness, arching a dark eyebrow. "Sibella, eh? Not Edward?"

"Either," Strathairn said offhandedly.

Brandreth's green eyes assessed him. "I don't know why you didn't marry Sib, Strathairn."

Strathairn offered him the decanter of whiskey. "Your sister has made a good match."

Vaughn held out his glass. "I'd have preferred her to marry you. Don't care for Coombe much."

"Just write that letter. Tonight," Strathairn said, refusing to be drawn. "And I'd rather you didn't mention I've given you the money."

"I shall have to tell Chaloner."

"Let's wait and see how well you do here."

"That's mighty generous of you."

"Not really. It suits me, that's all." Strathairn took a swig of his drink, savoring the delicate toasty honey flavor of good whiskey. "And if you find life here doesn't suit you, you are to let me know immediately. I'll not chastise you." He leaned forward. "But if I'm informed you are back at the racetrack, seeking out betting shops or Tattersall's, you'll be out on your backside."

Vaughn's eyes grew steely with determination. "I won't let you down, Strathairn."

Apparently, Vaughn meant it. At least for now.

AT LORD PETER and Aida's home in Curzon Street, Sibella attended Aida while her husband walked a distinct track in the corridor carpet. Finally, her sister gave birth to a daughter just before midnight. When the physician assured her that her sister was well and resting comfortably, Sibella returned wearily to St. James's Square. The clock struck two as she climbed the stairs. She found her mother still awake in the drawing room.

"The babe is born?"

"Yes, Aida has a daughter." Sibella removed her pelisse and hat and handed them to a footman.

"Both are well?"

"In excellent health. Peter is pleased and remains confident the next child will be a boy. Everyone is well. Do please go to bed, you look so tired."

Her mother followed her along the corridor to her bedchamber. "As do you. I don't know why Peter wouldn't let me stay to care for Aida."

"Neither Peter nor Aida wanted to risk your health," Sibella said diplomatically. Aida had begged her husband to convince their mother to go home. She preferred Sibella's calm practical nature to their mother's more forceful one.

They entered her bedchamber. "And the babe, did you see her?"

"Oh yes. I held her." She had studied the tiny hands, delicate features, and stroked the baby-soft skin. "She has the Brandreth's black hair. I believe her eyes will be green, too."

"I did fear she might inherit the drab coloring of Peter's family. Such a plain woman, his mother. Lady Wallace and the earl are traveling up from Dorset. I daresay they'll arrive first thing in the morning." Her mother pulled the bell. "I'm ordering hot milk. Please drink it." She stood behind Sibella who sat at the mirror removing the pins from her hair. "Where is your maid?"

"I told her not to wait up. I'm perfectly capable of getting myself ready for bed."

"What nonsense."

A rap on the door interrupted them. The bleary-eyed footman entered.

"Have hot milk and biscuits sent up, Bolt," Lady Brandreth said.

Sibella brushed her hair. There was no point in telling her mother she couldn't eat a bite even though she'd missed dinner. Her appetite had deserted her of late.

Lady Brandreth took the brush from her hand and ran it through

Sibella's hair. "You have not been at your best lately. Not at all like a woman about to marry."

Sibella closed her eyes, enjoying her mother's soothing touch. "I'm just tired."

"Are you not pleased to marry Lord Coombe? Is he not polite and attentive?"

"He is. But I don't love him."

"The love of your life isn't always the one you marry." Her mother put down the brush and gathered Sibella's hair into braids. "My dear, are you aware that I didn't love your father when we first married?"

Sibella met her mother's eyes in the mirror. "I wasn't, Mama."

"Not at first. I was desperately in love with someone entirely unsuitable."

"Was he a rake?"

"Oh yes. Lord Bascom was a rake of the first order."

Sibella swiveled to face her. "Did you ever regret not marrying Bascom?"

"Goodness, no. Do keep still. Bascom wed one of the Kirkpatrick twins. The poor lady died after only two years of marriage. Not from a surfeit of his company, I gathered. He was known to be seldom at home as gambling and mistresses were his favored pursuits." She smiled into the mirror. "But his eyes were like melted chocolate and his physique quite startling…" Shaking her head, she laughed. "All the ladies were smitten with him. I clearly remember that he wanted me as desperately as I did him."

Sibella studied her mother objectively. Age had thickened her waist and threaded white through her black hair but had also enhanced the fine bone structure of her face. "I believe many men did, Mama."

"Yes, but your father was the best of them. We made an excellent match in the end. Just look at our progeny!"

Sibella rose to remove her dress. Her mother came to help her, undoing two buttons just out of reach. "Foolish to spoil your maid. She will grow lazy and useless."

A footman brought in the hot milk and biscuits on a tray. The drink warmed her cold insides, but somehow the warmth failed to banish the chill which had lodged in her heart.

"I trust you will come to love Lord Coombe, my dear," her mother said. "After you become intimate, everything changes."

"I do hope so." Sibella was too tired to argue. The image of John's face as they stood on the pavement that last time swum into her mind's eye. Was that misery darkening his eyes? It hardly mattered, he had made up his mind. So infuriatingly noble. But yes, she admired that about him, too. She sighed. But had he found Vaughn?

Her mother tucked her in bed and left the room. Sibella blew out the candle and lay staring into the dark. Her sister's tiny babe was perfect. She wanted one of her own. She banished Coombe from her thoughts and indulged in the memory of John's hair like rough silk beneath her fingers. A deep sigh escaped her lips as her senses came alive to the slide of silk nightgown against her thighs. Exhausted and sensually disturbed, she drifted off to sleep.

Chapter Thirteen

FOUL AIR AND clamor greeted Strathairn when he arrived back in the city. Seated at his desk in the library, he dashed off a note to Edward explaining that Vaughn was safe and enclosing Vaughn's few lines addressed to Sibella explaining why he wished to remain at Linden Hall. He sprinkled sand over the letter, shook it, and folded it. Hesitating, he took a fresh sheet of bond, dipped his quill in the inkpot, and scrawled a brief missive to Sibella. *If you should wish to learn more, I shall be riding in the park tomorrow at noon.* He didn't attempt to examine his motives too closely, aware that seeing her wouldn't be helpful to either of them. But at least he had done what he promised and found Vaugh. Or Vaughn had found him. He instructed the footman to deliver the note before he changed his mind.

Strathairn rode into the park just before noon, with a glance at the sky. The rain held off but dark clouds threatened. Might she not come?

Sibella was too good a rider to favor the Ladies' Mile. She often rode earlier in the day before the *Beau Monde* gathered. He was dismayed by how pleased he was to see her riding with her groom. He rode up and reined in beside her. She greeted him, her green eyes alight with gratitude. "I can't tell you how relieved I was that Vaughn is safe at Linden Hall." He allowed his gaze to take in her green riding habit which matched her eyes. "I'm immeasurably grateful," she said. "You must tell me the whole."

"Your brother sought his fortune at the race tracks," Strathairn said. "I managed to persuade him to work in my stables. He seems keen to learn more about the stud. Always a strong interest of his as you know. And a far healthier endeavor than the life he pursued in London."

"Oh, how clever of you!"

"Not so clever. I shall gain from the arrangement. I can't be there as often as I'd like, and already, Vaughn shows some aptitude for the work."

"It's the perfect answer and most kind of you to take him on."

His heart warmed to see her smile. He noted the violet shadows beneath her eyes as he studied her pale face framed by her black riding hat. "Edward tells me Lady Aida and Lord Peter have a daughter."

"Yes, Catherine Ann. She's a perfect peach."

"She takes after her Aunt Sibella?"

Sibella steadied her mount as they grew closer to a couple riding ahead of them. "She has the Brandreth's coloring. She favors my mother."

"Then she will be a beauty."

"I expect so."

"And you have danced attendance on the babe and her mother? Day and night, forgoing sleep, I assume."

Sibella tilted her head. "Why, my lord? Do I not look my best?"

"You are as beautiful as ever, if a little tired around the eyes."

"You never were one to mince words." Sibella dropped her gaze to the reins in her hands. "My fascinating new niece does not tire me. There is a lot to be done in preparation for the ball and Maria's wedding. That is all."

"Lady Sibella?"

"Ah, here is Lord Coombe come to join us." Sibella's tone sounded overly bright, and he found her smile strained.

Strathairn stayed long enough to exchange pleasantries and then excused himself. The charmless Coombe obviously disliked finding him with his fiancée. He left the park and rode home, disappointed at having so little time with her. What a fool he was. Did he seriously believe that Coombe would permit their friendship once they'd married? He delivered his horse to the stable mews and entered the house, his shoulders tense. Was he being unfair to the man? He questioned his motives and found that he just didn't like the cut of Coombe's jib.

STRATHAIRN'S BUTLER, RHODES, delivered the mail on a silver tray. A letter bearing the Fortescue crest caught Strathairn's eye. He slipped his thumb beneath the wax seal and unfolded the letter scanning the contents. Guy had news of great interest. He would be there at two and hoped to find Strathairn at home.

Curious, Strathairn ploughed through the rest of his correspondence while listening for the door knocker.

As the clock struck the hour, a wild-eyed Guy burst into the room.

Strathairn pushed back his chair and rose to greet him. "My friend, were you not in the country? What has brought you to my door with such urgency?"

Guy threw himself down in a leather chair. "*Tiens*! You'll never credit it. Yesterday evening, I escorted my cousin, Eustace Fennimore, to Lord Bromehurst's gaming hell in the alley behind St. James's. You were with me when we found him in his cups a year or so back. Fennimore is an inveterate gambler who mixes alcohol with the laudanum prescribed for his gout to an alarming degree. When he asked me to accompany him, I agreed, because I feared he would be robbed, and possibly murdered for his purse. Hetty is fond of her godfather although why she does eludes me."

The butler entered carrying a decanted bottle of wine and poured them a glass each. Guy drummed his fingers on the arm of his leather chair. The door closed on Rhodes. "Please continue," Strathairn said impatiently.

"Forney's wife was there again," Guy said.

Strathairn sat up straight. "You saw her? Last night?"

Guy nodded. "As bold as you please, this time attired in a startling crimson affair, which caught my attention as I entered the room. I made sure she didn't see me. She had old Lord Crutchet hanging off her arm."

"That reprobate. I wonder what brought the countess to London. Did you manage to discover where she stays?"

"She is Crutchet's guest in his ancient pile in Richmond."

Strathairn put down his glass. "The deuce! If I leave now, I'll likely find her at home." He glanced at the clock as he moved to pull the bell. "Depending on the traffic, I can be there by four."

Guy's smile became bitter. "As her husband almost sent me to a watery grave, I'll accompany you."

The carriage made good time, and they alighted just before dusk in a leafy Richmond street close to the Thames. Lord Crutchet's grotesque mansion sat amid a grove of twisted cypresses. "While I speak to the countess, you make a search of the house," Strathairn said.

A butler almost as old as Crutchet answered the door. He dithered as he studied Strathairn's calling card, his eyes widening when Guy leaned toward him, his big hand on the door jamb. "The countess doesn't receive guests at this hour."

"She will see me." Strathairn pushed the heavy wooden door open. The frail, unsteady butler gulped audibly. "Please wait in the antechamber and I'll ask if the countess will grant you an audience."

Guy climbed the stairs as another elderly servant, dressed in Crutchet's livery with baggy hose clinging to his knobby knees, scurried into the hall. "Sir! You cannot go upstairs."

"Never mind, my good man," Strathairn said. "Either send Countess Forney to me or my friend will bring her down bodily."

He bent his head to enter through the low doorway into a musty, heavily beamed room. Velvet curtains at the narrow windows rendered the room as dark as night. The pair of candles on the mantle managed a feeble glow. The house reeked of dust, old age, and chamber pots. He couldn't imagine the countess enjoying her stay there.

Countess Forney swept into the room in a violet negligee which clung to her curves. "What is that man doing searching the house? On whose authority?"

"Mine, Countess." Strathairn remembered her as a woman who was aware of the power of her beauty and knew how to use it. She made little deference to widowhood. Her abundant dark hair flowed in loose curls down her back making her appear as if someone had just tumbled her into bed. It would not be Crutchet.

"I make no apology for my dishabille," she said haughtily. "I was dressing to go out. You have called without an appointment and must take me as you find me. And if you wish to discover where my husband is, you've come on a fool's errand." She remained standing and did not invite him to sit.

Strathairn folded his arms. "Where is Count Forney, countess?"

"He is dead. I assume you haven't come to offer your condolences." She tilted her head. "What, you don't believe me? It doesn't say much for your intelligence service, does it? You won't find him here. So, please, leave."

"I wish to learn the circumstances of his death, if you please." Strathairn leaned against the back of a chair, revealing no hurry to quit her company.

Her eyes narrowed. "His ship, bound for Marseilles, sank in a storm in the Mediterranean Sea near Palma."

"The name of the ship, Countess?"

She shook her head. "My, but your intelligence *is* inferior. The Sea Serpent. Not a large or particularly seaworthy vessel. But the best he could find at the time."

"How can you be certain he didn't reach shore?" Guy walked into the room with a shake of his head at Strathairn. "He might have settled down with another woman somewhere in Spain."

Her nostrils flared. "Forney would never have left me willingly." She studied the rings on her fingers. "One of the crew survived and brought me news of him." She moved toward the door. "Please go. I am still in mourning for my husband."

Strathairn glanced at the bright silk and blond lace barely concealing her bosom. He remembered Guy said she wore crimson, not black or deep violet in the gambling hell. "Nevertheless, I'd like you to return to Whitehall with us, Countess Forney. Please, would you dress?"

She stiffened. "I have an engagement this evening. There is nothing more I can tell you."

"Then we shall not keep you long."

THE DAY OF Sibella's betrothal ball dawned wet and dreary. The ballroom at St James's Square had been subjected to a flurry of preparation for days. Urns of flowers decorated every corner. Crates of champagne shipped from France were chilled in the cellars. The menu for a large quantity of delectable foods was selected. Rooms seldom used were prepared with toiletries in the dressing rooms for the ladies and gentlemen, and extra servants brought up from the country to attend them.

Sibella forced herself to appear happy in her mother's presence. When alone, she remained unsure of her ability to make Coombe happy, and whether she could be content. She was sure she would never love him. Every time she saw him she made a valiant effort, but always came away troubled. He was perfectly correct in his behavior toward her. She chided herself for being illogical and doubled her efforts to be nice to him. Even her mother found him personable. She had no avenue of escape. She had accepted that Strathairn would not step in and claim her. Her wedding to Lord Coombe was as inevitable as the seasons. She just wished he didn't unnerve her so. It was as if the real Lord Coombe had not yet revealed himself.

Chaloner had told her how proud he was of her. "You are a sensible woman, Sib," he said. "And I trust you will be very happy."

And you are a hypocrite, she'd thought, as she offered him her cheek to kiss. Tired of being called sensible, she was no longer sure it fitted her. Her emotions had been so confused of late. She sighed heavily and chewed her bottom lip as her maid pinned her dress of blush pink embroidered net over white satin. Her hair was pomaded and arranged in loops and pearls graced her throat and ears. She fiddled with an earring and her betrothal ring flashed. The ruby and diamond ring once belonged to Lord Coombe's mother. He had been at pains to reassure her that Mary Jane had refused to wear the ring as she disliked rubies.

At ten o'clock, the first guests began to arrive. Sibella stood beside Lord Coombe with her mother, Chaloner and Lavinia, to welcome them. In the ballroom, amid a profusion of candles and the glitter of spangles and finery, she danced the first waltz with her fiancé. He led her expertly through the steps, shoulders back, a satisfied smile on his lips. She tried not to compare him with Strathairn. But the differences were glaring. John's eyes delved deeply into hers when they danced, as if he wished to learn everything about her. Coombe seemed more concerned about the effect they had on those around them. He rarely showed interest in her as a person. Did he consider her an object, a possession?

Her mother said everything fell into place after husband and wife were intimate. She couldn't imagine the act, her mind closed in horror. Their relationship lacked tenderness and affection as if he only thought of her as a well-born wife with a generous dowry.

As they turned on the floor, her heart skipped a beat at the sight of Strathairn. He talked to Lord Fortescue and Hetty, but his eyes rested on her. She held his gaze until they spun away.

Lord Coombe's fingers flexed in her hand. "Do you and the Earl of Strathairn know each other well?"

"My brothers know him well."

"Are you ever alone in his company?"

"I imagine so, he often visits."

"Your friendship with that man is at an end." She watched in horrid fascination as a vein pulsed in his forehead.

A frisson of alarm spread through her at his sudden display of emotion. Was the real Coombe emerging before her eyes? "I don't expect I will see much of him."

"Never. I'm not asking you. I'm ordering you," Coombe said through clenched teeth. "Neither riding in the park nor dancing with him, nor seen to be talking to him at social gatherings."

Never talk to Strathairn again? She had at least hoped for that. She fought not to flinch and give him a reason to continue in this vein. "I don't like to be ordered about like a servant."

"Then behave like a respectable woman. I'm aware that affairs take place among the *Beau monde,* but please know that I will never countenance it."

She flushed and wanted to pull away from him. Never had she considered breaking her vows. Marriage was sacred. "I don't need you to tell me how to behave, my lord."

His fingers tightened as if he sensed her desire to end the dance. "You obviously do."

"What has angered you so?" She stared into his eyes, then dropped her gaze feeling as if she had glimpsed something illicit and disturbing.

"I saw how you looked at him. This is our betrothal ball. All eyes are upon us. We need to act with decorum. As every sober member of society should."

Sober! She screamed silently at the humorless man before her. Impossible to imagine him behaving in a spontaneous and joyful way. He was all about appearances. She had long suspected he hid his true character from her and gave her an unattractive glimpse of it now. She grew certain that it was not love that made him pursue her. Her mind whirled and she shivered as the music ended and he led her from the floor. When he gained control over her and her fortune, he would make her life a misery. A husband was able to lock a wife away or send her to Land's End or Northern Scotland under guard, or not let her out of the house without an escort. She would have a hard time escaping.

How well had he treated Mary Jane? If only she was able to discover more about his past. Uncovering the truth might set her free.

Chapter Fourteen

STRATHAIRN FOLDED HIS arms and watched Sibella dance with Coombe. They didn't look like a couple about to marry. Or even friends. She held herself at a distance from the viscount. "Have you had any dealings with Lord Coombe?" he asked Guy, who stood beside him, alone now, as his wife had left them to talk to friends.

Guy took a champagne flute from a footman's tray. "No, but Montsimon mentioned him."

"Go on."

"Apparently when he was in Paris, he met Lady Coombe's French cousin. He expressed outrage that Lady Coombe's death had been deemed an accident and demanded an inquest to be held."

Strathairn rubbed his chin. "And was there an inquest?"

"Yes. Lady Coombe's illness and her use of laudanum were blamed for her fall. And you have to admit the accident does sound feasible."

"Many things sound feasible." Had he been so intent on pushing Sibella toward a safe marriage, he'd discounted her good sense? She was perceptive and intelligent and might have good reason if she disliked the man. He searched the crowd. "I haven't seen Montsimon. Is he here tonight?"

Guy shook his head. "He's in Ireland visiting his estate."

The waltz ended and Sibella and Coombe left the floor. Sibella looked unhappy and Coombe angry. Strathairn's fingers curled into his palms, then loosened. It was none of his business, but he burned to hear what Coombe had said to upset her.

"Lady Forney was not seen to be a part of her husband's treacherous plot back in '16. But she might well have been," Guy said, drawing him out of his introspection. "Why was she treated so well at Bow Street and allowed to go free?"

"Irvine is to follow her. The more confident she feels about us losing interest in her, the better." Strathairn's gaze remained on Sibella as she and Lord Coombe moved through the crowded ballroom chatting to guests. He swallowed the bitter taste of regret. He never expected to fall deeply in love. Although he'd always admired women for their forbearance in putting up with men's unfaithfulness, as a youth, he'd been rather contemptuous when lovesick friends turned into fools. And after the war, well…

The Dowager Lady Brandreth approached them. "Strathairn, I must thank you for your dealings with my son, Vaughn. Sibella confessed he'd been missing for some weeks! I was led to believe he was still at his rooms and just being neglectful."

"I was pleased to, Lady Brandreth. He does well in Yorkshire. I received a letter from him today."

Her magnificent emerald eyes studied him. "You found him at the race track."

"Yes, that is true, but—"

"Then he must owe money. Quite a considerable amount, I gather, to send him running from London."

"No, he owes nothing as it happens, my lady."

A flash of humor lit her eyes. "I wonder how that can be?"

He rubbed a brow, adopting an innocent pose. "I suppose he has had a certain amount of success at gambling."

"You can't pull the wool over my eyes." She chuckled. "I shall find out the truth. I always do." She touched his arm. "I thank you sincerely for your generosity."

Strathairn bowed. "It has been to my advantage. Lord Vaughn is proving a valuable asset."

She began to walk away, then stopped, turning back to him. "Do you know Lord Coombe well, Strathairn?"

"Can't say I do, my lady."

The dowager's mouth grew pinched, but she said nothing more. Nodding, she left him.

Had she watched Sibella dance with Coombe and liked what she saw no better than he did?

DESPERATE TO REGAIN her composure, Sibella excused herself and left the ballroom to go to her bedchamber. She trembled with anger and distress.

Maria hurried after her up the stairs. "What happened?"

"I had words with Lord Coombe. He was quite horrid."

"What on earth did he say to you?"

"He accused me of being involved with Strathairn and forbid me to have any further contact with him."

Maria frowned. "He's noticed you have feelings for Strathairn and is jealous, dearest. One only suffers from jealousy when one is in love."

Sibella whirled around in fury. "Maria! He accused me of planning an adulterous affair with Strathairn! I admit I might have considered a liaison before marriage but never afterward! Have I given him reason to suspect I would be unfaithful? You don't understand the level of spite that man is capable of. He hides his true nature well behind a polite exterior. I shall be the recipient of his malice once we're wed!"

Maria's eyes widened. "What are you going to do?"

They entered her chamber and she shut the door. "I must return to his house to search for evidence that he mistreated Mary Jane. Can the leopard change its spots? I hope to find something—a diary or such like. I'll talk to the maids."

"But you can't go to his house unescorted. What reason would you give for being there?"

Sibella thought for a moment. "When do Harry's parents return from their trip?"

"The duke and duchess arrive home a sennight before our wedding. As you know, their stay in Italy forced us to delay it."

"They live close to Coombe in Chiddingston. When we visit them, I'll slip away and ride over to his house."

"Sibella! Ride across country alone? This sounds fraught with scandal. You might place yourself in danger. A gentlewoman alone and unprotected..."

"It is hardly Bethnel Green, Maria. I'm more likely to run afoul of a bull." She shrugged. "Anyway, I can outride any trouble."

"You're an excellent horsewoman. We were all taught to ride when we could scarcely walk, though it never appealed to me. But how shall I explain your absence to the duke and duchess? I do wish you wouldn't."

"I haven't decided quite how to go about it. Perhaps I'll plead a headache and beg to lie down in a darkened room." Sibella sat at the mirror and stared at her pale reflection.

She wasn't afraid of danger, and she was beyond caring about a scandal. Indeed, a scandal might be the answer to her problems. She would appreciate John's help, but he would never agree. At times, he was surprisingly straight-laced. No, a scandal wouldn't serve.

She chewed the inside of her cheek thoughtfully. If she could just convince Chaloner of Coombe's true nature, he would agree to her breaking the engagement. It would be done discreetly after Maria's wedding. He wouldn't be happy about it, but nor would he wish her to be married to a brute. "I'll ride across the fields and be as quick as I can. I expect it will take a little more than an hour there and back," she mused. "Coombe plans another trip to Bristol before your wedding. He will be away for a week. Can you speak to Harry and arrange for us to visit his parents during his absence?"

"There's already talk because you've delayed your marriage to Coombe." Maria sighed with a worried frown. "Older sisters are supposed to marry first."

"There's a good reason for it. Don't worry, I'll be most discreet."

Maria remained unconvinced. "I do hope you know what you're

doing."

"I can't ask Chaloner to call off the engagement. Coombe would sue for breach of promise. I must have proof! What would you do in my place?"

Maria rubbed her brow. "Probably what you're about to do," she said in a sober tone. "Such recklessness is unlike you, dearest. You were always the calm one in the family and the most sensible. You must see a great need for taking such a risk."

"I do." Sibella winced. Perhaps if she hadn't gone like a meek lamb to the slaughter, she wouldn't be in this position now. She rose and ushered her sister to the door. "Please promise you won't say a word about this to Harry."

"Well, of course not! Do you think I would?"

Sibella hugged her. "Goose!" she said in a soothing tone. "You and Harry are so much in love you share every thought. And it's quite right to do so. I hate asking you to keep this from him, but we shall tell him the whole story later."

"I do hope there's a happy ending," Maria said gloomily.

Sibella straightened her shoulders. There was nothing she couldn't handle, including Lord Coombe. Was she not a mature, competent woman?

Sibella and Maria returned to the ballroom, and Lord Coombe stiffly claimed her for a quadrille. To onlookers, he must appear the perfect fiancé. Considerate and attentive. Only she saw the unsympathetic light in his eyes when they rested on her. How his lips thinned.

As he believed her capable of committing adultery, she could say nothing in her defense. Her mother would put her emotions down to those of a nervous bride-to-be. She and Chaloner would blame Sibella's preoccupation with Strathairn as the cause. But she was now sure that her instincts about Coombe had nothing to do with Strathairn. Coombe was secretive in a way that John was not. She would never be able to trust him. She was about to be tied to him for the rest of her life! More evidence was needed of his true nature.

"If you behave in a manner proper to your station, we need never mention this unsavory topic again," Lord Coombe said. He glowered at her and scattered her thoughts.

She inhaled deeply. Why did he wish to marry her if he suspected her of being so deceitful?

Chapter Fifteen

WITH INCREASING DISQUIET, Strathairn observed Sibella hurrying from the ballroom followed by Maria. She was troubled, he could tell by the way she held her head. What had that blighter said to her? He gazed after her, distracted, and George Leadbetter, forced to repeat an amusing anecdote twice, demanded what ailed him.

When she returned to the ballroom, Sibella danced again with Coombe while her shoulders drooped. They barely spoke and said little to each other. A tiff? These things happened of course. When the dance ended, Sibella left Coombe's side to talk to Georgina.

Strathairn excused himself and wandered in that direction. On reaching them, he paused to exchange pleasantries.

"I do hope you'll dance tonight, John," his sister said. "There are ladies lacking partners. It is your duty after all. Lady Sibella will wish to dance with only one man tonight. Is that not so?"

"Indeed. I do hope you're both enjoying the evening," Sibella said with a faint smile.

"I trust you are, too," Strathairn said.

Sibella paled and fiddled with a bracelet. "But of course. You must excuse me. I believe Lord Coombe has the country dance in mind."

She hurried away.

"Why, what's afoot here, John?" Georgina demanded. "Lady Sibella seemed uncomfortable in your company."

"Nonsense, my dear. Where is Broadstairs?"

Georgina lifted her eyebrows and gestured with her fan to a group nearby. "My husband is not far away."

"He is never far from your side. He remains madly in love, I see."

Georgina jutted her chin. "As I intend he always shall be, but don't think your attempt to distract me has gone unnoticed."

He cocked an amused eyebrow as a group of her friends joined them. When he was able to excuse himself, he searched for Sibella among the couples advancing onto the dance floor, not being able to shrug off his concern. She was nowhere to be seen.

He turned to find Coombe beside him.

Coombe bowed. "I wonder if we might talk, Strathairn. On the terrace?"

The rain had eased, but pools of water spread across the stone paving, and the air was still heavy with moisture. Avoiding a puddle, he faced the scowling Coombe with distaste and gestured at the fine mist curling through the trees, dampening their clothes. "What is so urgent that it must be said in these uncomfortable circumstances?"

"I do not wish what I'm about to say to be overheard."

"What might that be?"

"I've seen the way you look at my fiancée. I know how thick you two were before Lady Sibella and I became engaged. And you still show an objectionable interest in her."

"In what way?"

"Your admiring glances."

"My dear fellow, half the men still old enough to care admire her. She's a remarkably attractive woman. You are a lucky fellow."

"I insist that you're never seen in her company."

"Impossible. The Brandreth's are friends of mine." No doubt, the man was jealous, but he wondered what provoked it. He was sure he would have learned nothing from Sibella.

"Friendship between a man and a woman of your age and circumstances is impossible without resulting in gossip. I refuse to have any such scandal attached to me."

Strathairn took a step closer fighting the temptation to punch the man in his arrogant face. "Attached to you, Coombe? I would have thought it was Lady Sibella's reputation you would be concerned about," he said with contempt.

"What affects me affects Lady Sibella and our future life together," he said stiffly.

The fellow *was* jealous. Well, he was familiar with that emotion. "There is no reason for gossip, Coombe. And I can assure you, I have nothing scandalous in mind," he said mildly.

"See that you don't."

Really, this was too much; the man was overbearing and rude. "Is that a threat? If I should offend you in some way, you'll challenge me to a duel?"

"I would not duel with you, Strathairn. That would be to your advantage. There are more subtle ways of dealing with such as you."

"And what would they be?" Strathairn studied the tight face of the man before him, as his concern for Sibella grew. He stared at him in disgust. "Don't threaten me, Coombe. That would certainly not be to your advantage."

Coombe narrowed his eyes. "I suggest you do not risk finding out."

"And I suggest you take very good care of Lady Sibella, who is a thousand times worthier than a mean-spirited individual like you," he said, as rancor sharpened his voice. "If you hurt her, you will feel my sword pinking your belly. I promise you."

Coombe's laugh was cynical, and his brown eyes burned with loathing. "An idle threat, my lord?"

"I never make idle threats, Coombe."

Coombe swiveled and strode back into the ballroom.

Strathairn strolled behind him with a desire to examine Coombe's innards splayed across the terrace. He had become interested in Lord Coombe. Very interested indeed.

STRATHAIRN, NOT WISHING to cause Sibella further distress, avoided approaching her again. He asked a young debutante to dance and spent the next twenty minutes attempting to put her at ease as she moved stiffly in his arms.

After the last dance ended, the musicians packed up and left the podium. Everyone began to say their goodbyes and moved toward the front door.

Strathairn was seeking his host and hostess when Guy approached him.

"I meant to mention that Mr. Eacock, the man you stationed in my street, reported seeing a woman outside my house," Guy said. "Probably nothing. She was dropped at the end of the street and on several occasions walked up and down before returning to her carriage."

"Did he describe her?"

"A dark-haired attractive lady stylishly dressed in a midnight blue cloak, so he said. She pulled the hood over her head as she approached my house. Eacock questioned her, and she said she was looking to buy a house in the area, and particularly admired mine. After I learned of it, I watched out for her, but she didn't come back again."

"Sounds innocent enough," Strathairn said.

"It does. She was French."

"French?" Strathairn didn't like it. "What are your plans?"

"The baby is with Hetty's aunt tonight with Eacock posted outside. I'm removing them to Rosecroft Hall tomorrow."

"A wise move. Hetty agrees?"

Guy's blue eyes grew steely. "For the baby's sake. An invitation arrived this morning for Lord Harrington and Lady Maria's wedding at St. Paul's which has set the cat among the pigeons. Naturally, Hetty is bitterly disappointed to miss it. We haven't announced it, but we are expecting our second child."

"That's wonderful news." He slapped Guy on the back. "Congratulations! But of course she would be disappointed. Poor Hetty."

"Still, it's very difficult for anyone to get into Rosecroft Hall past my butler and burley footmen," Guy said. "And no doubt you'll sort things out quickly."

He wished he shared Guy's confidence. "I'll miss you at my side."

"*Zut!* I hate not being in the thick of things. You must spare a few days with us at the hall when next you can."

"Not for some time, I'm afraid." The people ahead left the Brandreths and continued out the door. "I must say my farewells. I see Hetty converses with Lady Brookwood. Please convey to your lady wife how sorry I am to lose her bright presence from the social scene."

"I doubt I shall, Strathairn." He winked with good humor. "It will only add fuel to an already blazing fire."

Strathairn couldn't help but grin as he approached the Brandreth's. Chaloner looked mighty pleased with himself, the dowager fatigued, while Sibella beside her, laughed with what he suspected was false gaiety at something Edward said. Coombe glared at him.

He entered the square still troubled. Sibella had refused to look at him when he said his goodbyes. He hated to see her like this. She was ordinarily so bright and spirited. Whatever Coombe had said still upset her. Not a mere tiff then, but something far more troubling. He buttoned his coat while he tamped down the desire to question her more thoroughly about Coombe.

He gazed out the window of the carriage at the dark streets. Coombe had some business in the West Indies. He would make inquiries as to what it entailed, but surely Chaloner would have thoroughly investigated the man before he consented to the marriage.

When he alighted in Grosvenor Square, a man emerged from the shadows. "Lord Strathairn?"

"Billings, isn't it?"

"Yes, my lord. I bring unwelcome news. Irvine has been wounded."

Strathairn cursed. "How bad is he?"

"I don't know, my lord, but he lives."

"Take me to him."

Billing's explained what little he knew as the carriage raced full tilt through the dark streets. "It was while Irvine shadowed Countess Forney. Someone shot him."

Irvine remained unconscious in the surgeon's house in East London. Strathairn spoke to the grim-faced doctor who was cleaning his instruments in the next room. "How bad is he?"

"Not good. The injuries to his leg and arm are not life threatening if we can keep the infection down, but I'm afraid one shot damaged his liver. He lost a lot of blood on his way here."

"Take good care of him. Can he remain here until he's well enough to be moved? You'll be well paid."

"Certainly. If he survives. It's up to the good Lord now."

"Can I take a look at what you dug out of him?"

Dr. Pinkerton held out the bowl, and Strathairn picked a ball out, turning it in his hands. His scalp prickled as he wiped the ball of metal in his handkerchief, then shoved it in his pocket.

Driving past his club in Pall Mall, he was tempted to order the carriage to stop. He had more than one good reason to drown his sorrows. Instead, he removed the ball from his pocket and reexamined it as the carriage continued through Mayfair. In a few hours, it would be morning. He'd send a message to Parnham to alert the home secretary. This investigation was not over.

Strathairn prayed Irvine would be alive the next day. He decided to stay awake seeing it was close to dawn. A few hours' sleep always made him feel worse than none at all.

In the library, he took the tinder box from the mantel and lit the fire, then settled in the wing chair as his thoughts turned again to Sibella. He must pen a few letters to probe Lord Coombe's business dealings. And time grew short.

SIBELLA GLANCED UP as her mother entered her shadowy chamber. "No maid, Sibella? I will dismiss that lazy girl without a reference."

The air was smoky; the candles in the candelabra guttering, the fire reduced to a glow of embers. Slowly undressing, her limbs heavy with lassitude, she yawned and stretched, in no mood to argue. "I'd prefer you didn't. Sarah is an excellent lady's maid. I sent her to bed. It's almost dawn. I expected you to have retired by now."

"I'll sleep well past noon. I wanted a word."

"Oh?" Sibella laid her delicate gown carefully over a chair for Sarah to deal with in the morning.

"You looked beautiful tonight. Everyone said so."

"Thank you, Mama." Sibella pulled off her petticoat. Where was this leading? The urge to compliment her wouldn't ordinarily keep her mother from her bed. Such things would surely wait until daylight.

Her mother moved the dress aside and sat on the chair. "Of all my daughters, you are most like me."

"In nature?" Sibella rolled down a stocking. She doubted she would ever be as outspoken.

"No, Cordelia is like me in nature when she concentrates on anything other than her music. Sweet Aida takes after your grandmother. You inherited my figure and my cheekbones. I'm annoyed so many seasons have passed without you marrying and marrying well. We both know why Chaloner and I have pushed you toward this marriage with Coombe. You've been allowed far too much latitude in the choice of your life partner."

My, what had caused her mother to have such a bee in her bonnet? This was going over old ground, surely. Too tired and dispirited to discuss it, she pulled her lawn nightgown over her hips. "Maria is the beauty of the family."

"Maria looks just like my sister, Fenella. But you are like me."

Sibella faced her, curious where this was heading. "Oh, Mama, both you and Aunt Fenella took London by storm in your first season. I had only moderate success, and that was some time ago."

"Fenella and I were quite the rage for a time." Her mother's eyes grew thoughtful. "A heady time indeed." Her gaze cleared and focused on Sibella. "One must enjoy every moment of one's youth. It is fleeting."

"I am trying to." Sibella bit her lip to stop from protesting that if she'd loved her fiancé she would be happy indeed.

"I'm aware you don't love Coombe," her mother said as if reading her mind, "but what became obvious to me tonight is that you don't like him."

She was surprised, not by her mother's acuity, but that she should broach this now. She opened her mouth to tell her what had happened between her and Coombe but shut it at the sight of her worried parent. She hadn't noticed before that her mother grew older and had lost some of her strength and verve. Should she agree and send her parent off to bed deeply anxious? Her mother would take her side against Chaloner, who would consider her reasons ridiculous. She hated the idea of them arguing over her. She had made her plan and would solve this herself.

"Perhaps I pushed Coombe a little too far tonight. I am trying to understand him. He's not one to reveal his emotions."

"Some men can't." Did a little relief show in her mother's eyes? In most things, she was a pillar of strength and a font of wisdom, but it was too much to ask it of her now. "We can't always expect fulsome praise and showy acts of devotion. It doesn't mean they don't love us or care."

Sibella felt a pang of sorrow. For all her protestations, was her mother's marriage less than perfect? Her father had been a busy man not often in their company.

"I'll try to be patient with him." Sibella pressed a kiss to her mother's cheek.

"Good." Her mother pursed her lips. "You still have time, Sibella, to learn more about Coombe before you are wed."

Sibella stared thoughtfully at the door as it closed behind her parent. Her mother just offered her support if she found marriage to Coombe impossible. It *was* impossible! With a sigh, she placed all her hopes on her trip to Arrowtree Manor.

If only John would help her, but she could hardly ask him again. She hugged to herself all that was left of her shredded pride. Any feelings they had for each other lay in the past. She had to be careful though. Coombe observed her so closely she feared she would give herself away.

Chapter Sixteen

AFTER AN EARLY breakfast, Strathairn swore out a warrant at Bow Street and urged the constables to act immediately. Consumed with impatience, he prayed Irvine still lived as the carriage took him to Stepney.

At the surgeon's house, he found Miles Irvine not only alive, but conscious. "Milord." He weakly lifted his head from the bed. A bloody pad was fastened to his right side, his arm and leg bandaged.

Strathairn eased him down again with a hand on his good shoulder. "Easy does it. Can you tell me what happened?"

Irvine swallowed audibly, his eyes dark with pain. "We followed the countess to her dressmaker," he said, his voice faint. "I was stationed at the back entrance and had two men guarding the front."

"Yes, go on."

"She came down the back stairs several minutes later, dressed in a dark blue cloak, and hailed a hackney. I managed to keep her in sight as it took her to a ramshackle house in a street in Seven Dials. Left my carriage and crept to the house to see her talk to a big brute of a fellow with shoulders like a five-barred gate." He grimaced and laid his head back on the pillow.

"Take your time." Strathairn waited as Irvine's normally smooth-skinned face, was deeply furrowed in pain.

"Watched them through the window. The giant took metal parts from a crate—which fitted the description of the one Dawes brought ashore, milord! He assembled a gun on the table."

"Assembled it? Did you recognize the type?"

"Never seen the like. A double-barrel rifle, but nothing Thomas Manton has made." Irvine continued between gasps. "Brown lacquer, and the block, barrel and action parts fitted together like the fifth wheel on a carriage, real smooth like. It appeared to be breech loading..."

Strathairn's eyebrows rose. "*Hells teeth*!"

Irvine nodded, his eyes wide. "They talked for several minutes... I wasn't able to hear what they were saying... She emerged from the house without warning. I raced into the alley and fell over a pile of rubbish." He dragged in a shuddering breath with a cringe of pain. "They heard me. The countess boarded her carriage and took off, and I was left to run for mine where it waited down the road. He shot me before I reached it." Irvine gritted his teeth. "It was extraordinary, milord. He fired three shots in quick succession," Irvine grimaced, "and I'm afraid he got me with all three of 'em."

Strathairn stared at him. "There were no others there?"

"He was alone. The shots came from that rifle."

Strathairn read the concern in Irvine's eyes as they silently came to the same conclusion. It was a new style of gun not yet seen in England. "How did you manage to get away?"

"He came after me. While he was reloading, I managed to reach the carriage. Several shots struck the carriage as we took off, but they missed me and the jarvie who cursed me in fearsome fashion. Couldn't blame him. Good fellow, didn't desert me when most would have. Knew of this doctor and brought me here."

"Well done, Irvine." Strathairn nodded. "Do you wish me to inform your father?"

Irvine's mouth tightened. "We don't speak."

Irvine's father disagreed with his choice of occupation. Most fathers who cared at all did, including Strathairn's own. "Is there anything I can do for you? Anything you need?"

"No, I'm cozy here, thank you, milord. The doc says I can stay for a while."

"Get some rest. I'll return this afternoon to see how you fare."

Irvine coughed and closed his eyes. "Thank you, milord."

The door opened, and a young woman brought in a tray with a steaming bowl, spoon, and a plate of fragrant bread.

"This is my daughter, Miss Gresham, my lord," the surgeon said. "She is nursing Irvine."

The pretty freckle-faced brunette curtsied.

Strathairn smiled. "You have my utmost thanks, Miss Gresham. A pretty nurse is exactly what Irvine needs."

He left the house feeling a little more confident about Irvine. Was the countess here in England to take up her dead husband's cause? An act of revenge? But the man with the gun made him suspect there was a good deal more to it. This time she would not be so gently handled. She would expect Irvine to have been dealt with, and might have considered it safe to return to Richmond.

When someone banged on the door, Strathairn was catching up on his sleep in the library. He had visited Irvine again last night and found him a little better. Then he'd returned to wait for news from Bow Street.

It was too early for the butler and most of the servants to be at their stations. He opened the door and cool, lilac-gray dawn light filtered into the hallway. He recognized Clancy, a Bow Street runner he'd had dealings with in the past. "A note for you, my lord." Exhausted, the man drooped against the doorjamb.

Strathairn took the missive and nodded his thanks. "Do you require an answer?"

"No, milord."

"Care to come in? You look as if you could do with a drink."

Clancy's brows shot up. "Kind of you, milord, but I'd rather get home to m' bed."

Strathairn returned to the library fire where he scanned the missive from Parnham. Countess Forney had been arrested during the night in Richmond as she packed her things. She and Crutchet were taken to Bow Street for questioning. They would appear before the magistrate at two o'clock.

He rubbed his tight scalp. Were they finally coming to grips with the situation? He went upstairs to bathe and change. His valet had laid out his clothes for the day and the hip-bath stood by the fire in readiness. Hobson had been his batman during the war and almost knew what Strathairn needed before he did himself. Strathairn lay back in the bath and wondered what the day would bring as Hobson poured more warm water over him.

"You look tense, my lord," Hobson observed. "A massage will set you to rights."

"No time, Hobson." He stood, shedding water over the sides of the bath onto the floor, and stepped into the waiting towel. "After breakfast I must go out."

An hour later, he was on the road in heavy traffic. An hour after that, he pulled his phaeton up outside the surgeon's house. He alighted and threw the reins to his tiger, Jem.

Miss Gresham opened the door. She curtsied, a flush on her cheeks. "Good morning, my lord."

"How's the patient?"

"He is eating his breakfast."

Strathairn swallowed the gasp of relief, seeing Irvine propped up by several pillows. The bed linen, although heavily mended, was spotlessly clean. Morning sun flooded through the window onto the embroidered coverlet. The aroma of hot food filled the air.

"Good morning, Irvine." Strathairn drew up a chair beside the bed.

"Lord Strathairn." Irvine struggled to remove the tray from his lap, attempting to sit straighter.

"Eat your tasty breakfast while it's hot," Strathairn said. The pinched look around Irvine's mouth had gone, and while he still looked drawn, some healthy color had returned to his face.

"Take more than that to stop me." Irvine tucked into sausage and eggs with good appetite. "I'll be back at work in no time."

"Forget it." Strathairn shook his head. "Not until you're fully recovered. Is there someone who can care for you at home?"

Irvine winked at the young woman who brought in two cups of coffee. "I've been invited to stay until I'm back on my feet. Very generous of them it is, too."

"Indeed, it is." Strathairn nodded and took the cup and saucer from the young woman. She flushed an even rosier pink and tugged the edge of her apron. "Thank you for the coffee, Miss Gresham."

"You're welcome, my lord." She hurried from the room.

Once the door had closed, Strathairn leaned back in the chair and crossed his legs. "I'm sure you are eager to learn of the latest development."

Irvine paused, fork in the air, his eyes wide. "You've got one of 'em, my lord?"

"We've arrested Countess Forney. I'm on my way to Bow Street."

"She'd better talk."

"The constables will make certain she does."

"It looks like her husband is dead, doesn't it, my lord?"

Strathairn shrugged. "We seem to have a new enemy on our hands. And not one to take lightly."

"We must locate the rogue before he strikes. Do you have any idea what he and the countess planned?"

"No, but the time is ripe for sabotage. Your description of this man is circulating London and the environs. Spies are on the lookout for him. We've had a few false alarms, but so far, nothing."

As he left the surgeon's house, he suffered a frisson of foreboding. So much was at stake. Stories of unrest in the north filled *The Times*. It was the opinion of many that any activists who spoke out of turn and egged the people to riot should be hanged. Meanwhile, angry industrial workers in the midlands threatened to riot. The atmosphere was combustible. It would take little to stir up open rebellion, which could tip over into civil war.

IN LORD AND Lady Fenwick's drawing room, Lord Coombe solicitously arranged the shawl around Sibella's shoulders as they listened to *Ode to A Nightingale,* the latest poem read by the slight pale consumptive poet, John Keats. The beautiful ode pulled at the heartstrings, but Sibella had trouble concentrating due to Lord Coombe's ominous presence beside her. If he suffered regret for the way he had acted at their betrothal ball, he was not prepared to share it with her. Nothing more on the matter had been said, his manner coolly solicitous in the carriage.

He made her want to scream at him like a fishwife. His outrageous accusation warranted an apology or at least more discussion to clear the air. Worse, he made her feel guilt-ridden, although there was nothing she could do about her emotional state. She wasn't even sure what sparked such a heated reaction. Jealousy, a human failing, she might have understood, but she doubted that was it. She'd seen vehemence in his eyes not passion. Not given to hysterics, she did not trust him.

Maria hurried up as soon as Lord Coombe left. "I've spoken to Harry. We are to visit the abbey when his parents arrive home."

Sibella kissed Maria's cheek, aware how much her sister hated the idea. "Thank you, dear one." She couldn't wait. Nor could she consider the possibility of failure.

Chapter Seventeen

A NOISY, MOTLEY crowd packed the Bow Street magistrate's court. Prostitutes drunk on gin set up a din while thieves flinched nervously, their fox eyes darting about. Lady Forney stood in rumpled clothes before the magistrate, her gaze roaming around the room, as if surprised to find herself in such insalubrious company. Her shoulders sagged as her confidence vanished along with her well-groomed appearance.

Beside her, Crutchet looked a hundred if a day. He kept protesting in a high-toned wailing voice that he hadn't known the countess was involved in such extraordinary dealings. He jerked at the sharp rebuke and the deep scowl the countess gave him. Strathairn was inclined to believe him. Crutchet would never be a reliable member of a conspiracy. His mind wandered on occasion. His red-rimmed eyes blinked shortsightedly; the questioning, which had continued throughout the night, had reduced him to a befuddled and quavering state.

"What purpose took you to Seven Dials, countess?" the magistrate asked. "Mr. Irvine was shot when he followed you there."

Apparently, made of sterner stuff than Crutchet, she straightened, widening her eyes. "I know nothing of a Mr. Irvine, sir. He followed me? Whatever for? If he was shot, it was not by me."

"Why did you come to England?"

"How many times must I explain? While in Paris, I received a note from a man who said he had news of my husband, Count Forney. I hoped he might tell me the count was alive somewhere and unable to contact me, although in my heart I knew he was dead. When he wrote to me again in London, I went to meet him. It proved to be a ruse to persuade me to back him in some scheme. I refused and left."

"What scheme? What was the man's name?"

"He said his name was Smith." She faltered as chuckles and titters rose from the crowded court, then straightened her shoulders. Strathairn admired how quickly she recovered. "I didn't stay long enough to learn of his plan. I'm sure your Mr. Irvine, whoever he is, will confirm that I wasn't there above a few minutes."

"What had this Mr. Smith to say about the rifle he showed you?"

She shrugged. "I took little notice. I know nothing of guns, sir. I was disappointed and planned to return to France. I was packing when you brought me here."

She stood her ground under a barrage of questions.

It was time to test her further. Strathairn nodded to the prosecutor.

Mr. Eacock, the man employed to watch Guy's house and guard his child, took the stand.

"Is the woman you saw outside Lord Fortescue's house on more than one occasion here in the court?" the magistrate asked him.

"She is, sir." Mr. Eacock pointed at the countess. "Over there."

"It is noted," the magistrate said, "That the witness identifies Countess Forney."

"I hoped to speak to the baron. I thought he might know where Forney was," Countess Forney cried. She lowered her head and fell silent.

The magistrate banged his gavel and ordered the pair of them to Newgate to await trial at the Old Bailey. The countess crumpled like a marionette with its strings cut. She turned wild-eyed to point at Strathairn. "I will talk. But only to him."

The countess was brought to a room where Strathairn waited. She sat on the wooden chair and swept her untidy damp hair from her face. "I'm going to hang, aren't I?"

"Confess all and avert a serious crime, and it might go better for you."

Her eyes narrowed. "And spend the rest of my life behind bars? A short life, too, for I'll not survive long in that place."

"Where did the gun come from? What is Smith's real name? Where is he now?"

"I know nothing of the gun. Smith is a Frenchman. I never learned his real name. He kept his direction from me." She raised her eyebrows. "He would hardly take the chance that you'd torture me into revealing his whereabouts."

"Torture is an option, certainly." Strathairn dragged a chair up with his foot. He sat down, his knee almost touching hers. "Why don't you tell the truth?" he said. "It's your only chance."

Disturbed by his gentle tone and his proximity, her fingers worked at her hair again, busily tidying away the stray strands sticking to her damp forehead. "What will you do for me?"

"All that I can."

She snapped her fingers. "*Poof.* Nothing, in other words."

"You have little choice, for if you don't..." He let the words hang in the air.

"I don't know what else I can tell you!"

"I don't believe you, Lady Forney."

"Blood doesn't come from a stone."

Strathairn stood, hiding his anger and frustration. "Then we'll see how you feel after a few nights in Newgate Prison."

As the days passed, it became clear that the mysterious Frenchman, Smith, had gone into hiding. He'd failed to return to the house in Seven Dials. Inquiries as to the owner of the house had turned up a deceased estate. With no one to claim it, it fell into ruin.

Conscious of the urgency of the situation, Strathairn visited Newgate for another attempt at making the countess talk. Her wild gaze flew to meet his when he entered the crowded, putrid cell where inmates spent the daylight hours. Her gown was soiled, and her chin wobbled, but she stubbornly clamped her lips refusing to answer his questions. He reminded her of the inevitability of her fate and left, discouraged. He'd begun to doubt she'd crack. Was her determination to see this through to its dastardly end stronger than her need to survive? Or did she act to protect her husband? Could Forney be behind this?

While at Bow Street, Strathairn employed a runner to inquire into Lord Coombe's activities. Once home, he penned a letter to Governor Montserrat in Antigua and another to the authorities in Bristol. Coombe's sly threat worried him more than if the man had taken a swing at him or slapped his face with his glove. The man proved a disturbing mystery. No one of Strathairn's acquaintance knew him, so he sought out Edward who had introduced him to the family.

They met on horseback in the park that afternoon.

Edward, who worked as a solicitor rode into view on a roan. "I haven't long, Strathairn," he said. "I need to get back to see a client. Your note said you wished to discuss Coombe."

"Do you have any concerns about him?"

"Can't accuse him of being a charmer," Edward said. "And the poor chap hasn't a chance with you around."

Strathairn glowered at him as they trotted the horses down the Row. "You introduced him to Sibella. Did you or Chaloner feel the need to check the man out?"

"He was in the same year up at Oxford. Seemed a fairly conservative fellow. Not a close friend of mine, however."

"No, can't see you taking up with a conservative in those days," Strathairn said.

Edward grinned. "*Touché*. According to Chaloner, he's suitable husband material for Sib. Young widower, good breeding, plump in the pocket. Neat estate in Chiddingston. Sibella would be Maria's neighbor when her husband became duke. That should count for something."

"Would it? But what is your opinion of the man?"

"Honestly? Haven't warmed to him particularly on closer acquaintance. But I told Sibella not to take him until she was quite sure. No one has pushed her into this, Stathairn."

"Not forcibly perhaps."

"My advice is to let it go, Strathairn. Sib can't be happy while you're aways watching over her."

Strathairn raised his eyebrows. "I'm seen to watch over her?" Perhaps Coombe had a point.

"Your friends are aware how much you care for her, and if you don't, you're fooling yourself." Edward gave a half-hearted shrug. "I'd like to see you both happy even if it's not together. Dinner at White's Saturday evening?" He touched his hat and road away before Strathairn could reply.

Despite Edward's warning, Strathairn became more determined. He'd know this man inside out before he and Sibella tied the knot. If he proved to be all that he presented to the world, even if Strathairn didn't care for him personally, well he'd have to live with it. Meanwhile, he had a dangerous mission to get his teeth into.

With a hoy, Lord Montsimon rode up to him. Strathairn turned to greet him, relieved to have some cheerful company.

SIBELLA EYED THE thin-winged swallow gliding on the air above the trees. The soft mat of autumn leaves covered the ground and muffled the horses' hooves as they cantered along Rotten Row, steam from their nostrils rising in the cold air. She blinked as an icy breeze rushed across her cheeks and laughed at a witty observation Althea Brookwood had made, while riding beside her. Light of heart, Sibella was almost like her old self as Coombe had returned to his country manor to attend to business matters. She hated riding with him, disliking the way he handled his horse. He whipped the animal at the slightest provocation, which made the animal even more intractable.

Althea turned in the saddle. "Montsimon and Strathairn ride behind us."

Sibella resisted the urge to look over her shoulder as her heart began its cursed drumming. She gripped the reins tightly. Would she never be immune to Strathairn? Giving in to the impulse, she turned her head. Both handsome men looked very much at home on horseback as they approached. Enough to turn any lady's head. She cast a sidelong glance at Althea, but she had lowered her gaze.

"A chilly day, ladies." Strathairn reined in beside her. His gaze met hers with an odd intensity, making her start. As if he read her thoughts and discovered her plan. Even though he had no idea what she was about to do, he still unnerved her. She hated keeping secrets from him. Dishonesty didn't sit well with her. She had sworn Maria to secrecy, and thankfully, their paths would not cross until after she'd been to Arrowtree Park.

Montsimon's wavy dark-brown hair sprang back from a widow's peak when he pulled off his hat. Appreciation warmed his thickly lashed gray eyes. She guessed many women would find him attractive, doubly so, because he was fond of women and seemed relaxed in their company.

"You are both dressed for the cooler weather," he said in his soft Irish lilt. "And quite charmingly, I might add." His gaze lingered somewhat longer on Althea. She did look gorgeous in a royal-blue velvet habit trimmed with ermine, a matching hat perched on her golden locks.

"How gallant you are, Lord Montsimon," Sibella said.

Althea sagged in the saddle and put a hand to her forehead. "Sibella—my lords, forgive me, my head has begun to ache most abominably. I fear I shall have to return home."

Concerned, Sibella stared at her. How odd. She hadn't mentioned a headache before now. "That is indeed a shame, my dear. I'll accompany you, of course."

"No, please continue to enjoy the day. I'll be perfectly all right once I've taken a little willow bark and rested in a darkened room."

"Allow me to escort you home, Lady Brookwood," Lord Montsimon said.

"Kind of you, my lord, but entirely unnecessary." Althea's tone brooked no argument. "My groom will accompany me."

After Althea left the park riding with her groom, Montsimon's expression became abstracted. "I believe I'll ride on. Good day, Lady Sibella. Tonight at the club, Strathairn?"

"Does something go on between those two?" Sibella asked.

"No, nor ever likely to." Strathairn angled his fine stallion alongside her horse. "Lord Coombe doesn't ride with you today?"

"He's visiting his estate."

"Then may I see you home?"

"There's no need. Cordia and her husband, Viscount Barthe are here with friends." She glanced along Rotten Row. "I believe they're not far ahead of us."

"When does the family retire to Brandreth Park?"

"Tomorrow. Our stay will be short, however. We must prepare for Maria and Harry's wedding." She was careful not to hint at their visit to Harry's parents. "Coombes and mine follows soon after." She almost choked on the words when her chest fluttered like a frightened bird. She dropped her gaze to the reins in her hands afraid he'd see the dread in her eyes.

"I'm pleased I've found you alone."

At the tone of his voice, she tensed, and her gaze flew to his face. "Why?"

"What happened at the ball to upset you?"

Sibella bit her lip. Those handsome eyes of his missed little. "Upset? I hardly think… Well at one point, I was cross, I admit." She laughed and said in a careless tone. "Lovers will quarrel, you know."

Strathairn's eyebrows rose. "Lovers?"

"We *are* about to marry, Strathairn."

"Then what I witnessed was nothing of consequence?"

"A small disagreement 'tis all," she said airily, casting him a sidelong glance.

"Something's wrong. It's clear by looking at you." His lips firmed. Lips that had taken hers in passionate kisses she would never be able to forget.

"That's not flattering, Strathairn. Perhaps you require lessons in charm from Lord Montsimon. I was enjoying the day before you came."

He scowled. "*Dammit*! You're being evasive. I know you too well, Sibella."

"Nonsense. Men find women very difficult to understand. My brothers constantly tell me so. And being my friend does not allow you to curse in my presence."

"Then I apologize. Now, what happened to bring you so low?" He leaned toward her with intent in his eyes.

She shivered. If she didn't explain, would he whisk her off the horse and into the bushes?

She dropped her gaze. "Maria believes Coombe is jealous of you."

He nodded. "I believe he is."

She stared at him. "Did he say something to you?"

"He was angry."

She steadied her mount. "I'm sorry that happened. He's hard to understand at times," she confessed. Then immediately wished she hadn't, for Strathairn sat up straighter in the saddle.

"Your brother made enquiries into Coombe's past?"

"I expect so."

He eyed her. "I believe I'll do some digging into the man's history myself."

"Thank you, but really, it's not necessary. I'm quite capable of... Look, there is Roland. Cordelia is with him." Relieved, she nudged her horse's flank.

With a scowl, Strathairn made to grab her reins. "Sibella you're not going to—"

"Roland, Cordelia, come join us." She welcomed the disruption, fearing Strathairn would continue to interrogate her until he wrestled the truth from her.

It was his job after all, and she was sure he was very good at it. She would not allow him to become involved. Coombe had warned her, and even though Strathairn could hold his own in any company, she knew him to be honorable, and she had begun to suspect that Lord

Coombe was not. That way might lead to tragedy. She turned to talk to her brother as a sad little voice deep inside told her she would never know the thrill of surrendering herself to the hard, demanding, overpowering passion of a man like Strathairn.

Chapter Eighteen

STRATHAIRN HAD NOT had a chance to speak to Montsimon at Hyde Park concerning his time in Paris. He sought him at his club in St. James's, that evening, finding him in a heated discussion about politics with one of his cronies. Recently returned from France, Montsimon's smart coat featured a shawl collar.

"I see you're in danger of becoming a dandy," Strathairn said with a grin.

"I suspect I would fail miserably," Montsimon said with a laugh. "Dandies are devoted to elegance. They live before a mirror. I should become horribly bored."

He drew Montsimon away to a corner of the library, ordered wine, and questioned him about Coombe.

Montsimon tapped a long finger against his glass. "Lady Coombe's cousin suspected her death was not an accident, but he had no proof. He told me something of Coombe's activities on his plantation in the Caribbean. Said Coombe was a harsh master. Deuced unattractive that. I can't verify any of it. The fellow was clearly set against Coombe, but it might come down to the family estate, money and so forth. So often does. Coombe is a difficult man to read, is he not? Still waters run deep."

"'*Such men are dangerous.*'" Strathairn scowled as he quoted *Julius Caesar.*

"Quite so." Montsimon toasted with his glass. "Unlike you to go about quoting Shakespeare, Strathairn. One might think you were in love."

Accused twice in one day was a little too much. Strathairn moderated his expression and refused to rise to his friend's bait. "I never sleep well, and my father has a well-stocked library." True or not, the cousin's estimation of the man fitted with his own and tightened his gut. "I'll need to do some more digging on Lord Coombe, it seems."

A smile tugged at Montsimon's mouth. "Very solicitous of you. I would have expected her brother, the marquess, to find out all he could about the man before sanctioning the marriage."

"My thoughts exactly."

"More wine?" Montsimon signaled to a waiter. "The government remains concerned that we're on the brink of civil war," he said. "The menacing banners still do the rounds, and rancorous songs are sung in the alehouses. It would only take one forceful, charismatic leader to light the fire."

Montsimon narrowed his eyes against the smoky air. "I doubt it will be Henry Hunt. He's an accomplished speaker and popular, admittedly, but vain and irresolute, and not an advocate of violence."

"Let's hope it's like the barber's cat, all piss and wind. And once Sidmouth pushes through the Six Acts, the danger will pass."

"You are confident of that?" Montsimon looked unconvinced.

"Not entirely. I don't agree with the Blasphemous and Seditious Libels Act gagging authors and newspapers. Neither do the Tories. They won't pass this legislation."

Strathairn tossed back the dregs in his glass. Until then, peace was poised on a knife edge. One random act could shatter it. And somewhere, a ruthless murderer lurked, well-armed and with some evil design to bring chaos to England.

He left Montsimon at White's and walked down St. James's Street. Montsimon's comment about love turned his thoughts again to Sibella. She was never far from his mind these days. His lustful thoughts didn't surprise him; she was a beautiful woman, but he was surprised by the deep sense of longing. He'd never experienced such feelings for any woman. This was more than a passing fancy. It was soul-deep. Edward had the right of it, he did want to take care of Sibella. Of course, he'd relinquished any such right, and it was unlikely she'd ever confide in him again.

Society deserted London for the country now that the hunting season had begun, and parliament was in recess. Her family would soon vacate St. James's Square for Brandreth Park.

He had to keep his mind on the matter at hand, and would return tomorrow to the countess who might now be prepared to talk. Feeling hamstrung, he struck his cane against a lamppost, drawing a look of surprise from a well-dressed man passing by.

Strathairn shrugged with a smile.

"Some days are like that, aren't they?" the man said sympathetically.

"Indeed." With a slight bow, he turned to cross the road, tossing a coin to the street sweeper.

He arrived home to find a letter waiting from the Bristol authorities. Lord Coombe's conduct had never warranted scrutiny. It failed to set his mind at rest. Strathairn cursed, screwed the paper up, and threw it into the fire. He paced the length of the library as he scrubbed his hands through his hair. Something didn't smell right. He had an excellent nose for trouble, which came from experience and seldom let him down.

The next day he returned to the prison.

A heavy atmosphere of despair and an appalling rank smell of unwashed bodies, bodily functions and rat droppings greeted him. Lady Forney ran to him as soon as he entered. She had fresh scratches on her cheek. "Lord Strathairn! Can't you do something? I should not be in here with these prostitutes." She swung wildly to gesture at the women crammed into the narrow cell with her.

A woman with a hard face sneered at her. "Thinks she's too good for us and whines all the time."

Lines of tension had deepened in the countess's face, her eyes reddened.

"You have something to tell me?"

"Yes, if you get me out of this filthy hole in the wall."

Strathairn beckoned to the turnkey. When she was returned to her cell, he gestured for her to sit on the cot and offered her his handkerchief. She took the square of lawn and dabbed at the scratch on her face.

He signaled to the constable. "Fetch the countess water." He declined to sit on the flea-infested cot and leaned against the wall, folding his arms. "Now. Let's have it all."

"My husband didn't die when the ship foundered on rocks." She fussed with the handkerchief. "Forney was badly hurt though, escaping the wreck. He only lived for a few months."

"Where was this?"

"We took a house in Marseille. Many of his friends came to see him."

"Napoleonic sympathizers, I expect. Their names?"

She shook her head. "I shan't tell you that. But for Smith, they all remain in France. The cowards refused to join us."

"What is Smith's real name?"

"Philippe Moreau."

"Where is he hiding?"

She shrugged. "How should I know?"

He let out a heavy sigh. "You will have to do better than that."

"Moreau may have returned to Manchester."

He pushed himself away from the wall. "Has he been in Manchester before, stirring up trouble?"

"I believe so."

"Why go back there? What does he plan?"

She shrugged. "To cause trouble for the government, of course."

"Why? What drives him?"

"Moreau does as he pleases." She plucked at her bodice as if it was too tight although the gown hung loose on her slender frame. "He was a marksman in Napoleon's army."

He resisted shaking her. "Tell me more!"

"It's his plan to assassinate the Prince Regent."

Strathairn thumped the table. "When is this to take place? And where?"

She jumped in the seat. "I don't know," she cried. A little of her old fire returned to brighten her eyes. "Moreau will carry out his mission. He's prepared to die rather than fail."

"He will die. I assure you."

"You don't understand. He's a fanatic. British soldiers murdered his wife and children. With that gun and the element of surprise, no one can match him." She gave him a sly glance. "Your days are also numbered. You are on his list."

He ignored her jibe. "We'll find him and take away that element of surprise."

"He is not alone." She shrugged. "And as long as Bonaparte lives, emotions run high."

"Who else is with him?"

"Does he work with others?"

"No. This glorious attack will be all his."

"Why were you watching the baron's house?"

"When my husband lay dying, I promised him I would avenge him."

"By doing what, murdering Lord Fortescue? His wife? His baby?"

"I don't choose to make war on babies, but there's much more at stake."

He turned to gaze at the barred window. If he looked at her now, he would hit her. "Tell me where Moreau plans to strike," he said in a calmer voice.

"I cannot!"

"If that's the case, I can't help you." Strathairn decided to give her more time to stew over her future. He gestured to the turnkey to unlock the cell door. "We'll talk again tomorrow."

She twisted her fingers together, looking pale and curiously determined. "Do you enjoy seeing me so dirty and disheveled? I need my things." She jutted her chin at him. "I am a countess. Have them send my trunk."

Strathairn paused to think. With her things around her, she may be more inclined to talk. Remind her of the elegant life she had lost and might possibly regain. He turned to address her jailor. "Search the trunk first. I want any papers or letters you find. Remove anything sharp and keep an eye on her. I'll return tomorrow."

"Yes, my lord."

Strathairn stood in front of her, forcing her to meet his gaze. "You'll have tonight to think, Countess. I want to know what event Moreau has set his sights on. You had better come up with the right answers."

"They shall kill me whatever I say," her high-pitched voice echoed after him.

"Not if you give us the correct information."

Once home, he found the house too empty and went out again. He drank at an alehouse he hadn't been to for some time. Molly sidled up to him with a laugh. She ran her hands over his chest. "I've missed you, me lord."

Strathairn grinned down at her, appreciating her pretty face. "Have you, Molly?"

"Would you care to come upstairs?" She nudged her head toward the narrow stairs, which led to her attic room.

"Not tonight, Molly love. Allow me to buy you dinner." Strathairn smiled at her with the knowledge that he would never return here. Loving Sibella had stripped the habits of his old life away. He wasn't sure what lay ahead for him now.

Strathairn woke suddenly and rubbed his temples to ease the pounding in his head. After retiring late, he'd woken in the early hours drenched in sweat from another bad dream. He snatched his watch off the dresser. Barely seven. "Come!" he yelled at the brave servant who had knocked.

His butler, Rhodes opened the door and peered in. "Are you awake, my lord?"

"I am now, curse it! What's the matter?"

"A constable has arrived from the prison. He waits downstairs."

A shiver of apprehension ran through him. He threw back the covers and slid to the floor. "Show him into the library."

Strathairn shrugged on his banyan, pushed his feet into backless slippers and strode downstairs.

A man he didn't know stood ill at ease in the dim cold library. On seeing Strathairn, he hurried forward. "Grimsby, milord. It's Countess Forney. She killed herself during the night."

Strathairn cursed so fulsomely the man took a step back. "How the devil did she manage to do that?"

"A letter opener in her trunk. Quite sharp it was." He made a stabbing motion to his throat.

"Can't anyone obey orders?" Strathairn yelled. "You were to watch her! Her trunk was to be searched!"

"It was during a changing of the guard, milord." The man rose up on his toes. "We had searched her things, but the pretty thing looked like a trinket, in a brass scabbard it was, in among her jewelry..."

"Enough!"

The constable shuffled his feet and hung his head. "What's to be done, milord?"

Strathairn strode up and down, rubbing his hand across the stubble on his jaw. "Have the trunk sent here." He should not have trusted the fools. Now Moreau was free to go about his business unimpeded.

He had dressed, shaved, and breakfasted by the time the trunk arrived. It had been placed in the middle of the Turkey rug in the library. Strathairn threw back the lid. It was filled with expensive gowns, silk shoes, and fripperies. He kneeled and rooted through it. The jewelry box was empty. Perhaps the countess had used her jewelry to bargain for special privileges. More likely they had been stolen. One way or another, anything of value had found its way into the pockets of the prison guards.

He sat back on his haunches in disgust. Nothing. After easing his shoulders, he began again, taking out each item to study closely. He was losing heart and almost down to the bottom of the trunk when something bumped against his hand. "Fetch me a knife," he demanded of the footman who stood at the open door.

Strathairn took the knife and sliced through the crimson silk. He discovered a small book hidden in the lining. He sat by the fire to read it.

IN THE CONSERVATORY at Brandreth Park, Sibella pressed soil into a pot, glad to be back where she was at her most peaceful. She put the pot aside and took another as the scents of earth and fragrant lilies rose to soothe her.

"Sib?"

She spun around. "Vaughn!" She ran to hug him, drawing off her soiled gloves. "You appear well. Have you found Yorkshire to your liking?"

He grinned. "The weather is cold and it rains a lot, but it does tend to agree with me."

She drew him to a garden seat among the potted shrubs. "Do you plan to return?"

He straightened his shoulders. "Of course. Strathairn relies on me to help run things while he's away."

"I'm sure he appreciates all that you do."

"I wrote and told him I was coming to London because Mama wished to see me. He said he hoped to come down while I'm here. We have much to discuss."

Sibella tensed. "Strathairn is coming down to Tunbridge Wells?"

"I expect so, but he didn't say when."

Confident she'd be gone before he came, Sibella cast a fond look at her brother. "Tell me about your life at Linden Hall. What fills your days?"

Vaughn's recounting of his daily activities involved horses almost entirely. While sensing he was editing out anything she might disapprove of, Sibella's mind wandered. The duke and duchess were to return earlier than expected, and her visit was to take place the following Saturday. It fitted perfectly as Lord Coombe was to depart for Bristol on Sunday. Even if Strathairn arrived before they left, he was unlikely to find anything unusual about her visiting the abbey. If only she could be more confident of her own behavior under pressure. When suspicious, Strathairn's measuring gaze made her dreadfully nervous.

"And on Saturday evenings…" Vaughn was saying. "I attend the dances at the York assembly."

"You've made friends there?"

His roguish expression put her on the alert. The old Vaughn made an appearance. "I'd love to hear about them."

"The apothecary's daughter, Jenny, and I enjoy a dance. She has lovely fair hair and the bluest eyes."

"You will be careful, won't you, dearest? You can't toy with a girl from a respectable home."

He smoothed back his hair looking affronted. "Sib! You think so little of me."

"No, I don't. It's just that girls do take to you." She couldn't resist mussing his hair again. "You're such a handsome devil."

"Chaloner won't approve, but Jenny is a very sweet girl. You would like her, Sib."

"I'm sure I would." Sibella looked at him sadly. As the fourth-born son, it was unlikely he'd ever be heir, but marrying outside the beau monde was frowned upon. If his feelings remained constant, she resolved to help him persuade Chaloner to agree.

Chapter Nineteen

PARNHAM RAISED HIS head from the pages torn from the countess's book scattered over his desk. "We learn nothing of Forney from this."

They had learned much from the notes made by the countess, however, about the house in Seven Dials where they were to meet to discuss their future plans, her strategy to use Crutchet for her own ends, and details about the top-loading rifle Moreau had used to shoot Irvine and how it was brought to Liverpool from America. An American gunsmith had built the gun from the stolen plans of a man called Hall.

The gun was then smuggled aboard a boat to London where Dawes unloaded the crate. Moreau, the best marksman in Napoleon's army, planned to use the gun to assassinate the Regent and politicians. Lady Forney's personal vendetta to kidnap Guy's baby had thankfully been foiled. However, none of this told them when and where Moreau would strike.

Strathairn eased his tense shoulders. "What news from agents up north?"

"Nothing. The man's gone to ground." Parnham said. "The Regent is ill with pleurisy. He's not expected to make an appearance for at least another week. The next official function that draws both royalty and politicians together is the regent's patronage of Vauxhall Gardens Grand Gala. It's a perfect venue for him to strike under the cover of a fireworks display. The regent is determined to appear before the people. He is anxious to give a show of strength as he fears Princess Caroline, who remains popular here, will return to England." He paused. "The only other possible occasion would be the wedding of the Marquess of Harrington, but I shouldn't think—"

"What?" Strathairn jumped to his feet. "Sibella's sister, Maria's wedding to Lord Harrington? Who's invited?"

Parnham scratched his head. "The Duke is a favorite of King George, but the king won't be there, of course. St. Paul's Cathedral will draw quite a crowd with members of the *ton* and the regent attending, and possibly Viscount Sidmouth and Lord Castlereagh as well."

"We must take precautions," Strathairn said uneasily.

"The prince is well guarded and won't take kindly to us making an unnecessary fuss. His relationship with the people is bad enough. We'll throw all our resources at the gala." Parnham folded his arms. "Vauxhall Gardens has been advertised. Moreau will know of it."

"Still," Strathairn said thoughtfully, "with that gun, he could pick off the prince and several others right in front of the cathedral. He may even get inside."

Parnham's brows lowered. "The difficulty we have is that the prince never takes attempts on his life seriously. He will insist on attending, and the rest of the guests can hardly cry off."

"We could throw a net around the whole place and seal off all the roads," Strathairn said. "Check every carriage before it reaches the cathedral."

"How can I justify the expense of both venues when this madman might have decided his cover is blown and has gone back to France?"

"If Moreau turns up, I can get him," Strathairn said forcefully. "Don't you see? He may have both affairs in his sights. If he fails to strike at the wedding, he will try again at the gala, and maybe with some success."

"It will be on your head if all this expense is for naught," Parnham said. "We can hardly bring in the army. I don't know how I'm going to explain this to the home office."

"Let it be on my head." Strathairn pushed back his chair and stood. "If you don't need me for the following week or so, I'll take a sojourn to the country."

Parnham's brows flew up. "Yorkshire?"

"Kent. I'll alert the Brandreths. And I think a visit to advise the Duke of Lamplugh and his son is politic."

"I will send word. Better perhaps to handle this in person if you're down that way," Parnham said, drumming his fingers on his desk. "No sense in alarming them too much. Assure them that St. Paul's will be made secure. Tell them we have no concrete proof there will be any danger." He leaned back. "I can't say I like you being caught up in this, though. You have a personal interest in getting this man, which is never good—one can lose one's perspective. And this Moreau might be after you."

Strathairn grinned. "I didn't know you cared, Parnham."

Parnham gave a wry smile. "I just don't want to have to go to the trouble of replacing you."

Strathairn left the building. He had a more personal interest than Parnham realized. There was a lot riding on the success of this mission. The safety of Sibella and her family, revenge for Nesbit's death, and, if he was honest, the desire to have people respect and honor the work he did instead of viewing him with doubt in their eyes. He rubbed his neck. If he was wrong, he would come under serious censure.

He doubted the Brandreths would change their plans. Well, he would be there to take care of Sibella, whether Coombe liked it or not.

ON SATURDAY, SIBELLA and Maria journeyed to Lamplugh Abbey, as the duke and duchess were now in residence. Relieved to be at last actively tackling her concerns, Sibella attempted to ignore her irrational disappointment at missing Strathairn's visit to Brandreth Park.

Some hours later, the carriage traveled through a handsome park of chestnut, oak, and beech. "Lamplugh Abbey has a five-hundred-acre deer park," Maria said, gazing out the window.

The massive roof of the abbey appeared against the backdrop of a tumultuous sky. Maria turned to Sibella. "Storm clouds. You can't go in bad weather."

"I have to Maria," Sibella said through tight lips.

Maria sighed. "You will take a groom with you tomorrow?"

"I can't trust any of the duke's grooms to be discreet. Word is sure to reach him."

"Then take Manley. You can trust him. He's been with us forever."

Involving their groom in her scheme didn't seem wise, but Maria would fret if she didn't. "I'll consider it," she said, as they drove past an ornamental water feature graced with a majestic stone fountain.

Their carriage stopped in front of the building where four large wagons stood, with grooms at the horses' heads. Liveried footmen assisted a group of workmen as they carried crates up the steps and through the towering arched doorway. Some appeared to be very heavy.

A tall, slim figure emerged from the house. Harry came down the steps to greet them. He kissed them both on the cheek. "My parents have purchased all the statues and paintings in Italy," he said, his brown eyes smiling.

Sibella laughed. "I can't wait to see them."

"Father is like a boy at Christmas opening the crates. Mother sends her love and her apologies. She is resting as she is exhausted after the trip and will join us at dinner."

Harry led them through cavernous rooms filled with exquisite furniture, paintings, and tapestries to a huge echoing chamber where his father stalked about issuing orders to the workmen. More than a dozen paintings in gilt frames were lined up along the walls. Statues draped in white cloth stood around like ghosts.

The duke was an older version of Harry, tall and slim with greying brown hair. "My two favorite young women." He strode over with a glint in his eye. "Not one of these paintings can rival your beauty."

Maria stood on tiptoe to kiss him on the cheek.

Sibella gave him her hand to kiss. "Your Grace, you spoil us with your compliments."

"Impossible, my dear." He swept an arm around to encompass his new acquisitions. "What do you think?"

Sibella wandered along the row of paintings. Many of the artists were unknown to her. Some depicted historical battles. Yet not all were Italian. She spotted a delicious dainty Fragonard among them. "They are magnificent, your Grace."

"I'm glad you approve, my dear. Harry, ring the bell for tea. These ladies will be parched and require refreshment after their long trip."

After tea, Sibella left Maria alone with Harry. She went to the bedchamber she was to share with her sister. Too fidgety to do more than flick through a magazine, she gave up and went to the window to gaze at the grounds. Tomorrow, she would ride through those woods that separated them from Coombe's estate.

At dinner, Sibella entered the dining room on Harry's arm. She had always been interested in decoration and approved of the furnishings in this elegant room. The carpets and curtains were of rose and gold, the walls papered in soft mint-green damask, the cornices picked out in gold leaf as was the elaborately carved ceiling, from which hung a magnificent Italian chandelier.

The duke apologized for not providing more company. "It must be just a family affair because the duchess is still a little fatigued."

Some twenty dishes were laid out over the table, salmon at one end and a turbot at the other. Each was a masterpiece, the oyster sauce superb. Sibella sipped the delicious wine from grapes grown in sun-kissed Italian vineyards. Any other time she would enjoy the amusing and light-hearted conversation which took place. The duke carved the haunch of venison and the footmen served dishes on silver salvers. Maria looked beautiful in her gown of white silk and lilac net and seemed so much at home it gladdened Sibella's heart. It was good they had come, she decided, as long as tomorrow's escapade remained undiscovered.

The duchess spoke fondly of the Italian climate as plates of cheese and salad appeared, along with creams, a *Ragout a la Francaise* and pastries.

Sibella retired to the drawing room with the ladies, leaving Harry and his father to their port. The duchess, declaring herself refreshed from her rest, was keen to discuss the wedding with Maria.

The two men entered as Maria, with a shy glance at Harry, described her wedding gown made by the renown French couturiere, Madame Le Roy, to her future mother-in-law. While Harry attempted to overhear them, Sibella beat him at chess. He promptly demanded a return match. Fired up by masculine pride, he beat her soundly while Maria entertained them at the pianoforte. Her sister then joined them for a game of whist before they retired early, keeping country hours.

They picked up their candleholders. Harry dismissed the footman and escorted them up the carved oak staircase and along shadowy paneled corridors to their bedchamber.

Harry and Maria left Sibella at their bedchamber door. She said goodnight to Harry and as the door closed, Maria giggled. Harry must have stolen a kiss.

Sibella had just dismissed the maid when Maria reappeared with a blissful smile. She danced across the deep rose-pink carpet and perched on the edge of the bedcover of silk damask. Her expression grew somber. "Aren't you afraid you might arrive tomorrow and find Lord Coombe still there?"

"Not much chance of it. He must make an early start for Bristol. He'll be long gone by the time I arrive."

Maria plucked at a gold tassel. "What will you tell his servants?"

"That I hoped to see him before he left. That my groom's horse lost a shoe and had to return to the abbey."

Maria rose and turned her back for Sibella to untie her stays. "You're not taking Manley with you?"

Sibella's fingers paused. "I can't take the risk. Harry's parents must never learn of it. Your wedding is to be a splendid affair. Every important personage in the government as well as royalty will be there." She finished and stood back to study her sister. "Aren't you nervous?"

"A little." Maria wriggled out of her petticoat. "But I'm looking forward to it, the honeymoon especially."

Sibella laughed. "I'm surprised you two have been able to wait."

"Now we're under the same roof it becomes more difficult, especially as all the footmen are engaged in helping with the new acquisitions. Tonight, we were quite alone, and Harry pulled me into an empty chamber." She giggled. "He made me leave him there because he was…you know."

Sibella raised her brows. "Now how would I know?"

Maria scoffed. "You don't think you had the same effect on Strathairn when he kissed you in the garden?"

Sibella closed her eyes and gloried in the night they were alone in his house. Why hadn't he made love to her? "I didn't notice."

Maria made a rude noise of dismissal. "What about Henry? He has kissed you, has he not?"

"My dear, Henry Coombe's kisses are chaste!"

"That will change after you're married."

"I hope never to find out." She drew off her dressing gown and retied the ribbon on her lawn nightgown. When she climbed into the massive carved four-poster, she uttered a heartfelt prayer to that effect as she warmed her feet near the foot warmer.

Maria donned her nightgown and joined Sibella in the bed, pulling the curtains closed against the draft. "Dearest, what if you can't find anything there to aid your cause? What on earth will you do?"

A sob rose in Sibella's throat. She hastily swallowed it down and huffed with frustration. "As soon as you are wed, I will end the engagement. Then I might as well spend the rest of my days shut away in the country!"

Chapter Twenty

SIBELLA'S BITE OF toast stuck in her throat and she hastily took a sip of tea to force it down. "I fancy a ride over the grounds this morning." She warmed her hands around her teacup. "I simply must see more of the deer park." As the duke and duchess failed to make an appearance at breakfast, there was no one to dissuade her but Harry.

He glanced at the sky through the window. "I don't like that bank of dark clouds on the horizon. The wind's picked up, see how the trees sway? The storm will reach us soon."

"If I leave straight after breakfast, I can be back before the bad weather arrives."

"I'd accompany you, but I woke with a headache," Maria said, putting a hand to her forehead.

Harry eyed her anxiously. "Would you like me to ask mother for a restorative?"

"Heavens no," Maria said. "I'm sure I'll feel better soon."

"I'm sorry your head hurts, dearest," Sibella said sympathetically. "Please don't worry. I'll take Manley with me."

Maria cast her an anxious glance. "Good."

Harry signaled the footman to refill his coffee cup. "You'd best take one of my father's grooms. Then there'll be no likelihood of you getting lost. They know the estate whereas Manly doesn't."

"Manley has a wonderful sense of direction," Sibella said hastily. "I think I'd hurt his feelings if I didn't allow him to come."

Harry picked up his fork and drew on the white tablecloth. "If you follow the path, you'll come to the river. There's a bridge about a mile along. Cross it and keep to the east. You should have little difficulty. Then you can retrace your steps. The bucks won't give you any trouble this time of year."

"Are you sure, Harry?" Maria asked, her eyes like saucers.

Harry reached across and patted her hand. "Only in spring when they get frisky. I did hope to show you some of the estate, my sweet."

Maria laid a languid hand on her temple. "I couldn't manage to ride, but a walk through the gardens would be perfect. They are known to be glorious."

"Mother's roses gain first prize at the church fete every year, but this is not the best season to view them," Harry said. "But I can show you the hot houses."

"How perfectly lovely." Maria sent him a melting smile, and Harry grinned back.

Sibella worried that they might succumb to passion in a potting shed. She had certainly thrown opportunity their way. She stood. "I must go and change."

"I'll keep you company." Maria followed her from the room.

Upstairs in their bedchamber, Sibella pulled on a boot. "Do be careful of your behavior with Harry. Caught in *flagrante delicto* and facing a scandal two weeks before your wedding would scarcely be wise."

Maria laughed. "You are instructing me on appropriate behavior?"

"I feel entirely responsible. After all, I made you come here." She angled the black riding hat on her head. "I must see this through. I hope you understand."

"Yes, of course I do." Maria sighed. "Please don't worry about us. Harry is a gentleman. You have enough to deal with. I shall ask the duchess to give me a tour of the gardens."

Sibella grimaced. "I didn't intend to be a spoil sport." She picked up her crop.

Maria kissed her. "Please do take care, Sib."

"I will." She forced a smile on her face. "After all, I'm hardly walking into a lion's den." She wondered if she indeed might be, as she descended the stairs.

Sibella slipped outside without encountering the duke or the duchess and walked to the stables. Manley waited with a dainty chocolate-colored mare. The grizzled haired groom approached her, his weathered face cheerful. His presence calmed her, for he'd ridden behind her when she was a child. But this time it wasn't simply a matter of picking her up when she fell off her pony. "This is Clara, milady." He led the horse to the mounting block.

As Manley adjusted the stirrups, Harry walked into the stable mews. "Thank you, Manley," Sibella said after he'd assisted her to mount. "Saddle a horse. You shall accompany me."

"I have one saddled, milady."

Surprised that he'd taken it upon himself to ride with her, she walked her horse over the quadrangle to Harry. With a worried frown, he shaded his eyes and stared up at the sky. "Keep your eye on the weather, Sibella. Those clouds are marching toward us with the wind behind them."

"But the sun is shining. It's a heavenly day. Perhaps the storm will blow away before it arrives."

"I doubt it. But I can see there's no point in arguing with one of the Brandreth girls." Harry grinned. "We'll expect you at luncheon. Enjoy your ride."

When Manley led a tall gray horse out of the stables and leapt into the saddle, Sibella gathered up the reins. She walked the horse over the cobbles. "Take good care of my sister while I'm gone," she called over her shoulder. Harry's enthusiastic affirmation reached her as she and Manley rode away.

The horses broke into a fast trot. They rode through the park, the air perfumed with pine. Stately statues dotted the grass among magnolia trees. Sibella had questioned Coombe about the proximity of his property to the abbey during their last meeting, and he'd been only too eager to explain. His park wasn't large, but one corner separated by a stream ran with the southeastern border of the duke's estate.

Although the Lamplugh acres stretched for many miles to the north and west, the border of Arrowtree Manor was only a few miles as the crow flew, Coombe had told her, with a look of pride. She could not avail herself of Harry's instructions, she would ride east toward the morning sun, and should reach the stream. Once across, she would turn south, which would take her onto Coombe's land.

When Sibella took a path leading in an easterly direction, Manley rode up beside her. "His lordship said to ride north to the river, my lady."

So Harry had given the groom instructions. "I desire to visit my fiancé, Lord Coombe, before he departs on a trip and didn't wish to worry the marquess," she said to the groom. "I trust you to be discreet."

Manley nodded. "You know the way, Lady Sibella?"

"I believe I do, but it's quite a distance, so we must hurry." Sibella nudged her horse into a canter along a well-used bridle path.

Trees gave way to scrub woodland. Apart from the flutter of wings and the twitter of birdsong, it was quiet among the trees. The horse's hooves stirred the carpet of rotting leaves, releasing the smell of damp-leaf mold into the chilly air. She raised her eyes to confirm their direction, noting where the rays of morning sun flitted through the trees.

They rode steadily east. Almost an hour passed with no sign of the stream. It was further than she expected and time was passing. She gripped the reins. It appeared unlikely she could be back at the abbey until after luncheon and hoped no one would grow concerned. A branch caught at her sleeve as the bridle path narrowed and meandered down a slope. With a gasp of relief, she heard the rush of water. They pushed through bushes and came to the deep-sided stream burbling over rocks.

The horses splashed across the rocky bottom, climbed the mossy bank on the far side, and emerged into a glade.

"Where to now, Lady Sibella?" Manley's horse danced about, eager to gallop across the flat ground.

Sibella paused to get her bearings. The wind picked up and gold-edged gray clouds raced across the sky toward them, blocking the sun. A flash of lightning lit up the landscape and the rumble of thunder followed in an alarmingly short time. She tried to remember Coombe's description of his lands.

"I believe we are now on Arrowtree land. We must take a diagonal path across the glade and travel south," she called, praying she was right.

They rode over a plowed field bordered by hedgerow trees, the harvesting over. Another half hour passed, and gusts of wind began to tug at her hat. Rain-laden clouds caught up with them and loomed overhead. Lightning flashed again, the thunder deafening. She glanced up in dismay when a raindrop touched her cheek. "We must hurry," she called to Manley.

Sibella touched her mare with her crop and they galloped across a meadow and jumped a fence, surprising grazing sheep. She scanned the horizon and caught sight of smoke blown about by the wind. "There's the manor," she shouted, hoping it was Coombe's.

She set the mare at a wooden gate and cleared it easily. With Manley close behind her, she rode on through a copse of beech trees. Her thigh muscles aching. She'd not had such a long demanding ride in years.

Moments later, as droplets ran down her neck, they emerged onto the lawns of a small park at the stables of Arrowtree Manor.

Sibella dismounted as a stable hand rushed out to greet them. She nodded to the fellow and handed the reins to Manley. "Wait until I send for you." She hurried over the gravel drive to the house and circumnavigating it, approached the front door. She brushed the droplets from her damp green velvet habit as a maid answered the door. "Please inform Lord Coombe that Lady Sibella Winborne is here."

The maid curtsied. "The master isn't here, my lady."

"Oh, he's left already?" Sibella stepped through into the entry hall. "Then I'll speak to the housekeeper."

She was shown into the drawing room. Heavy rain beat at the windows and the trees swayed about in a gale. Her stomach roiling with nerves, she couldn't sit and strolled around, studying the room again. She had not cared for the house the first time and liked it no better now. Mary Jane seemed to haunt every nook and cranny. She rubbed her arms and took herself to task. She was being fanciful. What was the matter with her?

The housekeeper, Mrs. Elphick, appeared. "My goodness, Lady Sibella, you've missed Lord Coombe by several hours. Surely he wasn't expecting you?"

Sibella smiled. "No, it was a spur-of-the-moment decision, Mrs. Elphick. I rode over hoping to catch him."

"You rode, alone?" The housekeeper's eyes narrowed, although she fought to hide her disapproval.

"My groom awaits me in the stables. My sister and I are visiting the Duke of Lamplugh. Lady Maria is soon to marry his son, the Marquess of Harrington."

The mention of the duke worked, and a smile appeared on Mrs. Elphick's long face. "My goodness, all the way from Lamplugh Abbey. I'm sure you'll be wanting a cup of tea after your long ride. You've avoided the bad weather. But how shall you get home?"

"A bit of rain never hurt anyone, Mrs. Elphick."

"My good mother never recovered from a soaking. Came down with a chest complaint, and that was the end of her."

"I am sorry to hear it. But how annoying to have missed Lord Coombe. I wished to discuss with him several pieces of furniture my mother has gifted to me. I'm sure I can find a place for them."

"Lady Coombe furnished the house most carefully. I doubt there's a corner that hasn't been filled."

"Then some pieces must be replaced." Sibella walked around the room determined to put her mark on the house if only in her mind.

Mrs. Elphick nodded doubtfully. "Yes, my lady, if you'll excuse me, I'll see to the tea."

"I'll shall make a quick inspection before I take my tea. I wish to see the bedchambers. I have an excellent desk I plan to place in my bedchamber for correspondence."

Mrs. Elphick hovered at the door. "Oh? Yes, of course. I'll have a footman escort you."

"Not necessary, thank you. I know my way around after you so kindly showed me over the house the last time I came."

"Of course," Mrs. Elphick said again, looking so helpless Sibella had begun to feel sorry for her. "I'll see to the tea, I'm sure Cook has some of her excellent carrot cake to tempt you. If you'll excuse me?"

Sibella gathered up her skirts and climbed the stairs. With little effort, she located what must once have been Mary Jane's chamber, furnished in Chinoiserie silks. A delicate perfume still hung in the air as if she'd just left the room. The chamber was a riot of pattern and color, unlike the formal decoration employed in the rest of the house: embroidered cushions on the silk counterpane, a flowery carpet, and romantic tapestries.

Sibella had noticed some excellent French pieces about the house. Perhaps Mary Jane inherited them from her Huguenot ancestors. There was a dainty cylinder-top bureau with finely inlaid rosewood parquetry against one wall. Sibella hurried over and pulled out each of the three small drawers. All empty. She turned her attention to the rest of the furniture, but the room had been stripped of its former occupant's belongings. Nothing remained of Mary Jane except those small decorative touches and the hint of her perfume.

Relieved to find the corridor empty, Sibella dashed into the next chamber. Coombe's. His clothes in the clothes press confirmed it. A handsome boxwood *bureau de Pente* decorated with floral inlays stood by the window. The fall-front bureau was locked. Sibella rummaged through the drawers of a table by the bed but found no key. She bent down and pulled up the edges of the rug, then searched behind the curtains. Aware that the housekeeper would soon come to find her, she spun around. She bit her lip and examined the ornate brass keyhole; doubtful Coombe would have taken such a big key with him. Just supposing he wished to keep it hidden from the servants? Where might he put it? Her breath shortened as she searched every corner of the room with mounting panic.

Where could it be? She gazed around not prepared to admit she'd failed.

The bed! A feminine choice for a gentleman's bedchamber, elaborately carved, the header and footer painted cream and decorated with swags, ribbon motifs, and knotted bows. Under the mattress was a logical hiding place. She felt along under the soft mattress—nothing. She uttered a faint curse, a favorite of one of her brothers, and ran her hands over the surface of the mattress hunting for a hard object. Again, nothing. She straightened. That left the dome finials. She seized each one in turn. Three were fixed tight, and she was quickly growing disheartened until the last one moved in her hand. Endowed with panic-filled strength, she twisted the finial, first one way and then the other. Her heart thudding, the painted knob came free in her hand. With a gasp, she peered inside. A space was hollowed out. Nestled within was a brass key.

She clamped her lips on a triumphant cry, rushed to the bureau, and inserted the key in the lock. It turned and the fall-front opened. It was a complex piece of furniture, but luckily, a similar piece lived in her mother's dressing room at Brandreth Park. She'd played at the desk as a child, and could locate the hidden locked drawers, and now opened each one. Mary Jane's jewels were wrapped in velvet, as well as some documents, which a cursory glance showed were of no great interest. Deep within the desk, she found a sheath of letters written in a lady's hand. She held them to her nose, recognizing Mary Jane's perfume. With no time to read them, she raised her skirt and tucked them into the top of her stocking, securing them beneath her garter. She rustled when she walked, but it couldn't be helped. She just had time to lock the desk and replace the key, for a solid tread sounded on the stairs.

Sibella hurried from the room. "I see there are several nice pieces here already," she said, finding the housekeeper hovering in the corridor.

"Lady Coombe had excellent taste. Your tea is ready, my lady. I hope you have had sufficient time to look around at your leisure."

"How thoughtful, thank you. Now I could do with that cup of tea."

In the drawing room once again, Sibella sat on the velvet sofa. The maid brought in a tray. She unloaded the tea things, sandwiches, and a slice of carrot cake onto a rosewood pedestal tea table, scrutinized by Mrs. Elphick.

"You have a long, wet ride home." Mrs. Elphick gave a gloomy shake of her head, no doubt thinking Sibella mad to have ridden all the way there.

"I expect so. Could you arrange for my groom to be given something to eat? These look quite delicious."

As soon as Mrs. Elphick left the room, Sibella stood and removed the bunch of letters from her stocking. An eye on the door, she opened one. It was signed 'your loving wife'. Disappointed, she returned the letter to the pile. She poured the tea into the china cup and added milk. Taking a sip, she picked up another letter. She read it in its entirety without a twinge of guilt. Perhaps Mary Jane would approve.

The letter began ordinarily enough but with a pleading tone. What followed was shocking. The neat sentences grew longer and less well formed, degenerating into accusations. Was she merely ill and a little unstable? Sibella opened another and scanned the words. Similar to the first, but with each one, little by little, a story evolved.

His lordship had refused to come to his wife's bed. He made no secret of the female slave he'd brought to England and deposited in London, whom he visited whenever he wished. Apparently, he failed to hide his lack of desire for Mary Jane, telling her that her illness and the smell of laudanum made her unattractive to him. Each of her letters grew wilder, more enraged, and desperate. The final one dated twentieth May 1815, was addressed to him in the West Indies.

Mary Jane had found the slave he'd hidden in London. She learned from her how he mistreated the women at his plantation, having his way with them and begetting children, when he never came near her.

This last letter was so explicit, it turned Sibella's stomach. Mary Jane threatened to expose Coombe's behavior to society. England was turning away from slavery, she wrote, and even though he may escape prosecution, he would be condemned.

Oh, poor, poor Mary Jane. Sibella's eyes filled with tears. She wiped them away as anger churned her stomach. She gathered up the letters and stuffed them back under her garter. If this was not concrete proof that something evil had taken place here, it was certainly enough for Chaloner to see what a horrible man Coombe was and agree to put an end to their engagement.

She pushed away the cake, her appetite quite ruined, and went to ring for the housekeeper.

Mrs. Elphick appeared moments later.

"Thank you for the tea, Mrs. Elphick. I must be on my way." She straightened her skirts, aware of a crackle from the bulky letters. "When was it that poor Lady Coombe passed?"

"Just after his lordship arrived back from the West Indies on 22 August 1815. Such a sad day I will never forget it."

"Sad indeed." Sibella pulled on her gloves. "I'll walk to the stables."

"I do hope you have a safe journey home, Lady Sibella," the housekeeper said in a mournful tone. "But the rain…"

Sibella shook her head. "I'm a good rider. A little bad weather shall not bother me."

"I look forward to you returning as my mistress." The housekeeper escorted her into the hall where a footman stood waiting.

"How kind, thank…" The footman opened the door.

Lord Coombe stood on the step.

A groom held an umbrella over his head in the pelting rain. Horrified, Sibella watched the play of emotions travel over his face. Exasperation was quickly replaced by astonishment and then suspicion, which turned his brown eyes to stone.

Chapter Twenty-One

STRATHAIRN PUT UP at a coaching inn in Tunbridge Wells on his way to Brandreth Park. As he was shown to his room, he wondered how he would tell Chaloner and the family the news about Moreau without causing them alarm and anxiety. There was no way, he just had to tell them. He couldn't bear any harm to come to Sibella or indeed the rest of the family. He would stress to them the security arrangements that Parnham had made at the cathedral.

The next day, after a sleepless night, as thoughts of Sibella filled his mind, he drove his phaeton through the gates at Brandreth Park at mid-morning, eager to see her again.

The butler, Belton, assisted him out of his greatcoat. "The family are in the salon, my lord."

Strathairn entered the room where the dowager sat with Vaughn, Chaloner, Lavinia, and their children.

"Strathairn, you have arrived in time for luncheon," Chaloner said. "We received your note. What news do you have?"

"It may spoil your appetite, Chaloner. I wish I didn't have to tell you this." Strathairn took a seat as a stunned silence settled over the room as he talked.

Chaloner leaped from his chair before Strathairn finished speaking. "This is beyond the pale! We shall have to delay the wedding. Or hold it in another church. St. Georges, Hanover Square perhaps."

"I doubt the duke and duchess would agree to that," the dowager said, seemingly unruffled by the news. "They planned their son's wedding at St. Paul's the day he was born. And you can hardly ask the Regent to order a change in his itinerary."

"It's your decision, naturally," Strathairn said. "It's the opinion of the home secretary that if the assassin does strike, it will be at the Grand Gala held at Vauxhall Gardens, under the cover of Signora Hengler's fireworks display."

"Surely that must be the better choice of the two," the dowager said. "I read of it in the *London Times*. Madame Saqui plans an astonishing ascent on the tightrope, amidst a brilliant display of fireworks."

It sounded feasible, but Strathairn remained uneasy. "If the wedding takes place, rest assured, St. Paul's will be surrounded by guards and more will guard the interior. Discreetly, of course."

"Well, it sounds like pure conjecture to me." Vaughn leaned back and crossed his arms. "I say we allow the duke to make the final decision on the matter."

"That's sensible, Vaughn." His mother directed a fond smile at him.

Vaughn pushed himself to his feet and stretched, puffing out his chest. "If you can spare Strathairn, I need to discuss business with him."

Strathairn stood. "After which, I'll say my farewells and continue on to Lamplugh Abbey."

"A noisy coaching inn for luncheon? Nonsense," the dowager said. "You'll eat here, of course."

"You must, Lord Strathairn," Lavinia said. An ethereal looking woman, fine-boned and delicate, but the look she gave her mother-in-law was sharp.

Chaloner nodded. "Yes, I'd welcome a chance to talk further to you on this."

Strathairn bowed. "Thank you. You are most kind, but surely, it's inconvenient. I expect the whole family is here."

"Sibella and Maria are not." The dowager fixed him with one of her challenging stares. "They are visiting Harry's parents."

"Then I shall have the opportunity of explaining the situation to them there this afternoon," Strathairn said.

"You won't scare Sibella," her mother said. "She wouldn't have Maria's wedding spoiled for anything. She is a game one."

He couldn't help smiling. "I'm aware of that."

"High time you were," the dowager said with a lift of her brows.

Chaloner grimaced. "Mother, please."

His mother ignored him, her eyes on Strathairn. "My son Bartholomew will journey from York to preside over Sibella and Coombe's wedding."

"You will be pleased to see your son again, my lady," Strathairn said, refusing to be drawn.

The dowager gave a sharp nod. "I shall speak to you before you leave, Strathairn."

"Certainly, my lady. I await your summons." He smiled slightly and bowed, then followed Vaughn from the room, wondering what the imperious dowager marchioness had in mind for him. Surely, it was a little late to chide him. Or was she as worried about Sibella as he was?

"BROWN, DON'T JUST stand there dripping on the step. Remove yourself and that umbrella along with you," Coombes yelled at the hapless groom.

"Henry!" Pulse racing, Sibella hurried forward to take Coombe's arm. "I thought I'd missed you. I rode over from Lamplugh Abbey. Mama has given me some lovely furniture and I hope to find places to put them." She drew back. "But, you're drenched through. You must change immediately. What has happened to prevent your journey?"

Coombe's dark inscrutable eyes wandered over her. Apparently, he liked what he saw for his brown eyes brightened. "The storm has caused chaos. Floodwater washed down from the north. A bridge is damaged and the road impassable. We were forced to turn back."

"How annoying for you." Sibella's mind whirled. She must get away from here before he discovered the missing letters. But how? "I'm sure you are in need of a hot drink." She nodded at Mrs. Elphick, who stood waiting, her hands clasped at her waist. "After you've changed your clothes, Henry, please join me in the dining room."

"I'm not as wet as all that," Coombe said. He put a foot on the stair. "Come and show me where you propose these pieces of furniture to go. What are they?"

She struggled to breathe normally as she mentioned several pieces her mother would never part with. "The Chippendale desk and a pair of Louis XV chairs which are quite exquisite. They would be perfect for my bedchamber which I gather is the room to the right of the stairs?"

"There's a perfectly nice desk in that room already," he swung around to look at her.

"Yes, but I wish some of my own things around me. You will allow me that, won't you?" She fluttered her lashes, hoping the effect pleased him. A flirtatious, shrewd woman would have better luck with Coombe.

"I'm not sure about Chippendale though," he called down, having reached the top.

Conscious of a rustle at every step, Sibella was forced to follow him to continue the conversation. "But Chippendale made beautiful things. Do you not agree?"

"In the right setting."

They reached the landing. Coombe walked along the corridor and threw open the door to Mary Jane's chamber. He stood aside for Sibella to enter.

She hesitated.

With a warm glance, he waved her in. "Well? Come in and show me where they are to go."

She stepped into the room but stayed by the door. "I thought to replace the small desk over by the window. I require something larger for the considerable amount of correspondence I write."

He took her arm and drew her into the room. "What's that infernal crackling noise?"

She flushed. "It's not very polite of you to mention it, Henry. It's to do with my underwear."

He raised a brow. "Is it? How intriguing."

"Not intriguing, I assure you. Too much starch. It's… embarrassing." She prayed he would leave the matter alone. "Now, shall we have tea?"

"In a while." His study of her became disturbingly possessive. "I must say, I'm surprised to find you here. Alone."

"My groom waits for me at the stables."

"Does he? Then he shall wait a while longer." She stilled when he took her by the shoulders, then slid his hands down her arms to pull her against him. He lowered his mouth to hers. Sibella's breath caught, she was conscious of the letters, which must press against his thigh as he pulled her against him, his hands roaming down her back. His breath hissed against her mouth, his kiss hard and possessive, and not at all like his previously chaste kisses. She tried not to gag at the smell of Makassar oil he used liberally on his hair. When she recalled what Mary Jane had written, she had to struggle with the desire to push him back.

He drew away, excited anticipation in his eyes.

"You surprise me." Her forced smile must have looked suitably strained. "being here like this is quite scandalous."

"I have kept myself on a tight rein where you're concerned," he admitted, causing a rush of horror to weaken her knees. "But we shall be married in just a few weeks, is that not so?"

"But still, alone in a bedchamber. Our conduct will be talked about in the servants' quarters. I confess I don't feel comfortable about it."

"My staff wouldn't dare." He sighed. "Very well. Go to the drawing room. I'll be down directly."

Relieved, Sibella hurried to the staircase. She wasn't sure he believed her feeble explanation for the rustling. Would he think to check that the letters remained in their hiding place? She fought to stay calm when panic threatened to turn her descent into an unladylike scramble.

"One moment, Lady Sibella," Coombe called from his bedchamber.

With a quick indrawn breath, she chose not to hear him. She flew down the last steps arriving in the entry hall in a fluster, and almost fell. The footman stared at her with concern. Above her, Coombe came to lean over the banister rail. "My, you are in a hurry. I merely wished to tell you I will drive you back to Lamplugh Abbey."

"Would you? Thank you, Henry, so kind." Relief made her voice catch. "I was meant to be there for luncheon. I'd hate to worry them."

"I could hardly send you out into the rain on horseback. What would the duke think of me?" He looked pleased as he tugged at his cravat, then disappeared.

Sibella hurried into the drawing room. She took an agitated turn about the room, twisting her hands together. Before long, Coombe entered, dressed in fresh clothing, his hair brushed back. Her gaze flew to his but failed to judge his mood. His eyes reminded her of her mother's jet necklace she always wore to funerals: gleaming, dark, and hard, and she looked away.

Chapter Twenty-Two

STRATHAIRN DROVE HIS horses along the road toward Lamplugh Abbey, reflecting on his conversation with the dowager. Lady Brandreth confessed to having observed her daughter become increasingly unhappy. Her worry grew stronger after detecting a certain coldness in Coombe she didn't much like and hadn't noticed before. It may well be that marriage could change this once they got to know each other, but she wished she could be sure of it. She wasn't asking for the impossible, but would he please try to draw Sibella out? They had been such good friends, she was sure her daughter would confide in him.

"I find myself somewhat helpless for the first time in my life, Strathairn." She eyed him anxiously. "She doesn't confide in me. My opinion no longer seems to matter."

"I will, my lady. But Lady Sibella knows her own mind." He tactfully declined to mention her brother's determination that she marry Coombe.

"I wish Sibella had married you, Strathairn," she admitted as he took his leave. "I could rest easy knowing she would be safe." She drew out her handkerchief and sniffed. "It is a mother's wish for their daughters to find a safe haven in this dangerous world."

He'd bowed, wishing the same. He had come away stricken by the grand, fierce lady's anguish, and his own troubled thoughts deepened.

He was no easier in his mind on reaching the abbey. The butler showed him into the blue salon. Dwarfed by the size of the room, the duke and duchess sat on cream satin sofas near the fireplace with Harrington and Maria.

He walked the length of the room, noting Sibella's absence with a frustrated tightening of his lips. As he greeted them, he noticed Maria's face looked pale and her worried gaze sought his as if trying to relay a message to him. *Sibella! Where was she?* He went cold.

"Welcome, Lord Strathairn." The duke rose to greet him. "As you see, we are a small party at present and in dire need of your conversation. We await Lady Sibella's return. After breakfast, she rode off with her groom to visit the deer park and did not arrive home in time for luncheon. The storm probably drove her to seek shelter."

"I'm sure that's what has occurred," Strathairn said in a confident voice. A confidence he didn't feel. With a deep uneasiness, he realized Coombe's estate was in the direction of the deer park. Surely not… He pushed the thought away." I'm afraid I bring you troublesome news."

Strathairn sat and explained the situation. The duchess, alarmed, cried out. "Don't say we must postpone the wedding!"

"What does the regent say to this?" the duke asked.

"He insists on attending, your Grace. I doubt anyone has declined."

The duke narrowed his eyes. "We English won't bow to repression of any kind."

Strathairn agreed while he kept an eye on the door for Sibella. Maria knew something the others did not, and he wondered how he might learn of it.

Harrington pushed himself out of his chair. "I'll visit the stables. They may have arrived back."

Strathairn stood. "I'll accompany you, Harrington."

"I shall come, too," Maria said quickly.

"Is it still raining?" The duchess peered through the long, mullioned windows.

"It appears the worst of the storm has passed," Strathairn said, noting Maria's stricken expression.

The rain had lessened to a slight drizzle as they left the house.

They walked with umbrellas along the drive beneath dripping trees skirting puddles.

On reaching the stables, they learned that neither Sibella nor Manley had returned.

Maria clutched her fiancé's sleeve. "Harry, I have kept something from you. I pray you'll forgive me." Her voice broke. "Sibella made me promise, but now that she hasn't returned I must tell you."

Harrington gazed tenderly at his fiancée. "Why what is it, my love?"

"Sibella rode to Coombe's house. She hoped to be back in time for luncheon, but the storm…"

"Why did she go there?" Strathairn's heart squeezed, his fears realized, he was caught between concern for her safety and the foolish irrational fear that she had tender feelings for Coombe.

"She hoped to find evidence which would convince Chaloner that Lord Coombe is not worthy of her hand in marriage. She suspects him of being cruel to his former wife, Mary Jane."

Strathairn set his teeth. "Will Coombe be there?"

Maria wiped away a tear. "No, he departed for Bristol early this morning."

"The creek becomes a raging torrent after heavy rain." Harry frowned. "They might have turned back. I'll ride out. I know where to look for them."

"Forgive me, Harry," Maria whispered. "I shall never keep anything from you again."

He patted her cheek. "My poor love, what else could you do? I'm surprised Sibella did such a rash thing. It seems most unlike her."

"She was driven to it," Maria said.

Strathairn's heart lurched as fear and anger threaded through him. *Let her be safe.* "They might take the road," he said, fighting to stay calm.

"I'd best come with you. Sibella might need me," Maria said.

"Would you allow me to take Lady Maria along with me, Harrington?"

"Yes, my lord, I trust you to keep my lady safe."

"I'll need two fresh horses."

"Of course." Harry strode to the stable.

Strathairn escorted Lady Maria to the house. She fetched her cloak and bonnet while he informed the duke and duchess of their plan.

"Harrington is a good man," he said, as they drove along the straight drive toward the massive abbey gates.

"Oh yes, he is," Maria said quietly. "I wanted the same for Sib." She glanced at him. "I'm so afraid for her."

"Sibella is a fine horsewoman."

"Yes, that's precisely why I'm afraid. Something else has delayed her return. She would never deliberately have placed me in this awkward position."

Strathairn guided the phaeton through the gates and onto the road. "Harrington is right. It is out of character for Sibella to behave like this." That she had come to him in the dead of night showed how distressed she was. And he had sent her back to him, fool that he was. He concentrated on a sharp corner, taking it faster than usual. "She must have been desperate to take such a risk," he said when safely round it.

"Oh, she was. She has been *so* unhappy."

He narrowed his eyes. If anything had happened to her at Coombe's hands, the man would meet his maker.

COOMBE DROVE SIBELLA in his curricle. Sibella's attempts at light chatter failed miserably and they traveled the road in silence. She wished he had brought a groom; she disliked being alone with him.

They left the Chiddingston cottages behind and traveled along a quiet country lane. "You were wise to order Manley to wait until the weather cleared," she said. "It would be difficult to ride through the forest after all this rain." When Coombe didn't answer, she glanced at him and suffered a frisson of fear. He was seething with anger. His jaw worked, and he held the reins in a tight grip. "Is something the matter?" she asked, afraid of his answer.

"You fool!"

"I beg your pardon?"

"I have been so careful to ensure this marriage came about. And you have ruined everything. I would have been lenient with you. You could have enjoyed all that I offered if you'd been obedient. But no, you're a nosey bitch, aren't you?"

Sibella gasped and clung to the sides of the curricle. He slowed the horse, then drove the vehicle into an overgrown lane pulling up in a clearing behind a copse of trees out of sight of the road. He secured the reins, then swiveled to face her. "I believe you have something of mine."

Sibella's stomach roiled, she was afraid she'd be sick. "I don't know what you mean."

He grabbed her wrist and twisted it. "Give the letters to me. Now!"

"You're hurting me." Her breath came in frightened gasps as she tried to pry his fingers from her wrist.

His free hand clamped over the bunch of letters under her skirt. "Tucked into your stocking, are they? I thought that rustling was suspicious. They are my property. Shall I retrieve them myself?"

"No!" Sibella shoved at his chest, but he barely moved, still holding her in a steely grip.

"Very well, then." His eyes burned fanatically as his grasping fingers gathered up the folds of her velvet habit, baring her legs above the knee.

"Lovely legs," he said dispassionately, stroking her thigh. "I have been longing to spread them. It wasn't easy keeping my lust under control. I'll enjoy you once at least. You deserve it, for you have been a very bad girl."

She punched at his arm. "Take me home! You cannot treat me this way. What will my family think of such behavior?" Terrified, she twisted within his grasp as the curricle rocked and the horse bucked and whinnied. Coombe's thin lips stretched in a leer.

"I imagine they will be somewhat distraught after learning you died in a dreadful accident."

She inhaled sharply. "Like Mary Jane?"

He sneered. "Easily done. She loved laudanum and took the large dose I gave her like a lamb. She was a weak, whining woman with no beauty. I shall enjoy you far more."

Cold sweat gathered at her nape. How long before he killed her?

He fumbled awkwardly with the thick folds of her habit and petticoat while clutching her wrist. Sibella grasped the edge of the seat and with the other hand, threw all her weight away from him. Her petticoat tore in his hands. The horse whinnied, and the carriage jerked forward. Coombe overbalanced and was forced to let her go.

She whipped the letters out from under her garter and tossed them into the air. The wind caught them, scattering paper among the shrubbery and into the trees.

"*Bitch*!" Spittle formed at the corner of his mouth. Coombe reeled back and hit her hard across the face.

The blow rattled her teeth and stung her cheek. White light flashed before her eyes. With a cry, she fell backward out of the curricle, her skirt catching with a loud ripping sound. She landed hard on the muddy soil fighting for breath.

With a snarl, Coombe raced around, snatching at the letters within his reach. He gave up trying to collect the letters and swung back to her, murder in his eyes.

Bruised and winded, she clambered to her feet, just evading his lunge. Her torn habit trailing, she skirted the trees and ran back to the road with him pounding after her.

Sibella sensed Coombe gaining on her and desperately hoped for a carriage to come along, but the road was empty.

Coombe's hand closed on her arm, pulling her back. Desperate to keep her balance, she twisted in Coombe's grip and broke free, then turned to escape as a two-wheeled wagon loaded with brewers' barrels came fast around the corner.

The wagon driver hauled on the reins. Barrels bounced over the road. One barrel struck Coombe a glancing blow, causing his feet to slip from under him.

As Coombe fought to keep his feet, he snatched at the horse's bridle. The frightened animal reared in panic. Unable to right himself, Coombe fell to his knees. A hoof struck him a glancing blow to the head, and his roar of protest abruptly ended.

Surprise in his brown eyes, he toppled onto his back, his arms and legs at odd angles beneath him.

As if watching a tableau, shocked, Sibella stood unable to move as the frightened horse plunged again.

Chapter Twenty-Three

LITTLE WAS SAID in the tense silence. Strathairn constantly searched ahead as the phaeton swayed along the country road. If he lost Sibella, he wasn't sure he could endure it.

Maria held on to her hat which threatened to fly off in the gusty breeze. "Wouldn't we have met them by now if they came this way?"

"Not necessarily. The storm would have delayed them." He was surprised at how calm he sounded when the sense of urgency made his blood pound through his veins.

She gave him a grateful glance.

They rounded a corner and Maria cried out. "There's Sibella!"

The breeze ruffled Sibella's torn skirt and bared her thigh. When she turned to them, her face was blank with shock.

Strathairn drew the phaeton to a stop. He leapt down, horrified at the scene before him.

SIBELLA LOOKED UP as Strathairn strode toward her, pulling off his coat, Maria behind him.

"Are you all right, sweetheart?" he murmured as he slipped his coat around her shoulders.

"I am now." She drew in a grateful breath of Strathairn's male scent and pulled his coat across her chest.

Held safe within Strathairn's arms, Sibella stared down at Coombe whose body lay sprawled on the road, surrounded by barrels. Blood seeped from his head. "Is he dead?" she whispered.

Strathairn gently turned her face away. "Don't look."

"As dead as a mullet in the fishmonger's window," the drayman observed, having steadied his nervous horse and climbed down. He removed his hat and scratched his head. "What the devil was goin' on here?" He eyed Sibella's torn skirt and tattered petticoat, the quality of her garments unmistakable, and raised his eyes to hers with a flush of embarrassment. "Beg pardon, miss. Was the blighter attempting to abduct you?"

"It's a family matter," Strathairn said in a tone which brooked no further discussion. "I am Lord Strathairn. Tell me your name, then I would like you to alert the constable at Chiddingston before you go about your business. I will ensure the authorities are made aware of the full story and that you are not to blame for the accident."

"Right you are, milord. Me name's Popperwell." He looked around at his barrels strewn over the road. "I'll clear the road. We don't want no vehicles coming helter-skelter around the corner and running into us, do we?"

"I'm sorry to have caused you such trouble," Sibella murmured. She sagged, relieved to have Strathairn take over, for her mind had gone completely blank, her throat tinder-dry.

"Maria, take your sister over to that log and sit her down. She's badly shocked." Strathairn rolled a barrel toward the wagon.

"Come dearest." Maria, her face strained, placed an arm around her and urged her forward.

Sibella sniffed back tears which hurt her throat. "I have to get the rest of the letters."

"We will get them, Sib, but rest for a while."

Unable to watch, Sibella wrapped herself in his coat and leaned against Maria. When she raised her head, Strathairn had moved Coombe's mangled body to the side of the road. The drayman was busy setting the last barrel in place on his wagon. He climbed onto the seat, touched his hat, and drove away.

Sibella tried to rouse herself to pull her gaze from the body.

"Let's get those letters." Strathairn took her hand in his big reassuring one and they made their way back to Coombe's curricle. The letters drifted over the ground like white butterflies, the horse still tethered to the vehicle, grazing on grass.

"I'll secure the horse to the phaeton, and one of the duke's grooms can return it. The curricle can wait." He placed a hand on Sibella's arm. "Maria will gather up the letters, sweetheart."

She shook her head. "No, I'll help." It gave her something to do and she must have the evidence to show how Mary Jane suffered and met her terrible end. She bent to collect a page fluttering on the ground and held it out to Strathairn.

"You must take good care of these," she said, her voice cracking with emotion. "They are proof that poor Mary Jane's death was not an accident. Coombe killed her. He admitted as much to me."

He gently pried the papers from her stiff fingers. "I'll take very good care of them." He glanced at the letters and shoved them into his pocket. "Did he hurt you?"

Sibella shook her head.

She shivered as the cool breeze touched her leg, suddenly aware that her skirt had been ripped almost to the waist and her petticoat was shredded, revealing her thigh up to her garter.

Strathairn tied the horse and helped Sibella and Maria into the carriage. Squashed into the phaeton which was only meant for two, Maria slipped an arm around her shoulders while Strathairn took up the reins.

"Lean against me," he said. "We'll have you home soon and get you warm."

Comforted by his solid, calm presence, she began to talk haltingly. Her voice died away after relating the horrifying account of how Coombe had admitted to killing his wife.

Marie gasped.

"Don't cry, Maria," Sibella said. "I'm all right. He can't hurt me now."

"No more now," Strathairn said. "You need a warm drink laced with spirits to counteract the shock. Then I must talk to the Chiddingston magistrate."

Sibella was ushered inside Lamplugh Abbey with Strathairn's strong arm around her. An hour later, the frozen knot still lodged in her chest despite the hot tea and fresh clothing.

She'd lost all sense of time. Was it an hour since Strathairn, Harry, and his father shut themselves in the library or a mere ten minutes? At some point, the duchess declared she needed to rest and left Maria alone with Sibella in the salon.

When Strathairn's tall figure appeared at the salon door, she'd wanted to launch herself at his chest and sob into his waistcoat. He had taken control of everything so easily it was tempting to lean on him, but she was determined not to.

Maria tactfully excused herself and left the room.

Without commenting on her appearance, Strathairn took a chair. His eyes had darkened like smoke. She could feel the anger coming off him in waves. "You won't be too hard on Chaloner, will you?"

He leaned forward and took her hand and raised it to his lips. "Coombe is the only one I wanted to kill, and I'm frustrated not to have been able to do it."

Strathairn would have sent Coombe swiftly to Hades, Sibella had no doubt. She chewed her lip. His intent and unwavering gaze would unnerve most people, but only served to warm her. He made her feel safe. And in a few minutes, he would be gone again. She wished she could go with him. When she poured cups for them both, she spilled some in the saucer. She mopped it up with a napkin annoyed that her hand wouldn't stop shaking.

"Thank you." He took the teacup and saucer from her with a worried look. As he held the cup in his big hand and sipped the drink, she remembered how he hated tea.

She grimaced at the unpleasant taste of whiskey in the tea and replaced her cup in its saucer with a clatter of china.

He searched her face, his eyes filled with concern. "The duke and I examined the letters. The man was a monster."

"Yes, a monster," she repeated faintly as another shiver passed through her. The cup rattled in its saucer.

She leaned back on the sofa cushions and allowed herself to watch his deft movements as he stirred more sugar into hers. "Try it now. Sugar is helpful after a shock."

She took another sip and nodded. "Better, thank you."

"Lady Coombe's relatives will have to be informed."

She put a shaky hand to her throat. "The letters must be sent to them. Mary Jane deserves to have her story heard."

"Yes, she does."

Maria appeared at the door. She came to sit beside Sibella. "Are you all right, Sib?" Maria asked, stroking her arm.

"I will be soon. I just want to go home."

He returned his cup to its saucer. "I'll be back tomorrow. I'll drive you, if you wish."

"Yes, do go, Sib," Maria said. "Harry will take me back later."

"Thank you." Her whole body ached with exhaustion. She would lean on him. Just for a moment until she was herself again. "Will you explain what happened to the family? I don't think I can speak of it again."

He made as if to move toward her, then abandoned the idea and sat back. "I'll take care of everything. You mustn't worry."

Maria stood. "I'll go and ask Harry."

"I'm proud of you," he said when they were alone again. "You were brave, Sibella. And mighty resourceful." He left the wing chair and dropped down beside her. "Sibella, I've been a fool…"

"Please don't." She dropped her gaze from his eyes filled with life, pain, and unquenchable warmth. She could not let him rescue her.

He stood. "Very well."

The door opened and Maria returned on Harry's arm. "Would you like to change for dinner, Sib?"

"Yes, of course." She was sure she would be dreadful company and could not eat a bite.

"Will you stay to dine with us, Strathairn?" Harry asked.

"Thank you, but no," Strathairn said. "I must get this matter dealt with at Chiddingston. I'll return in the morning to take Sibella home."

Chapter Twenty-Four

After settling the matter with the Chiddingston magistrate, Strathairn spent the night at a rowdy inn where his sleep was constantly disturbed, but he wouldn't have slept much, anyway. When he'd listened to Sibella haltingly explain what she had endured, his teeth had clamped to prevent the curses on his tongue. Filled with helpless rage, he wanted to sweep her into his arms, to take her away. Far away. To Yorkshire. No one would ever hurt her again.

One thing he knew was that somehow, he and Sibella would marry. He no longer cared what Chaloner said. Once this business with the Frenchman was dealt with, he would leave this work to someone else.

At cock's crow, he was back on the road and arrived at Lamplugh Abbey after breakfast, finding Sibella waiting for him dressed in a blue pelisse robe that reminded him of spring and irises. During their drive back to Brandreth Park, he tried gently to introduce the possibility of their marrying sometime in the future. But she shook her head and refused to discuss it. It was the wrong time; he wasn't usually so insensitive. He mustn't put his own desires first. While aware that Sibella needed her home and family at this time, more than she needed him, he still fought the urge to pull up the horse and take her in his arms.

She began to talk about Coombe. How she had doubted him from the first. Her voice was strained. She was so hurt, he could only guide his horses along the road and quietly listen.

"I intend to remove myself from society after Maria's wedding. I know Chaloner will agree. It's the right thing to do."

While he didn't agree, he realized it wasn't the time to try to argue the point. That would come later. "For how long?" His voice sounded rough. With the reins in his right hand, he took hold of hers with his left, entwining her gloved fingers with his.

"Until the whispers die down and I feel able to pick up the threads of my life again."

The pain in her voice made him close his lips on another plea. "Take all the time you need. I'll be waiting."

She huffed out a sigh and extracted her hand from his. "John, this doesn't mean… That's all behind us now. Please don't feel you have to…"

"Don't get used to being a maiden aunt, Sibella. If you take too long, I'll be coming for you."

She darted a glance at him. "What would you do if you did?"

He grinned. "Throw you over my shoulder and run off with you?"

She gave a shaky laugh. "You are not to give up your work because of me. You would only come to resent me for it. And you won't leave it, will you?"

Pleased that he'd made her laugh, he turned to look at her. "I plan to. But not yet, Sibella. Remember this while you wander the gardens of Brandreth Park, I have never doubted my feelings for you."

Much as he wanted to hold her and comfort her, he concentrated on the road. Chaloner must be made to understand how close she came to death at Coombe's hands. What a tragedy it would have been had she'd married the man.

He was prepared to fight Chaloner if it was he she was trying to placate by burying herself in the country.

They approached Brandreth Park as the sun slanted long shadows over the lawn and warmed the fine old redbrick and sandstone house with its tapestry of ivy on the walls. The family was shocked at the news, the women rallying around Sibella. Her mother and sisters whisked her away, leaving him alone with Chaloner in his study.

Strathairn eyed Chaloner over his paper-strewn desk, and his anger removed any desire for tact. He was brutal and unsparing when he related what had happened.

Chaloner blanched and appeared shamefaced as well he might. "After the wedding, Sibella says she will retire to the country until this dies down."

"I think Coombe's devilry should be shouted from the rooftops!" Strathairn thundered.

"Well…it's not how I wish to handle it," Chaloner replied. "Sibella is sensible, I'm sure she will agree. Let Lady Coombe's relatives take up her cause."

Strathairn ground his teeth. Sensible Sibella had agreed to marry a man she disliked, a veritable monster, to satisfy the demands of her family and society. He stared at the marquess and his anger, also directed at himself, exploded, leaving a sour taste in his mouth. He thumped the desk, causing the silver inkpot to dance and two quills to roll over the surface. "Surely you still don't believe you know what's right for your sister!"

Chaloner leaned back, surprised by his onslaught.

"You more or less forced her to become engaged to Coombe," Strathairn continued ruthlessly. "And obviously, did not investigate the character of the man thoroughly enough."

Chaloner shifted in his seat, a flush staining his cheeks. "Should I have encouraged a marriage between you two? You, who showed little inclination to marry? You, who preferred the society of a tavern to the *ton*, John? You, who commits shady acts on behalf of the government? God knows what that entails? Best we don't go into that!"

Strathairn eyed him coolly. "A single man lives as he chooses."

Chaloner cast an accusatory look at him. "I have never imbibed or lost money at the gambling tables."

Strathairn, thinking Chaloner might have handled Vaughn better if he'd lived a little before he married, arched an eyebrow. "No, you never did."

"I wished for a happy life for Sibella. She spent too long daydreaming about a man who wouldn't marry her. Would you not have done the same in my place?"

Strathairn refused to acknowledge the truth of Chaloner's words. He had been very poor husband material after the war, and before it, if he was honest. That wasn't who he was now. "I would have let her choose her husband. And never considered a man she hadn't warmed to. You should have valued Sibella's intelligence."

"She made up her own mind in the end. And on the face of it, Coombe was eminently respectable being an heir to a title with a tidy fortune. It would have been nigh impossible to discover what lay beneath the persona he presented to the world."

What made Coombe attractive to Chaloner was best left unsaid. Strathairn had to agree that he'd failed her, too. But he wouldn't let guilt cause him to lose his focus. He intended to be there when her lovely eyes shone with the pure joy of living, no longer inhibited by family obligations. He folded his arms. "So now you're happy for Sibella to waste her life hiding away at Brandreth Park?"

Chaloner sighed. "I've never wanted that kind of life for her. That's why I urged her to marry. But I will admit, I did get that badly wrong."

"You'll get your wish. I intend to marry her if she'll have me. I don't much care whether you approve or not."

Chaloner paused, concerned eyes searching his. "John, you could be dead and gone any day. We both know that."

"When this mission ends, I shall ask her."

"After this mission ends, you say. As if you are employed to make a survey of the roads! I pray you find this devil quickly and emerge in one piece. You are a valued friend of this family. We will always be grateful for what you did to help Vaughn. And yes, I failed there, too."

Strathairn suffered a surprising wave of compassion for Chaloner. He looked so defeated. "When you resign from your position with the military, you have my permission to ask Sibella for her hand in marriage."

Strathairn wasn't about to disclose his plans. He disliked being dictated to. His fingers dug into his palms. "A murderous scoundrel has killed one of my agents. I'll see him hang."

"Then you must concentrate on that, John. There are lives at stake as well as yours. Maria might even be in danger at her own wedding if this scum isn't caught."

Strathairn pushed back the chair and rose. "It's back to London for me. You will say my goodbyes?"

Walking to the door with Strathairn, Chaloner shook his hand. "I pray all goes well. And when you are free of this, I would be honored to welcome you into our family."

His throat tight, Strathairn gave him a thin smile. "Then please speak favorably about me to Sibella."

Chaloner shook his head and a rare smile lit his eyes. "I believe you will do that admirably yourself when the time comes."

It couldn't come fast enough. He was never good at waiting. But he saw the sense of leaving her with her family although he didn't want to. He didn't want to at all. Strathairn left the house, biting down hard on his impatience.

THE SKY LIGHTENING to gray told her it was almost dawn. Sibella tugged at the bedcoverings, which were in a hopeless tangle. She had been lying awake for hours reliving the horror of the past few days. Why had John left without saying goodbye? Would he, as he threatened, come to claim her? She remembered his fierce declaration and thumped her pillow as a quiver raced through her. But he had important work to do. Dangerous work. She shivered.

When the morning sun rimmed the curtains, she darted out of bed, pulling on her cambric gown and sturdy half boots. She wrapped a shawl around her shoulders and tucked her hair beneath a cap. The servants had just begun to stir as she walked through the house and left by the French windows.

The garden was hushed and still, the flowers fading. Sibella drew the shawl closer around her. She had always enjoyed this time of the year; the air tinged with the scent of dew-drenched grass, the wisps of mist swirling away through the trees. But today, she found no joy in it. She tried not to dwell on the last few days but thought instead of her crushed dreams and the lonely time ahead. The dreary reflection brought a sigh to her lips.

She hurried across the lawn trying to lighten her mood. Maria needed her now. The wedding loomed and should rightly be a thrilling day, but the event was shrouded by the dark cloud of Coombe's death and the shocking news that a madman might strike as everyone gathered at St. Paul's Cathedral.

The first rays of sunlight penetrated the chestnut's canopy of leaves above her, but there was little warmth in it as she walked on, the fallen leaves crunching underfoot. She retraced her steps to the house before she was missed.

Once she'd dressed she went down to breakfast. Chaloner entered the breakfast room. "You're up early."

A footman pulled out her favorite chair near the window. "I could not sleep."

"Poor Sib. You've been through the mill." His eyes looked shadowed as he drew out the chair and sat opposite her. "I am to blame. I wish I could make it up to you."

She reached across and touched his hand. "Don't be silly. You just wanted the best for me."

"I still do."

"Have you read the letters?"

Chaloner scrubbed his hands over his hair. "Yes. It made fearsome reading. Made my blood run cold." He swallowed. "That I might have talked you into marrying him, horrifies me."

"Was John very angry?"

"Seething. I think there's a dent in my desk."

Her eyes widened. "You weren't to know. It would have been hard to discover any of it. Not unless you sent someone to the West

Indies, and even then, the truth about Mary Jane would not have come to light. Coombe kept his secrets close."

"Still. I'm devastated, Sibella. It's my dearest wish to see you happily settled."

She nodded absent-mindedly as Belton came in. "Coffee, Lord Brandreth? Lady Sibella?"

When the butler left again, Chaloner said, "I promised Strathairn I'd speak to you. He plans to ask for your hand when he is free to claim it. I gave him permission."

Her breath quickened and her cheeks became warm. "I expected he might. But I can't."

Chaloner threw up his hands. "I declare, I'll never understand women. Don't you want to marry him?"

She had always wanted to marry John. Desperately. But now… "I believe he wants to rescue me."

"From what? The danger from Coombe is at an end."

"He has become very protective of me."

"Not such a bad trait to have in a husband."

"It is self-sacrificing." She pushed back a lock of hair that escaped from her cap. "I don't want to come between him and his work. It would be awful if he just gave it up for me."

"I did not get that impression. He was quite forceful. Quite passionate in fact."

"I practically threw myself at him, Chaloner. And he talked good sense back at me."

Chaloner's eyebrows rose. "You did?"

She sucked in a breath. "Did he say he would resign?" If only he'd been like this before. Could she really believe him now?

"Not exactly. But I made it clear…and I gained the impression that he intends to."

"He wants to?" She shivered, remembering a pair of determined gray eyes. "Or does he feel he has to?"

"I know he's a hardened soldier, but beneath the bravado I suspect he has a soft heart."

A rush or warmth spread through her. "Yes, he does."

"But nothing can occur while this dangerous affair hovers over us."

Her heart started to beat hard. "Of course not."

"Strathairn vows to find this man who has killed his comrade. I think it has become personal."

"Oh no!" Sibella cried out.

"Have some faith in him, Sib." Chaloner leaned back in his chair and smiled. "So, you're not interested in marrying him then?"

"I need to speak to him."

"Not a good idea right now. Wait until after the wedding."

"Yes. You're right." She stirred her coffee as the footman brought the toast to the table.

Chaloner finished his coffee. He leapt to his feet and rubbed his hands together. "Enough of this. I'm hungry." He crossed to the sideboard and lifted the covers on the hot dishes. "Mmm. Kidneys."

Sibella buttered a piece of toast and added strawberry jam. She took a bite. "The strawberries were excellent this year," she uttered inanely. "I must compliment the cook." She put the toast down barely touched and left the table. "I shall eat later, Chaloner. I'm not hungry."

As the footman opened the door, Chaloner called to her. "Don't worry, Sib. I'll wager Strathairn's been in trickier situations than this in the past."

She walked along the corridor, fear churning her stomach.

Chapter Twenty-Five

In Manton's gun shop in Davies Street, after a careful selection, Strathairn chose a small muff pistol, its silver handle decorated with delicate filigree work. He weighed the small gun in his hand. Like all of Manton's, it was superbly balanced. In the shooting gallery upstairs, he greeted two men who practiced their marksmanship, shooting at paper wafers attached to cast-iron targets in the acrid smoky air. Although too small for his hand, the flintlock pistol proved efficient as Strathairn fired two shots into the target. It would serve its purpose.

Downstairs, he paid the gun dealer and placed it in his coat pocket. In the street, he glanced at his watch. Nearly two o'clock. The Brandreth's would be receiving. A hackney trundled past, and he stepped out onto the road to hail it. He directed the jarvie to St. James's Square.

On the way, his thoughts drifted to the many arrangements being put in place at St. Paul's Cathedral. While desperate to catch Moreau, he fervently hoped the blighter wouldn't choose Maria's wedding to unleash his mayhem.

In St. James's Square, the whole family had arrived for the wedding, but Sibella came alone to the salon dressed in a severely cut gray gown, her hair dressed in a simple style which emphasized her high cheekbones and delicate features. He drew in a breath; unadorned, she was even more beautiful.

"I'm alone today. Mother and Maria are shopping, and Chaloner and Lavinia have taken the children for ice cream at Gunter's."

"Good. I need to talk to you."

She pressed a nervous hand to her high collar.

"Not about us. That can wait," he said quickly, dismayed to find relief in her eyes. "I would like to know how you are, however."

"The strongest emotion is relief, John. And gratitude. I must thank you for coming to my aid."

"You did remarkably well on your own."

"Chaloner has read the letters. He's quite shocked."

"So he should be," he said dryly.

"You weren't too hard on him, were you?"

He shook his head. "I treated him with kid gloves. I hope to have him as my brother-in-law one day."

"John I can't..."

"No. Not the right time. I accept that." He drew the small pistol from his coat pocket. "I want you to take this with you to the cathedral."

She inhaled sharply and waved it away. "I hate guns. I accept the necessity of them, but I don't like shooting things. When I ride to hounds, I'm never at the kill."

"This is important. You may need to defend someone you love."

Her finely arched dark eyebrows drew together. "I certainly hope not."

"Shall I show you how the pistol works?"

She shook her head. "With four brothers as well as my father, I could hardly avoid an understanding of how guns work."

"However, a little practice might be in order. Come with me," he said. "Well go outside via the kitchens."

On the way to the servants' entrance, Stathairn purloined two empty glass bottles from the bemused cook.

They left the house and made their way to an area of lawn adjoining the kitchen garden where Strathairn set up the bottles on the garden wall. He walked back to where Sibella stood and loaded the gun.

"Is this entirely necessary, John? Isn't it a matter of just squeezing the trigger?"

He laughed. "It's more complicated than that as you will soon find out." He took her arm and drew her back. "Perhaps we should try from a distance of fifteen feet. Don't worry if you miss the bottles. Practice makes perfect."

She eyed him. "Do you really think I'm so helpless?"

"Not at all, it's a skill to be learned like any other. Let's get to it."

He took her hand and pressed the weapon into her palm, resisting the urge to pull her toward him, and folded her fingers around it. Then he raised her arm toward the first bottle. "Keep your arm straight and your head steady." He stepped away.

Sibella fired the pistol. The glass exploded, shards flying into the garden. A flock of birds erupted from a nearby tree.

Strathairn gave a bark of laughter. "Well done."

"Isn't that enough?" she asked, handing him the firearm. "Shall we go inside?"

"Not yet. Beginners luck perhaps." He reloaded it and handed it to her. "One more bottle."

"I think I've got the hang of it, John." Sibella raised the pistol. The second bottle shattered. She turned to him with an amused expression. "Do I need any more practice?"

He grinned at her. "You'll do just fine. I only hope you're never angry with me. Before we go inside, I'll reload it and show you how to put the safety catch on. That's if you need to be shown?"

A smiled teased her lips and she nodded. "Please do."

They walked back to the house where the kitchen maids were clustered around the door, staring out.

"Nothing to worry about," Strathairn said. "Just a bit of practice. Not that her ladyship needs it."

The maids retreated, tittering among themselves.

"Tuck this into your reticule," he said when they were alone. "You can give it back to me after the wedding if you don't wish to keep it."

She laughed, the old Sibella making a brief appearance. "I think I will keep it, thank you. It makes me feel safe." She eyed him anxiously.

"You won't take any unnecessary risks, will you, John?"

To know she cared warmed him. "I have no intention of being shot by some madman. But I can't be everywhere at once."

She examined the finely made little firearm, turning it in her hands, then moved away to place it carefully on a table. "You must guard the regent, of course."

He came to stand beside her and tipped up her chin with a finger. "I'd rather guard you."

"Don't worry about me. You must rid us of this fiend."

"I have every intention of doing so," he said. "I'd hate to ruin the wedding celebration, but we must take precautions, you do understand?"

"Yes, of course. We are all very grateful."

"I must go."

"Stay safe, John," she said, her voice soft.

He attempted to judge her mood and took her hands to press a kiss into each palm. "I hope to see you soon."

She rubbed her arms. "Don't say it like that. It's as if the Fates will decide."

"I don't believe in fate."

Damn it all, he couldn't leave her like this. Who knew what tomorrow would bring? He wanted to tell her he loved her, but he held back. Instead, he took her slender shoulders in his hands and lowered his head to cover her mouth with his. She murmured a half-hearted protest, but he slipped an arm around her waist and pulled her close. At the touch and scent of her skin, he felt more alive than he had in weeks. Her objection turned into a soft moan, and she kissed him back, driving him to deepen the kiss.

Sibella's hands flattened against his chest and she pushed him away. Her green eyes had darkened, the pupils dilated. She drew in a ragged breath and touched her bottom lip with her tongue. "We mustn't."

From somewhere, he found the strength to release her and made for the door. "Don't forget the gun," he said over his shoulder.

An hour later, intent on visiting his wounded comrade, Miles Irvine, Strathairn drove to Pinkerton's Stepney house. His partner had decided to retire and become an apothecary after he married the doctor's daughter.

Irvine rose to greet him, leaning heavily on a crutch. Although obviously still in some pain, he appeared contented, surrounded by books on herbs and potions.

After they settled in the small modestly furnished parlor, Strathairn acquainted Irvine with the latest developments. He then asked for a more detailed description of Moreau. "He's like a phantom," he said. "You're the only one who seems to have set eyes on him."

Irvine eased his sore leg on a cushion. "A giant of a man, more broad than tall, long hair, black as a sweep's. I'm afraid that's all I can give you."

"It will help," Strathairn said.

Irvine looked doubtful. He shook his head. "Better if I could be there."

"Well, you cannot," Strathairn said. "And really, why would you?" With a grin, he jerked his head toward the kitchen where Irvine's intended sweetly sang as she prepared their coffee.

AT BRANDRETH COURT on the morning of the wedding, a welcome late summer burst of sunlight cheered everyone. While returning again and again to Strathairn's kiss and the fear she held for him, Sibella visited the cook, ensuring the food prepared would satisfy the dietary requirements of her brother Bartholomew, his wife Emily, and their three children. They had arrived from Yorkshire the previous evening.

The wedding breakfast was to be held in the ballroom with music and dancing. Sibella walked through the reception rooms taking in every detail of the gleaming house, scented with fragrant blooms sent up from the hot houses at Brandreth Park. After the housekeeper assured her everything was progressing smoothly, Sibella sought Maria in her chamber.

Maria stood before the Cheval mirror, her eyes shining while her maid knelt at her feet, fussing with the hem of her wedding gown. The white-figured gauze over a slip of white satin, was ornamented with rows of broad silver lace, the white satin sleeves slashed *à l'Espagnole.* Their mother's lustrous oriental pearl and diamond necklace and earrings decorated her throat and ears.

"You look divine," Sibella said, her throat tight with emotion. Her younger sister was to be married, and would leave their home to begin her new life with Harry. It was thrilling, but she would be sorely missed. "Your wedding gown rivals poor Princess Charlotte's. Harry will be struck dumb at the sight of you."

Maria giggled. "As long as he can manage to say I do."

"How long will you be away in France?"

"A sennight. We are to stay at the Le Meurice on the Rue De Rivoli, right in the heart of Paris. The hotel has just been built."

"Sounds divine, dearest." Sibella moved toward the door. "Everything is in readiness downstairs. I must go and dress."

An hour later, Sibella picked up the skirts of her white crape frock and stepped into the waiting carriage with Maria and her mother, who was dressed in ruby silk. Behind them Chaloner and Lavinia, with their son, Freddie, entered their carriage along with Bart and Emily. Sibella smiled encouragement at her beautiful sister as the coachman directed the horses to walk on.

Her stomach tightened with nerves when the carriage rattled through the streets toward St. Paul's Cathedral as pedestrians stopped to stare.

Chapter Twenty-Six

STRATHAIRN ARRIVED AT St. Paul's Cathedral several hours before the wedding and wasn't happy with the situation. He'd come under some criticism while arguing for more men to secure the roads around the cathedral and feared there were gaps in their net.

A clamor rose from the crowd gathered along the west front. Workmen, shopkeepers, men of the cloth, and families with children stood twenty-deep along the barrier, waiting for the prince regent and distinguished guests to arrive.

Strathairn roamed along the line of constables. The surrounding streets were blocked off with only one entry point at Ludgate Hill where occupants of each carriage would be checked before passing through the barrier to let down passengers at the cathedral steps.

He circumnavigated the massive domed cathedral, following the fence from St. Paul's church yard to Paternoster Row. Confident that New Change, Carter Lane, Dean's Court, and Creed Lane were secure, he made his way back to the west entrance to find the crowd had grown larger and strained against the barrier. Then he entered the cathedral through the massive great west door, making his way down the aisle beneath the huge dome to the nave, his footsteps echoing on the tiled floor.

Guests waited in their finery, their voices hushed in the hallowed space. His eyes roamed every shadowy corner, locating the constables attempting to appear inconspicuous. They guarded the quire, the stairs to the dome, and the crypt. Some peered down from the whispering gallery and others lurked in the chapels. All seemed in order, but how could he be sure?

When he returned outside, the crowd had grown even larger. The constables and Bow Street patrollers among them were as hampered as he was, with only a brief description of the man they sought. Blinking in the sunlight, he scanned the faces for a dark-haired giant. He could only fall back on his keen eyes and his instincts, which seemed nowhere near enough. What if Moreau was here, and he failed to find him in time?

The Marquess of Harrington stepped from his carriage and raised a hand to Strathairn before disappearing inside the cathedral with his best man. The duke and duchess' gleaming coach followed, drawn by six matched white high steppers.

Moments later, a dark blue carriage bearing the Brandreth crest was admitted. The footman put the steps down and the dowager, Lady Brandreth, alighted, her two youngest daughters following. The bride looked undeniably lovely, but Strathairn's gaze rested on Sibella in her white dress with a wreath of red and white roses in her hair. She nodded to him with a smile.

Strathairn swung around as the constables moved the barricade to admit a man. Astounded, he strode toward the limping figure. "Irvine!" His wounded comrade leaned heavily on a crutch, deep lines of pain and strain aging his young face. "You should not have come."

Irvine panted from the effort. "I want to be of help if I can. As you said, I'm the only one who has seen the devil."

"I'm relieved to find you here and very grateful," Strathairn said. "It's imperative we get to him before he can fire off that gun of his. Can I ask you to walk a little? Search for him in the crowd?"

Strathairn withdrew one of his pistols from the bandolier beneath his coat and held the gun out to Irvine. "If you run into him, use it, but I'd prefer to take him alive."

Irvine shuffled away toward the people jammed up along the barrier while Strathairn had a word with the constable. The regent would soon arrive.

When he joined Irvine again, the injured man shook his head. "He's not here. Maybe it is to be Vauxhall."

"Keep looking. If you see anything, no matter what, give me a sign. I'll be watching," Strathairn said. "I will return in a moment."

Sibella waited at the top of the steps at the cathedral entrance. He ran over the ground and climbed to meet her, his appreciative eye roaming over her. "How beautiful you both look."

"Has anything happened?" She curled her fingers around her reticule, her eyes wary.

"Not so far, I hope..."

Out of the corner of his eye, he saw Irvine limping back toward him. Irvine raised his arm. "I must go." He turned and raced down the steps.

"I've found Moreau," Irvine said, gasping. "I'll swear it's him. He's here."

"Where? Don't make it obvious."

Irvine gestured over his shoulder with a subtle movement. "He's just appeared down Ave Maria Lane."

Strathairn turned his head toward the lane. A big solid dark-haired man stood among the crowd. "You're sure that's Moreau?"

"I'll never forget that hulking brute. He marked me indelibly."

"Alert the constables," Strathairn said. "Tell them to follow me. But with stealth. We don't want to lose him and neither do we want a stampede!"

He left Irvine's side and walked over to the barricade as another carriage carrying more wedding guests passed through.

The regent's cavalcade appeared and advanced in stately fashion down Ludgate Hill, flanked by guards on horseback. Strathairn pushed into the throng, patently aware that if the people panicked, many would get hurt. The tightly packed, excited mob pushed back at him, struggling to keep their position which made movement frustratingly difficult. He chose not to draw his gun while he kept his eye on Moreau's dark head. A shooting match would be disastrous.

Strathairn was a few yards from the Frenchman when Moreau saw him and whipped the rifle out from beneath his coat. Those around him who saw the weapon cried out and tried to get away.

Exclamations of horror and rebuke followed Moreau as he fought his way back toward Ave Maria Lane with Strathairn coming fast behind him. Strathairn could hear his French curses and threats as he pushed people aside. His gun now drawn, he warned people to let him through, but their terror impeded him as they struggled to put distance between themselves and the two men with guns.

Moreau shoved several people to the ground as he pushed on toward the lane. A woman carrying a child fell heavily.

"Help her up!" Strathairn called with a curse. He couldn't get a clear path, and Moreau had almost reached the edge of the crowd. If he made it to the end of the lane, he'd have a good chance to get away.

Moreau burst out of the mob as Strathairn gained on him. He broke free and sprinted after the Frenchman. Behind him, the two constables following were jammed between those surging against the barricade to glimpse the prince regent, whose cavalcade was only minutes away, and those attempting to flee the scene.

Strathairn wanted this mongrel captured alive. A quick death wasn't good enough for Moreau. Drawn and quartered, his head on a pike would be the only justice and deterrent for others with the same aim.

Moreau took off up the lane, but the heavy man was slow on his feet. Strathairn took aim and brought him down with a shot to the thigh. Like the felling of an oak, he crashed onto the pavement with a roar of rage, the rifle flying away. Strathairn reached him as he staggered to his feet, bleeding heavily. Strathairn did not expect the weight behind the mighty punch, which sent his head reeling. When his foggy gaze cleared, Moreau was lurching for the gun, and Strathairn leapt after him. Before Moreau's hand could grasp the rifle, Strathairn kicked it away.

The big Frenchman charged again, butting Strathairn in the chest, which knocked the air out of him. Strathairn staggered, then leapt forward and attacked him with his fists. All the pain and fury he carried for Nesbit and Irvine and past events that had nothing to do with Moreau lay behind every loaded punch.

Despite being crippled and weakened from the loss of blood and Strathairn's blows, the big man still fought back. A ham-fist connected with Strathairn's cheek and his ears rung. Their labored panting reverberated around the narrow lane while the shocked crowd uttered barely a word. Strathairn managed to plant a good facer, rocking the man back on his heels. As Moreau shook his head, Strathairn danced forward and delivered a right to the giant's stomach and followed it with an elbow to the jaw. Moreau's head twisted, a trail of spit flying from his mouth.

Moreau was all muscle but unschooled. Strathairn got the big man in a headlock. The rifle was too far away for him to reach. He had to disable the Frenchman to get to the weapon. When he brought his knee up into Moreau's groin, he cried out in pain.

Moreau spat out a string of French curses as Strathairn drove his fist continually into the Frenchman's stomach. The devil wouldn't go down.

A monk approached them. He picked up Moreau's rifle and pointed it at the Frenchman.

"Give me the rifle," Strathairn said, surprised that a monk should display a penchant for violence.

The monk threw back his hood.

Strathairn choked and went cold. Forney! The count sneered, his face thin and pasty. He altered the trajectory of the gun to Strathairn's heart.

"An eye for an eye. You killed my wife," Forney cried, his strange wolf-like eyes wild.

With a shriek, Moreau broke free as Forney fired, the ball striking Moreau in the head.

Forney let out a howl as the Frenchman went down. With a sense that fate may have caught up with him, Strathairn stood helpless as the count aimed the gun at him.

He pulled the trigger.

A bright flash and Forney staggered back as the rifle exploded in his face. He crumpled, his habit smoldering.

Strathairn knelt beside him as he fought to breathe. It seemed that fate had favored him today. He climbed to his feet as Sibella emerged chalk-faced from the stunned onlookers, the muff pistol in her hand.

"Give me that." Strathairn grabbed the gun from her as the two constables closed in on the stricken Forney who was prostrate on the ground, his blackened face hardly recognizable.

"Is he dead?" Sibella asked, her voice oddly flat.

"No, he still breathes, but not for long." Strathairn stood looking down at the conspirator they had thought to be dead. No question that death would claim him now.

He put his arm around Sibella. "My God, Sibella. I should be angry with you. What in God's name are you doing here?"

She struggled out of his grasp. "I was desperate. I wanted to help if I could. So I followed you."

He took her hand. "You're missing your sister's wedding."

"They'll wait for me."

"Prinny doesn't wait for anyone."

Sibella sagged against him and he led her to the church, through the crowd of subdued people. They gasped and murmured and parted like the Red Sea to let them pass. He half expected to see the prince emerge from the cathedral in a rage.

"See what happens when you give me a gun?" she asked as they crossed the forecourt. "I don't ever want it back."

"I'm not about to give it back." She might have been hurt, or worse... "Everything is all right now." He swept her up the steps.

"Who was that man in the monk's garb? I saw his eyes. He would have killed you," she whispered.

At the entrance, he raised her gloved hand to his lips. "Count Forney. He won't kill anyone now. Thank you for being so brave, my love."

She pulled away from him. "The wedding. I must go."

"Sibella..."

She shook her head sorrowfully at him and disappeared into the interior shadows of the cathedral.

THE WEDDING PARTY gathered in the nave.

"Where have you been, Sibella?" Cordelia asked in a low voice. "You are holding up the wedding. The Prince of Wales will be angry."

"He isn't," Chaloner said, briskly, silencing Cordelia with a gesture. "Mother sits next to the regent and is keeping him amused. What happened out there, Sib?"

"The assassin has been killed," Sibella said.

"Oh, thank heaven." Maria clapped her hands.

Chaloner nodded. "Then may we proceed?" He held out his arm to Maria and nodded to a church alderman. In a moment, the organ music swelled.

Sibella took her bouquet of red roses from their footman, then walked down the aisle ahead of Aida and Cordelia in their white gowns with Chaloner and Maria following behind.

Familiar faces greeted her as she walked, from family to politicians and princes.

She took her place beside her sisters. Relief that John was safe made her tamp down a shudder while she watched Maria join Harry at the altar and the ceremony began.

When she'd followed John as he made his way through the crowd, it hit home to her the extent of the danger he faced. How strong and competent he was, yet he still came within a whisker of dying. It would not be the first time, of that she was sure. He would never give it up. Not for her or for anyone. It was in his blood.

As Maria vowed to love and obey Harry, Sibella bit her lip to suppress the anguish which came with the knowledge that he was lost to her. Her sister's voice seemed almost distant in the vast echoing space, perhaps because of the heavy thud of Sibella's heart in her ears.

The ceremony over, Maria and Harry went to sign the marriage lines. Sibella returned her mother's smile with trembling lips. Since Coombe died, her nerves seemed to lie close to the surface. In her quiet moments, she relived the terrifying expression in his eyes, his determination to rape and murder her, and the awful moment when he was killed.

When John spoke to the man with the crutch and entered the crowd, she was compelled to follow him with an overwhelming urge to do everything she could to help, to turn what fate might have in store into a victory.

The monk had pushed past her and pulled back his habit. She saw the mad, murderous look in his eyes, which had chilled her to the bone. What made men so wicked? It shook her to the core to know such evil existed. Her sheltered life had left her unprepared. John must have witnessed many terrible things. How close he had come to death, yet he seemed so calm.

She'd sought solace in his arms for one fleeting moment, and she would always be grateful for that. She admired his bravery and his dedication, but at the same time, she wanted to beat him on the chest and rail at him for this work he did. What a fool she was to love him for precisely what he was, a brave man prepared to risk his life for his country, and yet wish to change him, to subject him to a life of quiet domesticity. She wouldn't ask it of him.

Chapter Twenty-Seven

STRATHAIRN SAW MOREAU'S body and that of Forney, who was now deceased, off in the wagon. The ceremony over, the guests filed out of the cathedral with murmurs of disbelief as news of what had taken place spread among them. The crowd remained, ten-deep behind the barricades, waiting for any crumb of information.

When the regent descended the cathedral steps, a hush came over the crowd, but for a few, faint-voiced protestors. What they had witnessed seemed to subdue even the most vocal. Strathairn stood with Irvine while they organized a carriage to take his wounded colleague home. "So much for prototypes, eh?" Irvine said.

"Not properly tested," Strathairn said.

"Thank the lord for that." Irvine patted him on the arm. "I can't tell you how pleased I am to see you standing here. Tried to get a shot off from the barricade, but too many people were in the way. I felt bloody helpless watching that unfold." He shook his head as he handed Strathairn his pistol. "Too close for comfort, milord."

"Indeed." Strathairn could only be grateful that he hadn't been reduced to a bloody mess in front of Sibella. *Sibella!* Why did he fear she was moving away from him? Had he lost her?

Before mounting the steps of the royal carriage, the regent sent his aide to fetch Strathairn.

He praised Strathairn's swift action. "If we had more like you in the royal guard, I would sleep better at night," he said, his plump face breaking into a smile. He granted Strathairn the title of Marquess of

Strathairn in principle.

Shocked, Strathairn thanked him with a bow.

"I shall expect to see you take your place in the House of Lords," he said before climbing into his carriage.

The procession began to wend its way past the dismantled barricade as the crowd rallied to boo and cheer. There was no way of refusing the regent, and Strathairn found he didn't want to.

By the time he arrived at St. James's Square directly after visiting Parnham, the guests had partaken of the wedding breakfast and had repaired to the ballroom.

When Strathairn entered the ballroom, Maria left her new husband's side to greet him. She curtsied low enough to please the regent.

"Lady Harrington, please. That is hardly necessary." Strathairn took her hands and raised her to her feet.

"My family is eternally grateful for what you did today Strathairn. You are a very brave man."

"You should caution your sister not to take such risks."

"I have done." She studied him carefully. "She is very bold and daring isn't she. I am in awe of her."

"Yes, and courageous."

She eyed him anxiously. "Sib would make you a fine partner in life."

"She might not agree with you."

"Oh, she does, never fear," Maria said gently. "But this business with Lord Coombe has affected her. Sib needs time to recover."

He doubted time was what Sibella needed. She needed distraction and to feel safe, both of which he was happy to provide. "You make a beautiful bride, Lady Harrington. Your husband is an extremely lucky fellow."

Her eyes sparkled up at him. "I am blessed to have Harry." She glanced over his shoulder. "Here is my sister. Please excuse me, I must return to my husband."

She walked away, leaving him alone with Sibella. After one glance at her pale face, he took her arm. She did not resist as he drew her out into the corridor. A footman shut the ballroom door on the buzz of conversation.

Sibella's eyes looked bruised as they searched his. She chewed her bottom lip. "I'm sorry if you're angry with me."

"I'm not. Why would I be?"

She shook her head. "It was foolish of me. I might have got in the way."

"I wish you hadn't witnessed it, that's all."

He wanted to kiss her, to convince her that the future was theirs if only she would trust him. But the footman stood to attention by the door, making a valiant effort not to gaze in their direction.

"Maria thinks we make a good pair," he said, his voice gruff. He wanted her to love him, but this was hardly the time to plead his case. There was so much more he needed to explain to make her understand what he'd only just realized himself. Now with Forney dead and the regent's commendation, he felt freer, lighter than he could remember. It was a profound experience which almost left him reeling.

"Now that Maria has left home, Mama is having the dower house prepared. She plans to move in as soon as it's ready."

He hesitated, measuring her for a moment. "Your mother will be quite comfortable there?"

"Yes, we both shall be."

"You'll stay with her until she is settled?"

She refused to meet his gaze. "That part of the garden has been neglected. I look forward to the undertaking."

"This is what you want?"

"Yes." She took a deep breath. "It is time Chaloner and Lavinia had the house to themselves. Lavinia has been remarkably patient."

"That's not what I asked you." He took a step closer.

Lady Brandreth entered the corridor. "Sibella?"

"Yes, Mama?"

"We are charging our glasses. Wales is about to make a speech." She nodded at him. "Strathairn. I believe we are indebted to you yet again, but come, we cannot insult the prince."

Frustrated, Strathairn followed them inside. He accepted a flute of champagne from a footman. There was no chance of pursuing his conversation with Sibella. Today, she belonged to her family and he must dredge up some patience from somewhere.

"To the bride and groom!" The regent raised his glass to the married couple, and everyone responded. He launched into a speech about his father's close friendship with Harry's father, the Duke of Lamplugh, and how sorry the king was he had not been well enough to attend.

"The king cannot walk and isn't aware that his wife is dead," Vaughn said at Strathairn's elbow. He gained a fierce look from his mother.

After Lord Liverpool added his sentiments to the occasion, as eloquent as always, then the musicians tuned their instruments for the first dance.

Strathairn sought out Sibella when the music began. She refused to dance, so he sat beside her. "When do you return to the country?"

"In a few days."

"I will visit you there." Her smooth brow creased, and he hastened to add, "I shall be busy for a while, however." He had no intention of forcing his suit upon her. Maria was right; she needed time.

Late November, Tunbridge Wells

SIBELLA MADE A mental note to tell the gardener that the rhododendrons beneath the drawing room windows had become too bushy and were shutting out the light. On her garden ramble, frost crunched under her half boots, the fountain frozen over. Gardeners raked up piles of papery brown leaves from beneath the skeletal trees and burned them, smoke rising into the cool gray-blue sky, the color of Strathairn's eyes.

When she recalled the warmth and determination in those eyes, her body tingled. Her memories of him invaded her thoughts constantly. She twirled the stem of a yellow autumn crocus in her fingers and wandered on, cutters in hand, bending to trim a branch here and pluck a spent bloom there. Twitch, a brown and white terrier puppy from the stables, followed her about on his short legs, deserting her only to chase off the birds. She wanted to make a pet of him, but her mother refused, because he barked at her cat.

In the two months since the family had returned to Brandreth Park, she had busied herself making improvements to the garden. After conferring with the head gardener, they worked to restore the neglected corner surrounding the dower house while inside, workmen hammered and sawed, the smell of paint drifting out. She had chosen the color schemes for the paint, wallpapers, and fabrics for many of the rooms, as her mother seemed a little subdued and disinterested. "I miss Maria's gay laughter," she'd said on more than one occasion.

"I do my best, Mama," Sibella said for the umpteenth time. Not even the most celebrated comedian of their time would rouse her mother to laughter. But Sibella was gentle with her, aware that her mother was having trouble with the move and adjusting to losing another of her chicks.

"Shall we have a family dinner on Saturday evening? I'm sure Maria and Harry will come."

"Mm. Perhaps." Her mother stroked the cat and sat eyeing the reams of wallpaper on a table. "Are you sure that color will suit?"

"You did agree to it. I'm sure you'll like it when it's finished."

After she and her mother moved in, Sibella threw herself into organizing the servants. When the house functioned the way she wanted, she allowed the formidable housekeeper, Mrs. Huxley, to manage it.

Her days free, she rode, employed her needle, wrote letters, or read. Thoughts of John, his laugh, the warm grip of his hand in hers, and his kiss made her fidgety. Did he still love her? She re-read a letter from him, smiling at his description of the puppies. His first letter had thrilled her, and now they came regularly, telling her news of his life, but he wrote like an old friend and not a lover. Disturbed by the lack of any declaration of deeper feelings, the days began to drag, except when the weather was fine and her nieces and nephews came to entice her to play cards or shuttlecock on the lawn. She grew annoyed with herself. She really must accept the inevitable.

At least her mother had finally settled. Keen-eyed as ever, she was less sharp-tongued. "I don't know why I waited so long to move here," she confessed to Sibella one evening as they sat by the fire and listened to the rain lashing the windowpanes. "How pleasant it is to have one's own home again, even if it is a humble one."

Only a select few would call the dower house humble. Built during George III's reign, it was more modern than the mansion, featuring a pleasing symmetrical exterior with elegant columns and shuttered windows. The rooms were snugger than the big house where the drafts lifted some hall carpet runners when the wind blew fiercely.

Lavinia had grown in confidence as mistress of the house, and even Chaloner seemed more at ease when they called to discuss Christmas, now only a few weeks away. Christmas was always a big affair at Brandreth Park.

Christmas! The crocus fell from her nerveless fingers as she wandered the garden paths. Would John come before then? Would he come at all? Or was there a lady in his life he'd failed to mention? At night, she lay awake thinking about him. He appeared in her mind as she worked in the garden. The horror of Coombe's death and that awful day at the cathedral faded with time, but the memory of John's ardor only grew more vivid. When she'd walked away, had she destroyed what he felt for her?

She could examine her feelings with honesty and acknowledged it was John's physical beauty and the inexplicable aura of danger that surrounded him which first attracted her. She had looked upon him as an escape from her mundane existence. At that moment, when she feared she would lose him, her deep love for him shook her like a powerful ache.

A carriage rumbled through the gates, the wheels clattering over the gravel drive. Maria! Sibella ran, clutching her bonnet, the dog yapping at her heels.

Her sister waved from the coach window, a stylish ermine cap over her dark hair as the duke's carriage came to a halt outside the dower house.

A footman in the duke's magenta and light blue livery helped her sister, resplendent in a fur-lined pelisse of olive green, down the steps. Sibella rushed across the frosty lawn to embrace her. "Dearest, what brings you here?" Maria looked as a young bride should, happy and well loved.

"We have been visiting Harry's Aunt Agatha and spent last night a few miles from Tunbridge Wells. I had to come and tell you..." Maria glanced at the footman and took her arm. "Come inside."

After Sibella ordered tea, they perched together on the blue sofa in the drawing room, now papered in marine blue and cream stripes, blue silk damask curtains at the window.

"I like your color scheme," Maria said, gazing round. "Where is Mama?"

"She is still abed. I've sent the footman to tell her you're here."

Maria clutched her hands together. "She should hear my news first, but I cannot keep this to myself a moment longer." Her eyes glowed. "Sib, I believe I am with child."

Sibella hugged her. "Are you sure, dearest? It's so early."

Maria rested her hand on her flat stomach. "I just know. And I have missed my monthly courses."

"Mama will be pleased. Another grandchild," Sibella said. "The very thing to cheer her after such unsettling times."

A maid brought in the tea things. She breathed in the fragrance of a new tea she had been trying. Maria took a sip and put down her cup. "Delicious. How are you, Sib?"

Sibella straightened the lace edging on her cuff. "I am well. Why? Don't I look it?"

"Mmm." Maria tilted her head. "The strain has gone from your face, but..."

"But what?"

"A certain restlessness in your manner has replaced it."

Impossible to keep secrets from Maria. "Perhaps I am a little restive, now everything is in order here."

"After Christmas when you return to London..."

Sibella pressed her lips together. "A season does not appeal."

"No, but I thought..." Maria shook her head and her eyes turned sad. "No word from Strathairn?"

"Yes. He writes often."

Maria smiled. "Does he? Well then."

"He is ensconced in his Yorkshire estate, deeply involved with his horses, he writes as an old friend," Sibella said. "He might have met someone else."

"You know as well as I do that isn't possible. He's in love with you, Sib."

Sibella's chest tightened. "I thought so."

"He has stayed away deliberately. I advised him to."

Sibella stared at her. "You did? You might have told me."

Maria's cheeks flushed. "You would have sent him away forever. You needed time to think."

Sibella poured them both another cup. "That is true."

"When he does come, everything will fall into place."

"If you are wrong, and he fails to appear, I shall be perfectly happy to remain here with Mama," she lied, with a defiant toss of her head.

Maria grinned. "You don't believe that any more than I do."

"I threw myself at him once and he rejected me." Sibella shrugged. "I shall accept friendship if that is what he offers me. I have my pride."

"Don't let pride stand in the way of happiness."

"I've been trying my darndest to forget him."

"I'm sure you've succeeded. When he comes, you'll treat him like last season's hat." Maria laughed. "He's such a big handsome fellow with his gold-streaked hair and stubborn chin."

"Not stubborn," Sibella said, rushing to his defense.

"Ah. Is that so?" Maria laughed again.

"You can be *so* annoying." Sibella smiled. "As you are with child, I shall ignore you."

"Maria! Where have you come from?" Chaloner walked into the room. "How is Harry?" He threw himself into a chair and they were soon catching up on news.

Chaloner interrupted their chatter. "Would you mind leaving us for a moment, Maria? I need to talk to Sib."

Maria wrinkled her nose. "What can you possibly tell her that I'm not privy to?" When he frowned, she held up her hands. "Very well, I want to see Mama, anyway."

Sibella handed him a cup of tea. "Whatever is the matter?"

"It's about Strathairn," he said.

"What about him?" Her heart began to thump wildly.

"Not bad news, nothing like that."

She edged forward on her chair. "Thank heavens!"

"I need to make a confession. Last year at Strathairn's hunt ball, I ordered him not to become too interested in you. At that time, I believed he was not a suitable husband for you. And he wasn't. He did agree, Sib."

"Yes, he would have."

Chaloner sat with his hands on his knees, his dark head drooped, so filled with remorse she instantly forgave him.

"John always avoided talk of marriage. Spies should not marry, you see," she explained.

Chaloner straightened. "Ah, you understand."

She perched on the arm of his chair. "I know you had my best interests at heart."

He rested an arm around her waist, gazing at her with his slow smile. "But everything has now changed."

"Why?"

"I've had a letter from him. He has resigned from military intelligence. He says he intends to settle down, and I have good reason to believe him."

She gasped. Strathairn hadn't mentioned it in his letters. "I was thrilled to hear the news of his investiture. No one is more deserving than John. But to leave the military! I never expected that."

"Becoming a marquess brings more responsibly." He stood and patted her head. "I'll go up to see Mama."

She rose and walked with him to the stairs. "Thank you for telling me."

"That's not the only news I bring." A gleam lit his eyes. "I've invited him down for Christmas. Sent Edward as an emissary."

"My goodness!" She put her hands to her cheeks.

Chaloner grinned at her shocked expression and turned to go upstairs.

Chapter Twenty-Eight

Winter in Yorkshire began early and could be bitter, but the day was pleasantly mild as Strathairn rode his horse across the paddocks to the stables. Strange, but he didn't miss the excitement of Whitehall, although Parnham tried to tempt him back. Their intelligence network had discovered that while Forney lay ill after his rescue from the sinking boat, he was already plotting to return to England and tried to engender interest from his old colleagues.

Most had lost their taste for it and considered Bonaparte a spent force. All but Moreau turned him down flat. When the count regained his health, he traveled to England. He landed in East Sussex where he remained for some months on a Frenchman's farm. After, taking the Frenchman into custody, with some persuasion, they learned how the plan was formulated. Countess Forney and Moreau first arrived in London to set their plan in motion while Forney remained out of sight. Moreau traveled north to stir up the people, and Countess Forney set about abducting Guy's baby. Forney came up to London to witness the Prince of Wales's assassination at Moreau's hand and to watch Strathairn suffer defeat on that day before Forney shot him.

Strathairn felt more at ease and his troubling dreams of the war seemed to have vanished. He did not attempt to delve too deeply into the reason. It was enough that he slept well and woke looking forward to the day. All he needed now to make his life complete was for Sibella to be here with him. And he must woo her. So, he began to write to her, telling her about his day, the horses, the beautiful place in which he lived, how Vaughn's romance was progressing or the lack of it, and the puppies' antics. He talked about Linden Hall, how it sorely needed a lady to care for it.

Men were not domestic creatures, and he hated such a beautiful house to go unloved. He kept his letters light in tone, filling them with humorous situations and descriptions. He resisted waxing lyrical about how much he loved her, nor tried to draw a declaration from her. And he did not say he was coming to see her. Why he wasn't sure, but perhaps he feared that she would hastily reply and end their association. Time, he thought was on his side. She had loved him, he'd been sure of it. Did she still?

And her letters were much in the same vein as his. About her garden, her mother settling into the dower house, news about Maria and Harry. And how much more relaxed Chaloner seemed, which she put down to Lavinia liking to have Brandreth Park finally under her control.

Strathairn rode across the cobbles of the stable block and found Edward patting a horse and talking to his younger brother. He dismounted and threw the reins to a stable hand. "Edward! How good to see you."

Edward shook his hand. "I must address you correctly, my lord marquess! Chaloner witnessed your investiture by the Privy Council."

"Let's not make a fuss over nothing," Strathairn said with a grin. He hadn't expected to care, but found he did. The work he'd performed over the years had in some way been ennobled, and his contribution to his country valued. Work, considered objectionable by most gentlemen of the *ton,* which had seared his very soul. He only wished his father could have witnessed the formal ceremony in the Lords and heard Prinny's fulsome praise.

"I've been visiting a friend in Edinburgh," Edward explained. "How are you both? Still getting on?"

"We've become a trifle dull." Strathairn winked at Vaughn, "And welcome your company." He resisted mentioning Vaughn's flourishing relationship with the apothecary's daughter in the village, although he wrote Sibella about it, because Vaughn told him she knew. He doubted Chaloner would agree to them marrying.

The companionship of the two Brandreths caused him a pang of yearning. If Chaloner had not warned him off marrying Sibella, he might have given in to the impulse last year. But he'd conceded that at that time. Chaloner had been right. He would not have made Sibella happy. But he was confident he could now, and was keen to convince her he longed for hearth and home with her at his side. He seethed with impatience to advise her of it. "Time for a drink, I believe. You will stay of course."

Edward chatted about that which he'd found inferior in Scottish society compared to the English as they walked along the gravel drive to the front of the hall where his butler waited dwarfed by the entry. "Lord Edward will be staying, Rhodes. Please inform the housekeeper."

Edward's carriage stood on the circle, and Strathairn gave orders to have it driven to the stable mews.

"So, what news is there from home?" Strathairn asked, as he led them inside.

Edward grinned. "That is one of the reasons I am here. Chaloner has invited you to spend Christmas with us."

WHEN SHE THOUGHT she spied snow clouds hovering on the horizon on Christmas Eve, Sibella gave an anguished gasp. It was too early for snow, surely. If it should snow, would John be able to reach them tomorrow? Her emotions rose and fell like a gusty breeze after Edward told her John had accepted their invitation. She kept busy organizing every detail while conferring constantly with Lavinia, who was even more nervous than she was to have full control of organizing a family Christmas, and very grateful for her help.

The entire Brandreth clan gathered in the salon where the Christmas log blazed in the fireplace. Promised a pantomime tomorrow,

Nurse ushered the noisy, excited children who had eaten too much marchpane and gingerbread away to bed.

Maria played *While Shepherds Watched Their Flocks by Night* on the pianoforte while Harry turned the pages. Cordelia and Roland accompanied her on harp and cello, while Aida and Peter sang along. Sibella admired the room swaddled in greenery and brightened with red holly. A tall yew tree stood in one corner decorated with candles, gifts, dried fruit and nuts, a custom her mother had taken up after hearing of it from Queen Charlotte. Sibella ticked over the list in her mind. In the kitchen, the plum puddings were prepared, a turkey, goose, and a ham dressed in readiness along with various other meats. Piles of fresh vegetables plucked from the kitchen garden. Wine, champagne, and ratafia brought from the cellar. The servants' boxes were ready for tomorrow while foxhunting was planned for Boxing Day, unless a bout of unseasonable weather put paid to it.

Earlier, carolers arrived to sing at their door. After a chorus of *Deck the Halls* and *Here We Come a-Wassailing*, they were fortified with mulled wine and mince pies.

In the warm salon, the Christmas hymn ended. With a lot of laughter, Harry kissed Maria beneath the mistletoe dangling from the chandelier, and Chaloner captured the protesting Lavinia to do the same.

The knocker rang out again. Sibella expected a tenant offering a tithe. Her breath hitched when Belton announced the Marquess of Strathairn. John walked in with his valet following, his arms laden with boxes.

"Just a few things from the home farm, some cheeses, apple brandy, and so on. Hobson, take them to the kitchen." He smiled at everyone. "Merry Christmas."

Oddly breathless, she hung back as the family crowded around him. He was handsome in his dark gray coat, pearl-colored silk waistcoat, and dark trousers, but somehow different.

Might it be her imagination or was there a more settled look about him, a new maturity in his face. Whatever it was, the sight of him made her breathless. He bent over her hand and she went still at finding such passion in his eyes.

"Lady Sibella." John eyed the mistletoe above their heads. A smile curled his lips. He dipped his head and kissed her. Everyone gasped and broke into applause.

"If you'll excuse us for a moment," Strathairn said. "I should like a moment alone with Lady Sibella."

"Oh, yes. Perhaps the conservatory?" Sibella led him among the plants where they could be alone. When she turned to face him, he took her hands in his. Shocked, she realized the brave man was nervous. "You must marry me now that I've kissed you in front of your family," he said, with an endearing grin.

"That's not a very romantic proposal." She was shaky herself. "It's more of a demand."

He swallowed. "I love you, Sibella. I want to share my life with you. Will you accept if I go down on bended knee?"

"Oh no." She laughed and drew him close. "You will dirty your fine clothes."

He needed little encouragement, wrapping his arms tight around her, his breath hot against her ear. "Will you?" he whispered against her hair.

"We must talk," she protested weakly, her body turning warm and heavy as his lips trailed across her cheek.

"We have a lifetime to talk, do we not?" he whispered against her mouth.

His hands explored the hollows of her back. She put her arms around his neck and gave in to the kiss, relishing his touch as she breathed in the smell of clean male. The kiss ended and left them both breathless as she clutched his coat. "I will marry you, John. As soon as the banns are read," she said, her voice unsteady.

"No need for that. I've had the license for a while," he said, his husky voice and loving gaze making her sigh. "A bit creased in one corner, but I'm confident it will suffice."

Chapter Twenty-Nine

THREE DAYS LATER, Strathairn nervously raked his hand through his hair as he stood with Edward beside the salon hearth. Before them, Bartholomew looked suitably solemn as he held the family Bible. The rest of the family gathered in the room, the dowager marchioness in deep blue was seated on the sofa with Lavinia, Aida, and Cordelia, in their pretty, violet, yellow and blue gowns, while the men stood. The children were hushed by their nannies as the doors were flung open by a footman. Sibella entered, stunning in the white dress she'd worn to Maria's wedding with lace at the neck and around the hem. White blossom graced her wealth of dark curls.

He caught his breath as she walked toward him on Chaloner's arm. Maria in pale blue, followed holding the hand of a little blond gentleman. Five-year-old Randal took careful steps across the carpet as he carried the ring on a royal-blue velvet cushion, which wobbled in his chubby hands, while his father, Roland, Viscount Barthe, silently applauded.

Sibella took her place beside Strathairn and smiled tremulously at him. Her green eyes, tinged with blue like the finest of emeralds, were alight with unspoken emotion.

He squeezed her hand.

Edward took the lopsided pillow from Randal and winked at him, and his mother came to draw him away.

Bartholomew cleared his throat and began the ceremony.

Moments later, Strathairn slipped the diamond-studded wedding band he'd purchased from Rundell, Bridge & Rundell, jewelers, on her finger, relieved that the ring fitted, it's size taken from one Edward had purloined from Sibella's jewelry box.

"Darling." She smiled up at him.

"My own." He lowered his head to hers and kissed her as the room erupted in joyful clapping, the children released to run amok.

As Edward slapped him on the back and Chaloner shook his hand, Strathairn exhaled on a long sigh. He felt like he'd awoken from a long dream. He'd wanted this lovely woman from the first moment he saw her across a crowded ballroom before he went off to war, but never considered himself worthy of her and doubted this day would come.

She was his.

THEIR FIRST NIGHT together was to be spent at the Crown Inn in Biggleswade on the way to Linden Hall. John often stayed there and introduced her to the proprietor, Job, and his wife, Mary. A splendid repast was served to them in their private parlor.

Sibella sipped her wine. It had occurred to her that John would have regretted his sisters not being at the wedding. Lady Georgina and the duke were on the Continent, and his sister, Lady Eleanor, had been unable to come from Devon to be with them.

"As your sisters could not attend our wedding, shall we hold a wedding ball?" she asked as he poured her another glass of wine.

"A splendid idea."

"We could invite all our friends, too."

"Indeed we could. But not until the cold weather has left us. Can't expect them to brave the winter roads."

"We'll make it just before parliament sits? A weekend affair," she mused. "An orchestra of course, and dancing." She smiled at him. "Something for us to remember."

He reached across and took her hand, running his thumb over her palm, his gaze as soft as a caress. He released her hand and pushed back his chair. "Shall we go?"

John left her to go to a separate chamber from hers to bathe and change.

Sibella slipped inside the one they were to share, with her maid.

The innkeeper's wife had thoughtfully placed a bowl of yellow jasmine on the table. Its sweet perfume blended with the aroma of apple tree wood burning in the fireplace. Sibella washed as best she could with a basin of hot water and a towel, then Sarah helped her into her nightgown and dressing gown and brushed out her hair before the mirror.

She dismissed the maid and perched on a chair while she waited for John. Her big noisy family and the familiar homes that had made up her life ever since she could remember were no longer its center. She eagerly embraced her future but admitted to being nervous. Her skin tingled at the sight of the bed with its patterned cover. This was really where their marriage began. Where they truly became man and wife. She tried not to dwell on the fact that John would have known many women, but the thoughts crept in. Would she please him?

John entered and shut the door. He smiled and turned the key in the lock. She rose from the chair and crossed to him, wanting to touch him.

Freshly shaved, his hair damp, he smelled of the woody soap he favored. He had discarded his coat and the crisp white linen shirt open at his neck displayed a tuft of dusky hair.

He smiled. "Hello."

She smiled back and her nerves slipped away. "Hello."

John leaned back against the door and held her loosely in his arms, searching her eyes. "We've come a long way today. Are you tired?"

"No. It's just... I don't know...a bit odd to have left my family."

"You miss them?" A pulse beat in her throat. "Maybe I can help?" He brushed back a lock of her hair that coiled over her breast.

Her bottom lip trembled. "You already do."

"Will you mind living so far away?"

"I'll miss Maria. But I expect she will visit us often."

"And your mother, too," he said with a smile.

She laughed. "No doubt you will see more than enough of my exhausting family."

"I'm on excellent terms with your family," John said. "Even your mother has sought my advice on more than one occasion."

"Has she, indeed?" She stroked his hair back from his forehead. "I want you to myself for a while," she whispered, "to enjoy long quiet days when we can do as we please."

"And the long nights," he said gruffly.

He framed her face and pressed kisses over her cheeks, her chin, and then took her mouth in a passionate kiss, while she leaned into his hard body against the evidence of his desire pressing against her belly. "Your heart beats as fast as mine," she whispered when he drew away.

"You aren't too tired, are you, sweetheart?"

Sibella needed no gentle awakening to passion. She had yearned for this since the night she'd gone to his home and came away frustrated and saddened. She'd never believed this day would come. Joy bubbled up in her laugh. "A little. But I shall sleep later."

"*Sibella.*" He tightened his arms around her and pressed his mouth in that sensitive spot below her ear. He eased her away from him, his eyes dark with emotion. "I love you."

Her throat tightened and she could hardly speak. "I love you, too."

His lips teased at hers, his breath smelling sweetly of wine. "I thought of this lying in my bed at night and ached from wanting you." His voice took on a delicious raw and husky tone.

If only she had known it. "I had a few interesting dreams of my own," she confessed, reaching up to trace the smooth edge of his jaw.

Amused eyebrows rose above heavy-lidded eyes. "Would you care to describe them?"

"Later perhaps, we can compare notes." She swallowed. "But I'm sure yours will eclipse mine. My knowledge being somewhat limited."

He drew in a sharp breath and lowered his head. His lips devoured her in a hard, possessive kiss, and his tongue invaded her mouth, tracing its interior. She stilled at the sensual pleasure of it, and curious, pushed his tongue aside to delve in to taste him. The startling effect shot erotic heat to her nether regions and made him groan.

He slid off her gown and threw it onto a chair. She stood in her nightgown while his hands framed her body. He traced the outline of a nipple through the thin fabric with a thumb and his broad shoulders heaved. "You eclipse my imagination."

Her nipple firmed and deepened the throb between her legs as if some invisible thread linked all the erotic parts of her body together.

John breathed raggedly, kissing the soft skin beneath her ear, while his hands skimmed over her bottom and down her legs, bunching up the material to bare her thighs. When he edged her legs apart, her face grew hot.

His warm gentle fingers parted the folds of her sex and she pushed against him as an almost maddening need built within her, just beyond her grasp. She shut her eyes as his clever fingers stroked her and his tongue invaded her mouth. Overwhelmed, she sagged against him.

With a murmured endearment, John lifted her into his arms, carrying her to the bed. The hard ridge of his erection prodded her side. She was curious to discover more and breathy with excitement.

She knelt on the bed and tugged his shirt out of his trousers, exposing his rigid, flat stomach. He made an appreciative sound when she slid her arms around him and pressed her lips against satiny skin and the hard muscle beneath. He moved away and began to undress.

She lay back, amazed at the play of his muscles across powerful shoulders as he stripped off his shirt and tossed his boots to the floor. A dusting of hair arrowed down from his broad chest to disappear into his trousers. She gasped. "I never thought…"

"Thought what?" he prompted, as his fingers worked at his buttons.

"That you'd look like Michelangelo's *David*."

With a surprised grin, he dropped his trousers. His erection burst free from a nest of dusky hair.

She eyed the size of him with a nervous giggle as his stockings joined his boots. "Well perhaps not so much."

He walked unashamedly naked to the bed. The mattress dipped under his weight. She became aware of his big body lying beside her, so powerful he made her feel safe. In one swift movement, her nightgown was gone and she was naked. He threw it on the floor. *Not so safe.*

"Mmm." He trailed soft kisses along her shoulder, while his hands glided over her back, her waist, and hip. By his reaction and his murmured response, he appeared to like her body. His held a total fascination for her and she reached out to touch him.

He groaned and with a strained smile, took her hands away. "Later, sweetheart." He held her hands on the counterpane above her head as his hungry, lustful gaze swept over her body, stretched out before him and he lowered his head to her breast.

Chapter Thirty

JOHN CUPPED HER perfectly shaped breast in his hand and took a nipple in his mouth. Sibella gave a mew of approval. Her obvious pleasure set him on fire, and his balls tightened. He gave equal attention to the other breast, then as she wriggled and gasped, kissed his way down over the soft skin of her belly to the vee shape of dark hair at the juncture of her thighs.

Her thighs tensed beneath his hands. "Oh, John, no!" she protested. With a ragged breath, she seized fistfuls of his hair.

Ignoring her protestations, he swirled his tongue over her sensitive button, until he got the reaction he sought. She wriggled, fought him, shivered, and with a moan of surrender, pulled him to her. He slipped a finger inside her while gently thumbing the hard pearl of flesh, the center of a woman's pleasure. She drew in a sobbing breath and thrust up her hips as the climax took her. "Oh, how lovely," she whispered.

"Yes." It was pure heaven to watch her.

She was wet and ready for him, and he would go mad if he couldn't enter her soon. But he had never deflowered a virgin and discovered he was nervous. He wasn't small, and she was so slender. What if he hurt her? It would have to be quick this time. And, perhaps in a day or two…

A PULSE BEAT a tattoo at the base of his throat. That she could have such an effect on him quite robbed her of breath. She gave herself up to him. She was his, in her heart, mind, and body, and longed to please him. "I want you inside me," she whispered. She buried her face against his neck, flushed by her boldness.

"My love, I want that, too."

"I am not made of delicate china, John."

He grinned and cupped her breasts. "Strange that I'm not thinking of Wedgewood right now." He pushed her legs apart and settled between her thighs. "It might be uncomfortable at first."

"My sisters told me to expect it," she said with an anxious swallow. "But only at first."

"Yes, only at first."

Her breath hitched when his erection nudged her entrance, warm, hard, and insistent. She grasped his shoulders as he eased his way inside her with a deep groan of ecstasy.

A flash of pain made her gasp. She was tight and uncomfortable as he stretched her, and she couldn't hold back the small mew of protest that escaped her lips.

It was enough to make him pause. "Shall I go on?"

"Yes." She hugged him closer. There was no stopping now. He wanted her. Even if it hurt dreadfully, she wasn't about to fail them both.

He pushed deep inside her and withdrew, continuing with rhythmic thrusts. The discomfort began to ease. She loved that they were together, perfectly connected. The pleasure increased, erotically charged, amazing sensations raced through her. "Ooh, John."

"Yes." He breathed the words. She pressed her lips to the cords of strain in his neck. He grasped her bottom, and his thrusts grew harder, going deeper, his gaze sliding somewhere away from her, his breath ragged. The raw urgency of his passion and the friction of his body, moving deeply within hers, overwhelmed her. Completed her. The room filled with the slap of their bodies coming together and their rasping breaths.

John groaned, and a burst of heat warmed her deep inside. He lay panting for a moment before easing himself off her. "I hope you're not hurting, sweetheart."

There had been very little pain. Utterly content, she shook her head and curled into the curve of his body with her eyes closed as sleep hovered close. She was quite taken with the fact that she was now truly a woman. That she was possessed with a womanly power which made John moan. It opened up all sorts of fascinating avenues of exploration. "How often does one make love?"

With a deep chuckle, he dragged the covers up over them, tucking them around her shoulders. "As often as possible and as soon as your body recovers."

"I'm quite all right, really, just a little sleepy."

He leaned over, ran a gentle finger down her cheek, and pressed a feather-light kiss on her lips. "Sleep then, darling."

"Mmm. I love you, John."

Almost asleep, a sudden thought brought her awake. She propped her head up with her elbow. "We arrive at Linden Hall the day after tomorrow?"

"Yes." He opened his heavy-lidded gray eyes, so sensual she drew breath.

"Do you have a good staff at Linden Hall?"

"I do."

"I'm glad." She laid her head on the pillow. Another quiet moment passed as she listened to his even breathing. They would always share a bed, no separate bedchambers for them. "Are any rooms in need of renovation?"

"I'm sure you'll discover them. Sibella, will you go to sleep? We have a full day of travel ahead. We can discuss this in the carriage."

"I've always wanted a bedchamber papered in cerise moiré. Do you think you could bear it?"

He shut his eyes. "I suspect I may have to."

Her lips curved in a smile and suddenly sleep deserted her. This gorgeous man lay beside her and she wasn't done touching him. She leaned over him and traced the bump on the bridge of his nose. "How did you get this?"

He raised dusky lashes to reveal a gleam in his eyes. "A disagreement."

"Pooh. What sort of explanation is that? And the scar on your thigh?" She lifted the blankets.

He gave a gasp of exasperation and pulled her atop him. She lay there, skin-to-skin, looking at him in surprise. "What?" His erection nudged her belly, and she smiled into his eyes.

Epilogue

Linden Hall, York
Late spring, 1819

SIBELLA DESCENDED THE staircase to the marble hall where John waited, a hand on the banister smiling up at her, his dark evening clothes and crisp cravat a perfect foil for his fair hair. Their recent stolen moments still warmed her as she smiled back at him.

"You are beautiful, my love," he said, tucking her arm through his. "Shall we await the arrival of our guests?"

"I am assured everything is ready, but you did distract me from making a final inspection," she scolded.

"You weren't complaining at the time," he said with a wicked smile.

Sibella raised her eyebrows. "You are far too good at distraction, my lord." A smile tugged her lips as she picked up her emerald green silk skirts and crossed the marble floor to Rhodes who stood in his black butler's garb casting a stern eye over the footmen and the tittering maids.

The first to arrive were John's sisters. Sibella kissed Georgina's cheek. "How radiant you seem. You are well?" The exquisite cream lace gown perfectly concealed the early stages of her pregnancy.

"I am, thank you. You should always wear that shade of green to highlight your eyes."

"A little too much artifice, perhaps?" She curtsied to Broadstairs. "Your Grace."

"I quite agree with my wife, Lady Sibella. You're stunning in green," he said with his gentle smile.

Sibella greeted John's older sister, Eleanor dressed in lavender. Sibella was pleased to find she'd cast aside her mourning clothes.

"How do you find Devon?"

"Suitably quiet," Eleanor said. "I miss of the hubbub of London at times, however."

Sibella was tempted to play matchmaker, for a woman as lovely and interesting as Eleanor should not languish as a widow forever.

The rattle of carriage wheels sounded on the driveway, and a moment later, bright chatter flooded into the hall as Hetty and her husband, Guy, Baron Fortescue, entered.

"How good to see you both," Sibella said, as John shook Guy's hand. "Congratulations on the birth of your daughter. What did you call her?"

"Genevieve, after Guy's sister." Hetty said. "Genny for short. I look forward to your company when you have a quiet moment, Sibella," she said as more guests came through the door. "There's Lady Eleanor. I simply must speak to her. I wish to convey my condolences for her loss. I missed Lord Gordon's funeral."

Sibella smiled to herself. The conversation would turn to poetry, for they shared an interest.

She walked forward to greet a new guest. "Althea, how exquisite is that gown. And how it suits you."

Althea Brookwood smiled and hurried to kiss her. "Thank you. Marriage agrees with you. What a sly pair you two are marrying in secret."

"We decided to marry and saw no reason for delay." Sibella had been aware that the *ton* believed her to be pregnant at the time of their marriage, but as time passed, the gossip died away.

"How very romantic."

The diminutive blonde widow was dressed fetchingly in midnight blue. Would she ever seek love in another man's arms? Sibella certainly hoped so.

John was laughing with a tall handsome gentleman. He brought the elegant Irishman, Lord Montsimon to Sibella's side, where he bent over her hand. "Charmed, my lady. Would you grant me a dance tonight?"

"Please don't flirt with my wife, Montsimon," John said with a grin. "There are many beauties here tonight."

Montsimon glanced at Althea who had excused herself to speak to Hetty. "Indeed."

An hour later in the ballroom, dancers formed graceful patterns as they weaved across the dance floor. The music of the orchestra lilting, Sibella was content to watch the dancers as she fanned herself in the warmth from the two huge fireplaces at either end of the room. She was very pleased with her efforts. She gazed around the elegant room, the columns, the chandeliers, the scents of early spring flowers on tables mingling with the ladies' perfume. Beyond the tall windows the moon shone down, veiling the manicured gardens in a silver net.

Ladies chatted on sofas while men clustered together discussing politics and no doubt, planning a visit to the stables on the morrow with a ride across the moors. The guest suites were in readiness, the menus to her satisfaction. This would rival one of her mother's parties, and she hoped her parent would approve. As she moved through the crush, she smiled at her mother where she held court among a group of dowagers. She seemed content with her life, but you could never be sure with her mother.

Maria waved as she danced past in Harry's arms. They'd left their baby son, Adrian, at Lamplugh Abbey with the besotted grandparents.

Chaloner and Lavinia swirled past laughing at something. How content they now seemed.

John came to find her. "You did promise me the waltz. I hope no other gentleman has claimed it?"

"As if I would waltz with anyone else," she scolded.

He shook his head with a grin. "I need to keep an eye on Montsimon."

"No you don't. And anyway, he has his eye on another lady."

"Much good it will do him."

She gazed up at him with a loving smile. "The ball goes well, doesn't it."

"It's perfect." His smoky blue gaze always made her tingle to her toes. "As you are, my love."

THE END

Printed in Great Britain
by Amazon

24654362R00152